ESCAPE TO THE WEST
BOOK THREE

THE
WAYWARD
HEART

NERYS LEIGH

PROLOGUE

May, 1870
Ithaca, New York

"Please don't cry, Mama."

Mrs. Cotton gave Lizzy a watery smile. "I'm just happy for you, darling. I know how excited you are."

Lizzy *had* been excited, up until they reached the station and the reality of leaving her family set in.

She wrapped one arm around her mother's shoulders and rested their heads together. "I'm sure you'll barely even notice I'm gone."

Mrs. Cotton sighed. "How do we even know it's safe?"

"We've talked about this, Mama. It's all arranged by the marriage service, and the pastor there vouched for Richard. And once I get to New York City I'll be travelling with four other women. I'll be safe. You don't have to worry about me."

"I'm your mother, of course I have to worry about you."

"Remember," Nathaniel said from where he lounged against the wall of the station waiting room, arms folded, "if anyone tries anything, you just kick him right in the..."

"Nathaniel Sebastian Cotton!" Lizzy's mother exclaimed, rounding on her youngest son. "There will be no mention of where your sister is to kick anyone."

His gaze flicked to Lizzy as he fought a smile. "Yes, Mama."

"She knows precisely what to kick without having to use

1

vulgar terms, don't you, Elizabeth?" She looked back at Lizzy, eyebrows raised.

Lizzy grinned. "Yes, Mama."

Mrs. Cotton nodded. "Good."

Nathaniel pushed away from the wall and walked over to them, winding his arms around Lizzy and drawing her close. "It's not too late to change your mind, Liz," he whispered into her ear. "You don't have to go."

A bubble of pain rose in her chest and she had to blink back tears. Being only a year and a half younger than him, of her three brothers she was closest to Nathaniel. But she was determined not to cry until she was safely on the train.

"I know. But this is what I want."

He sighed, his breath tickling her neck. "I'm going to miss you so much."

"Me too."

Through the haze of unshed tears, she noticed a pretty young woman walk past them. Nathaniel shifted slightly.

"You're watching that woman, aren't you?" she said.

"No."

"Liar."

His body shook as he chuckled and he drew back to look into her face, gently brushing aside a stray dark curl and kissing her forehead. "You know me far too well."

"All the luggage is on board." Jack, Lizzy's oldest brother, walked up to them. "There shouldn't be any trouble. Not like they can lose five bright yellow trunks."

She let go of Nathaniel and Jack held out his arms to her.

"Don't forget," he said as he held her, "if you need us for anything, just send a telegraph and we'll come right away. For *anything*. And if this Richard fellow doesn't treat you like the princess you are, you tell us and me, Fred and Nathan will come over and set him straight."

She snorted a laugh against his jacket. "Princess?"

He drew back to smile at her. "Not to us, of course. To us you're still our pain of a little sister. But to everyone else you're a princess." He kissed her forehead. "And don't you ever forget it."

Before she could reply, she was pulled from his embrace, turned round and engulfed in a huge hug.

"My turn," Freddie said as her middle brother's massive arms wrapped around her. "Hey, squirt," he murmured into the top of her head.

"Hey, goliath."

"If he doesn't make you happy, you come right on home. Promise?"

She nodded against his chest. "I promise."

"And if he does even the smallest, tiniest thing to make you unhappy, you tell me and I'll come over there and pound him into the dirt."

She giggled at that. Despite his size, she knew Freddie wouldn't hurt a flea. "No you won't."

"For my baby sister, I will."

"I've arranged for them to transfer the luggage at New York," Lizzy's father said.

She looked up to see him approach from the direction of the baggage car. "Thank you, Daddy."

"Now, I've looked into the marshal at that town you're going to and he seems like a trustworthy man. Name's Lee Cade and he fought for the Union in the war. Got several commendations for valor too. So if you need help, you go to him."

"Yes, Daddy."

"And if you want to come home for any reason at all, you send us a telegraph and we'll wire you the money right away. For any reason, even if it's just because you're homesick."

"Yes, Daddy."

3

He huffed out a breath and shook his head. "I don't know why I ever agreed to let you do this."

She left Freddie to walk into her father's embrace, wrapping her arms around his waist and laying her head against his chest. "You agreed because you want me to be happy and I want this more than anything."

His chest rose and fell in a sigh. "I never could say no to my little girl."

"I'm not a little girl anymore, Daddy."

He kissed the top of her head and whispered, "You'll always be *my* little girl."

Lizzy clamped her eyes shut, but no amount of blinking could stop the tears from coming at that.

The sound of the guard's whistle squeezed at her heart. As much as she'd been looking forward to this for months, having to leave her family was turning out to be almost more pain than she could bear.

Forcing herself to step away from her father, she looked around at her family, wiping at her tears with her fingers. "I love you all so much."

Jack solemnly handed over her bag, they followed her to the train, and after one final family hug she climbed on board, finding a seat where she could see them from the window and waving as the train pulled away from the station. Pressing her cheek to the glass, she watched them until the station was lost in the distance.

She stayed like that for a full minute, letting the cool of the glass against her skin sooth her doubts and fears. Then she faced forward and wiped her tears away with her sleeve.

She wasn't going to be sad, not now her journey had begun. This was her dream, to travel across the country, see new places, have thrilling adventures, and fall madly in love with a handsome cowboy in the wild west.

And it was going to be the most exciting experience she

could imagine.

She just knew it.

CHAPTER 1

"Can you see them?"

Lizzy bounced on her seat, her excitement threatening to get the better of her. After months of correspondence and a week on the train, she felt like if she didn't get to see Richard soon she'd explode.

In front of her, Jo hooked her elbow over the back of her seat and stared out the window. "There are so many people, how do we know..."

The train slowed as it pulled into Green Hill Creek's station and up ahead a small cluster of men came into view. Lizzy jumped from her seat. "Over there! That must be them!"

Louisa took her hand and tugged her back down onto the seat beside her, looking embarrassed.

Lizzy spared her a brief smile before returning her attention to the men outside. "Oohhhh, they're all so handsome. I can't even decide which I want to be mine."

Jo twisted round and rested her chin on her hands on the back of her seat. "Calm down, Lizzy. They're only men."

"They're not just *men*," she said, "they're our husbands. Or will be soon. Aren't you excited to meet Gabriel?"

Jo shrugged and glanced out the window. "I guess."

She placed a hand on Jo's arm. "Don't worry, it's all right to be nervous. I'm sure he'll be handsome and wildly romantic and you'll be madly in love in no time."

A smile pulled at Jo's lips. "Don't ever change, Lizzy."

6

She laughed. "I'm not sure if I could, even if I wanted to." Her mother had tried to encourage her to become a proper, refined lady for as long as she could remember, but even she hadn't managed to restrain Lizzy's perpetual enthusiasm for life. There was just too much out there to do and see without having to worry if people thought her behavior was appropriate.

"I don't think I can see Jesse," Louisa said, leaning forward against her to peer through the grime the glass had accumulated during the train's week long journey from New York.

Lizzy returned her attention to the group of nervous-looking men. "He said he has light brown hair, didn't you say?"

"That's right, but I don't see light brown hair. I see three with dark hair and one blond who must be your Richard. Then there are two older men, but neither of them can be him."

Lizzy stared at the man with pale blond hair she'd somehow missed before. Louisa was right, it had to be Richard. *Her* Richard. For a moment she couldn't do anything but gaze at the man with short, neatly combed hair and a trimmed moustache. "He's so handsome," she murmured to herself.

"What if Jesse's not here?" Louisa said. "What if he's changed his mind?"

"Wouldn't surprise me," Jo muttered.

Lizzy wrenched her gaze from her intended to shoot Jo a reproving look as she wrapped her arm around Louisa's shoulders. "He absolutely wouldn't. He must be hidden behind the others or maybe he's been delayed or something. He'll be here, I know it. No man in possession of all his faculties would pass up the chance to marry you. You're one of the nicest people I know, and so pretty. Isn't that right, Jo?"

7

Jo sighed. "He'd have to be an idiot all right." She stood as the train finally drew to a halt. "Might as well get this over with."

Louisa watched her walk along the aisle, mingling in with the other passengers. "Anyone would think she didn't want to be here."

"She's just nervous. You know Jo, she likes to act tough." Lizzy picked up her bag and took Louisa's hand. "Come on. Let's go and get married."

Outside, the station was already filling with passengers stretching their legs or boarding/leaving the train. Lizzy and Louisa followed Jo in the direction of the group of men who were standing back a little from the tracks, out of the way of the crowd.

Lizzy glanced back to check on Amy and Sara, the final two members of their group, who were following a little way behind them, before turning forward again to fix her attention on Richard. A couple of months before, he'd sent her a photograph of himself along with his proposal of marriage, but seeing him in the flesh, not to mention in color, was a whole different experience. Not that he'd been at all unattractive in the photograph. She had to admit, to herself at least, that the image had prodded her answer towards the affirmative. That and the fact that he owned a ranch and was a real life cowboy.

What could be more exciting than living on a ranch in the wild west with a cowboy for a husband? Nothing, as far as Lizzy was concerned.

Louisa suddenly jerked her hand from Lizzy's. "Ouch! Not so tight."

"Oh! I'm sorry, I'm just so excited."

"I guessed that," she said, smiling. She took Lizzy's hand again. "Just try not to break any of my fingers."

Lizzy clasped her friend's hand with more care. "I'll do

8

my best."

Lizzy and Louisa joined Jo where she had stopped, facing the small group of men. Their husbands-to-be were darting glances at them, all except for Richard whose eyes were fixed on the ground. In front of him he clutched a tan colored cowboy hat so tight that the brim looked to be in danger of being irreparably squashed.

One of the older men stepped forward. He was well-dressed and looked to be in his early fifties. "Ladies, welcome to Green Hill Creek. I'm Pastor Simon Jones and this is my wife, Irene."

The only woman in the small gathering gave them a broad smile. "We're so thrilled to welcome you all. I'm sure you will be happy in our little town."

Lizzy pressed her lips together to stop herself from blurting out that she knew she would. She had a habit of saying things without thinking and she was trying very hard to act like a lady while meeting Richard for the first time. She did what her mama had told her to do when she was feeling overexcited and began a slow count to ten.

One... two... three...

Her attention drifted back to Richard and she lost count, only half listening to the pastor explain how he would be introducing each couple in turn and then they would go to the church for the marriage ceremonies. Goodness, but Richard was handsome. Her future husband wasn't overly tall, the two dark-haired, clean-shaven men in the group were taller, but he looked strong. She imagined the physical effort of working with the cattle on his ranch kept him healthy and fit. She longed to see his eyes, which he'd said were blue, but he was still staring at the ground.

Then the pastor said something that made the others laugh, what it was Lizzy had no idea, and Richard looked up. His eyes met hers. For a few seconds, neither of them moved.

"First, Elizabeth Cotton."

Lizzy blinked at the sound of her name and dragged her gaze from Richard to look at Pastor Jones. Was she supposed to be doing something?

Richard stepped forward with a small, uncertain smile.

"Miss Cotton," the pastor said, waving a hand towards Richard, "may I introduce Richard Shand."

He held out his hand. "Ma'am."

With a squeal Lizzy rushed forward and threw her arms around his neck. It was a few seconds before she remembered they were in public. And she'd forgotten to count.

Shrugging off a twinge of embarrassment, she stepped back and smiled up at him. "I'm so pleased to meet you, Richard. You're very handsome."

He looked slightly stunned, which she couldn't really blame him for. "I'm pleased to meet you too, ma'am. And thank you."

He offered her his arm and they stepped back to join the rest of the men as the pastor called Louisa's name.

She adored Louisa, but Lizzy couldn't help feeling a little envious of her as she stepped forward. She always looked so well put together, with her sleek, perfectly styled auburn hair and green travel dress that she somehow kept immaculate even in the dust and dirt that permanently hovered around the train.

Lizzy always seemed to look like she'd been rolling around on the floor, even when she'd only just got dressed. And her thick, dark, wavy hair was the very definition of unruly. Just like her.

She glanced up at Richard and wondered if he would mind unruly. Since he spent most of his day on horseback among the cattle on his ranch, she hoped he'd be happy with a little wildness.

"Louisa, this is Peter Johnson."

10

Lizzy stared in awe as the other older man in the group stepped forward and pulled off his hat. Even though he must have been in his late forties, he was huge, his shirt straining across his wide chest and broad shoulders. He was also taller than anyone else in the group. Even her brother, Freddie, would have had to look up at him.

"Miss Wood," he said to Louisa, "I'm Jesse's father and I'll be taking you to meet him, if that's all right."

A small frown of confusion marred Louisa's face for just a moment. "Of course. I do hope he's not unwell."

"Oh no, miss. He'll explain when we get there."

Next to be called was Sara. Watching her gaze up at the man she'd been talking about practically nonstop since they'd left New York, Lizzy had to swallow a giggle. There was no mistaking that Sara was already in love with Daniel Raine. If anyone was going to be happy in her new life with her husband, it was her. And Lizzy herself, of course.

As Pastor Jones introduced Jo to Gabriel Silversmith, Lizzy stole another look at Richard. He glanced down at her, giving her a nervous smile when he saw her watching him. Her heart did a little skip and she was sure she must have blushed.

It felt so strange to be with him after they'd corresponded for so long. At least, it had felt like a long time to her, but Lizzy had problems being patient once she decided she wanted something. More than once as a child she'd been caught by her parents on Christmas Eve in the middle of the night carefully peeling open the wrapping on her gifts under the tree so she could see what they were before tying them back up again in the hopes that no one would be any the wiser. She wasn't good at waiting, so five months of writing to her handsome cowboy had driven her to distraction when all she wanted to do was come to California and begin her new life on the ranch. It had taken him so long

11

to propose that by the end she'd begun to wonder why he'd advertised for a wife at all. When the letter came in which he'd asked her to marry him, she'd leapt up from the settee and whooped, startling both her mother and Ellie, the family dog.

And now she was finally here, her arm linked with Richard's, about to become his wife. It almost didn't seem real. Was it as strange and exciting for him? All she saw in his face was nerves, but she couldn't fault him for that. She was a little nervous herself. Although mostly excited, as usual.

The last in the little group of women who'd travelled all the way across the country from New York was Amy. Funnily enough, after making it all that way she seemed to get lost in the final few feet, disappearing when the pastor called her name. But she reappeared a few seconds later and was introduced to Adam Emerson. Lizzy knew from Amy that he was Green Hill Creek's postmaster, although he seemed very young for such an important position. He also seemed nearly as nervous as Richard, but she knew he and Amy would be just fine. Amy was a lot of fun. Lizzy liked her very much.

"Well," Pastor Jones said, "now we're all sorted out, let's get the luggage and head to the church."

As they started for the baggage car at the back end of the train, Richard put his hat back on.

"Oh!" Lizzy exclaimed, without thinking.

He looked down at her. "Is something wrong?"

"Oh no. No, not at all." She suddenly felt ridiculous. "It's just... your hat. It makes you look so much like a cowboy."

What she really meant was he looked like one of the dashing heroes on the cover of her novels, all handsome and smoldering and ready to sweep the heroine off her feet. Just as Lizzy had imagined he would. Well, he wasn't smoldering that she could tell, but he was dashing nonetheless. It made her feel a little breathless.

"Well, thanks, I guess." He looked slightly confused, but he'd probably never read any of the dime novels that had so captivated her with dreams of coming to the west.

"I suppose cowboys are everywhere here," she said as they walked.

"You know about cowboys?"

"I've read a lot about them." Even though her knowledge was more or less limited to romance and adventure novels, they were very detailed. She felt sure there had to be some truth to them.

"Well, it's true some of them can be a bit rough, but if you stick around the ranch you'll be fine. The ranch hands are all good men. You'll be safe with them."

"Oh, I'm not afraid," she said, eager for him to know she was going to be a brave frontier wife. "I'm excited. It's all so thrilling."

His eyebrows rose. "Oh. Well, um, that's good then." They'd reached the growing pile of luggage near the back end of the train where the porters were unloading. "Which are yours?"

"The yellow ones." She and her mother had spent weeks painting the plain wood her favorite color. One had been covered with painted flowers by her parents and even her brothers. That was her favorite. It was funny how the trunks meant for carrying everything she owned had themselves become her most treasured possessions and she was glad to see they'd come through the journey relatively unscathed.

While Richard loaded her luggage into his wagon, Lizzy moved to stand beside Jo where she was watching Gabriel place her carpetbag and single, very battered trunk into his buckboard. "Are you ready to be a married woman?"

"As ready as I'll ever be."

Lizzy's own happiness dimmed a little at her friend's continued lack of enthusiasm. "Are you having second thoughts? You don't have to marry him if you don't want to. You shouldn't feel pressured into doing anything."

Jo smiled at her. "I'll be okay. Always am."

Lizzy wound her arm around Jo's. "What was Gabriel like in his letters?"

She looked into the distance as she thought. "We didn't exchange many. I don't think he's one for writing and it was all very quick. He tried though, I'll give him that. They may not have been eloquent, but they were very..." She cast about for the right word.

Lizzy couldn't help herself. "Trying?"

Jo burst into laughter, earning a startled look from her husband-to-be. "Thank you, I needed that."

Lizzy squeezed her arm. "It will be all right, you'll see. You just need to get to know each other. But if you need anything, anytime, you come right over. Richard's ranch is... well, I don't really know where it is, but it's around somewhere. I'll give you directions on Sunday, when I know myself."

Her friend gave her a speculative look, as if trying to work something out. "Can I ask you something?"

"Anything."

"Why did you come here? I can't think you would have had any trouble finding a husband where you were, especially with all those young students where your father is a professor. What did you say the place was called?"

"Cornell. It's very new."

"Well, surely there were any number of men competing for your attention there."

Lizzy shrugged one shoulder. "There were a few. Most of them were too scared of my father and brothers and a lot were far too serious. All studying and no fun."

"So there weren't any at all you liked?"

She kicked at the dirt, biting her lower lip. "Promise you won't think I'm silly?"

Jo pursed her lips. "I don't think I can promise that, but I can promise that if I do, I won't say so."

Lizzy smiled and looked at the ground, lowering her voice. "I wanted to marry a cowboy and live in the wild west. You know, where there's adventure and everything." After a few moments of silence she looked up to see if Jo was laughing at her. She wasn't, but she didn't look as if she entirely understood either. "You think I'm silly."

"I don't think you're silly. I think you should do whatever you want to. Why should only men get to have all the adventures?"

"Exactly!" Lizzy said, brightening. "Just because I'm a woman doesn't mean I shouldn't be able to go out and have adventures and see the world. Well, the rest of the country, anyway."

"But why come here and marry? Why not just come and..." she waved a hand to encompass the town, "see it?"

Lizzy's eyes went to Richard where he was loading the last of her trunks into the wagon. "Because one of the biggest adventures I can imagine is to fall madly in love." She returned her gaze to Jo in time to see her eye roll. "Wait, you think I'm perfectly normal to want to see the wild west and yet silly to want to fall in love?"

"I didn't say that."

"Your face did."

Jo chuckled and patted Lizzy's hand. "I think you shouldn't pay any attention to what I think. I hope it works out for you, I truly do."

"Oh, it will," Lizzy said, grinning, "I'm sure of it. Look where we are! We've already travelled across the whole country. It's already the biggest adventure I've ever had and it's barely even started yet."

With their luggage loaded into the men's various carriages, Louisa left with Mr. Johnson and the rest of them began the short walk to the church. Lizzy and Richard chatted as they walked, her arm through his. Well, she chatted and he responded with one or, if she was lucky, two word answers. She refused to be deterred, however. So he wasn't a great talker, or maybe he was just shy. Once they were more comfortable in each other's company that would surely change.

She was just asking how far the ranch was from the town when a commotion broke out behind them. She turned to see Amy lying unmoving on the ground and Adam on his knees beside her.

Sara, who had been walking with Daniel next to them, rushed to her side. "What happened?"

Adam touched his fingers to Amy's face. He looked terrified. "I... I don't know. She just fainted."

Lizzy hurried over, joining the rest of the group forming a circle around them.

"Oh my," Mrs. Jones said, "is she all right?"

"Give her some air," Lizzy said, although she wasn't sure exactly how one gave someone air. She'd read it in a book once.

"Amy?" Sara said. "Amy, can you hear me?"

Amy's eyes slowly fluttered open and she looked up at Adam.

"She's awake!" Mrs. Jones said.

"Give her some air!" Lizzy repeated, and then shook her head at herself. She wasn't very good in a crisis.

Sliding his arm around Amy's back, Adam helped her to sit. "Are you all right?"

She raised her hand to her head, looking dazed. "I'm sorry, I don't know what happened."

Pastor Jones crouched beside her. "You've obviously had a lot of excitement and stress travelling."

Amy hadn't seemed stressed at all on the journey, but maybe Lizzy had missed it. She'd been so thrilled to be seeing all the new places they were travelling through that she could easily have neglected to be mindful of her new friends. She determined to be more observant and caring in the future.

"I'm all right," Amy said as Adam helped her to her feet. "Truly I am."

She took a step and her legs buckled beneath her, Adam only just managing to keep her from falling.

"Maybe I should just take her home," he said to Pastor Jones. "Could we possibly have the ceremony tomorrow?"

"Of course we can," the pastor said. "That's a good idea. I'm sure all she needs is some food and a good rest."

Lizzy couldn't help feeling a stab of disappointment. She'd been looking forward to seeing each of her friends take their vows and now she would miss Amy's wedding. When they reached the church, she hugged Amy. "I wish I could see you get married. You must tell me all about it on Sunday."

Amy's smile seemed tinged with sadness, although Lizzy couldn't imagine why. "And you'll have to tell me all about yours."

With Amy and Adam continuing towards the town, Lizzy entered the church on Richard's arm, along with Sara and Daniel and Jo and Gabriel. She liked the Emmanuel Church immediately, with its white wooden walls, tall, arched windows and cheerful flowerpots outside the door. It felt friendly and welcoming. Pastor and Mrs. Jones led them past rows of wooden chairs to the front where a raised platform spanned the room.

Everyone took seats in the front row and the pastor stepped up onto the platform.

"Welcome to Emmanuel Church," he said. "Of course,

17

you don't have to attend, but we'd love to see you on Sundays. I'm contractually obliged to say that, but it's still true."

Lizzy laughed along with the rest of them. The pastor was funny. That boded well for his sermons.

"When my wife and I got in touch with the Western Sunset Marriage Service more than two years ago in response to the increasing need for wives for the unattached men around the town, we had no idea of the response we'd receive, and the number of marriages that would result. It has been a joy to be instrumental in bringing lonely men and women together and seeing the happiness it brings. I am truly honored to be joining you together as men and wives, and know that you will be continually in our prayers as you start your new lives together."

Mrs. Jones nodded. "Amen."

"Now, I'll keep things simple as I'm sure you're tired from the journey and you want to get to starting your new lives together," Pastor Jones continued. "But I know this can all be a bit overwhelming, so I want to ask you all to think on what you're about to do. Marriage is a solemn vow before the Lord and not to be entered into lightly. So just take a few moments to make sure in your hearts this is truly what you want. No one will judge you if you change your mind. This is the rest of your lives and you need to be sure. So we'll just have a quiet few seconds and if anyone is having second thoughts, just raise your hand."

As they sat quietly, Lizzy heard Richard shift next to her. For one panicked moment she thought he might have raised his hand, but when she looked both were clasped together on his lap. She berated herself silently for doubting him. He was the man for her, he wouldn't have asked her to marry him otherwise.

"Well, all right," Pastor Jones said. "Looks like we're all

ready. So without further ado, Miss Carter and Mr. Silversmith, would you join me?"

Jo and Gabriel's short ceremony seemed a remarkably unemotional affair to Lizzy. She wasn't sure what she'd been expecting, but it was sad to her that the beginning of a marriage should be so clinical. It was no wonder that Jo hadn't been happy to arrive. Now Lizzy saw the two of them together, she couldn't help wondering why Jo was marrying Gabriel at all. She prayed that God would fill them with love for each other. She desperately wanted all of her friends to be as happy as she was going to be with Richard.

Jo and Gabriel had returned to their seats and Pastor Jones called Lizzy and Richard up. Her heart was thudding so hard she was afraid everyone would be able to hear it.

"Elizabeth, Richard," Pastor Jones said as they stood before him, "marriage is a sacred vow before God and a pledge to each other to stand together, as one, for the rest of your lives. Whatever may come, you will never face it alone. It won't always be easy, but if you love and hold onto each other through it all, it will be right."

She glanced at Richard. His gaze was fixed somewhere near the pastor's feet.

"Do you have a ring?" Pastor Jones said to him. "It's fine if you don't. Not all men do."

He raised his eyes. "Uh, no."

It was much more practical to have the ring made afterwards so it would be the correct size, Lizzy told herself, so it was just as well he didn't have one. She'd always had unusually small fingers, although the rest of her wasn't so big either, only exceeding five feet by a couple of inches. Her father always said her personality made up for any lack of size.

"All right then," Pastor Jones said. "Richard, do you take Elizabeth to be your lawfully wedded wife?"

There was a moment of silence. Lizzy looked up at Richard and saw him swallow.

"I... do."

She was sure she'd only imagined his tiny pause.

The pastor turned his attention to her. "Elizabeth, do you..."

"Yes!" She gasped, covering her mouth with her hand as she realized he hadn't even completed the sentence. "Oh!"

Pastor Jones chuckled. "Well that's certainly the most enthusiastic yes I've ever had."

She laughed with everyone else. It would give her something to tell their children, the way she was so eager to marry their father she didn't even let the pastor finish speaking.

"Would you face each other?" he said.

Lizzy was extra careful with her vows, not wanting to get anything wrong and meaning every single word, even the part about loving him. She didn't love Richard yet, but she was certain it would happen soon. This was her dream, and everything was going to be perfect.

She just knew it.

CHAPTER 2

It came as a bit of a surprise to Lizzy when she emerged from the church on Richard's arm that everything was the same as it had been when they'd gone inside.

She knew it was silly, but she'd thought things should have changed somehow, that becoming a wife would make the world different, or maybe that it would make *her* different. But she felt exactly the same. It turned out that being a wife heralded no transformation whatsoever. Perhaps it would come later, when she was more used to her new status. Or when she and Richard... did what married couples do.

She blushed at the thought and glanced up at him, half expecting a knowing smile as if somehow he could read her thoughts now they were man and wife. But his attention was directed back up the road towards the station, which was probably just as well.

After bidding the pastor and his wife goodbye, the three couples made their way back to the station where they'd left the wagons and luggage. Richard, Daniel and Gabriel retreated to give the ladies some time together before they went their separate ways.

This was the part Lizzy had been dreading. She hugged both Sara and Jo.

"I'm going to miss you two so much," she said, wiping tears from her eyes with her fingers. "You're all my best friends now."

"Stop it," Sara said, dabbing at her own eyes with a handkerchief. "I'm already all emotional over getting married. Any more and Daniel's going to have a blubbing mess for a wife all the way home."

Jo shook her head. "You two are strange. We'll be seeing each other again in two days for church."

"But we've been together for a whole week," Lizzy said. "Aren't you going to miss us even a little bit?"

Jo pressed her lips together, doing a very bad job at hiding the smile trying to force its way onto her face.

Lizzy sidled up to her and nudged her shoulder with her own. "Admit it, you like us and you're going to miss us."

Jo's face broke into a grin and she gave her a playful push. "Of course I like you, silly."

"I knew it," Lizzy said, laughing. She glanced at the men who were talking by the wagons. "Do you feel any different? You know, now you're married?"

"I think it's going to take a while to get used to it," Sara said, "but I'm very happy that I am, I know that much. What about you?"

"I don't know. I thought I would, but I don't, not really."

"When you fall in love, that will make you feel different. Just you wait."

Lizzy looked at Jo. "Do you feel different now you're a wife?"

She snorted a laugh. "No. Not like the pastor saying a few words changes anything." Her smile disappeared as she looked at the ground. "Falling in love does change you though. Makes you lose your senses."

Lizzy was about to ask her if she'd ever been in love, but before she could Jo looked up and her usual confident grin was back.

"In a good way," she said.

Lizzy longed to ask her about it, but she knew she

wouldn't get a straight answer. Jo was an expert in talking without actually saying anything. Maybe she'd open up when they'd been friends for longer.

With a final set of goodbyes and more hugs, they climbed into their respective wagons with their respective husbands and set off for their respective new homes.

"Green Hill Creek seems like a nice place," Lizzy said as they drove north along the town's main street.

"It is," Richard replied, his eyes on the road ahead of them. "Lots of good folk here."

They passed stores of all kinds, the marshal's and doctor's offices, and the bank.

"Where is the post office?" She'd been searching for where Amy would be living with Adam once they wed but couldn't see it.

"Back the other way from where we turned onto this road. There are a few more businesses down there."

Lizzy nodded even though he wasn't looking at her. "Do you know Adam Emerson?"

"Not well but yes. He's a good man. He'll look after your friend."

She nodded again as they passed a three storey building painted a faded green. The large sign fixed to the second floor balcony proclaimed it the saloon. Lizzy gasped at the sight of two scantily clothed women lounging on chairs behind the sign. She knew there were such places where she came from, but they tended to be confined to certain streets, away from the more respectable areas, or else they were discreet. This place sat brazenly side by side with mercantiles and grocers. Not to mention the grand looking hotel at the top of the street. The juxtaposition of the scandalous with the mundane shocked her.

She wanted to ask Richard about it but didn't dare bring up the subject, so she looked away and tried not to think about it.

More than a few people stopped to watch them pass, mostly women.

"Is there something on my bonnet?" she whispered to Richard.

He turned towards her, his eyes moving up. "You mean apart from the flowers?"

"I mean anything that shouldn't be there."

"I don't think so. Why?"

She nodded surreptitiously at yet another woman looking at them. "I've seen a few people looking at me."

He stared openly at the woman and then shook his head. "Oh, don't mind them. That's just the Green Hill Creek gossip brigade. Five ladies arriving all at once to marry five local men sets tongues wagging, no doubt."

"Oh." Gossip had never interested Lizzy in the slightest. There were much more interesting things to occupy her time than speculating on what other people were doing.

The next woman to stare got a big smile and a cheerful wave, just to let her know that her nosiness wasn't going unnoticed but Lizzy was willing to overlook it and be friendly anyway. The woman, who was more than twice Lizzy's age and wearing a hideous pink calico dress with far too many ruffles, gave a tiny, somewhat startled wave back, making Lizzy giggle.

They soon emerged from the town into a rural idyll, the kind of landscape she had always dreamed of living in. It wasn't that she never saw farmland at home where she lived in Ithaca. Her family lived close to the countryside on the outskirts of the city and she often tagged along with her brothers into the fields and forests. But something about the Californian landscape made it seem so much more open and rugged and inspiring.

She took in a deep breath of clean air filled with the

scents of spring, wildflowers blossoming, and sunshine. Living out here was going to be wonderful.

"It's so beautiful," she said, gazing towards the mountains in the distance.

"That it is."

"Where's your farm?" She winced at her error. He'd corrected her on that after her very first letter. "Sorry, ranch."

He pointed towards the mountains. "Over there a ways. The house is beyond those trees and my land extends all the way into the foothills. Should take us another half hour or so to get there."

She tried to stay calm even though the thrill of being so close to her new home made her want to bounce in her seat. She didn't though because her mother always told her it made her look like an overexcited five-year-old.

"Can I see the cows tonight?"

"It'll be a bit late to go out to the beef cattle herd, but we have four milking cows, you can see them if you like."

"I'd like that very much." She'd never seen a cow up close before. She wondered if they were friendly and if they'd let her stroke them.

They rode on in near silence for a while. Lizzy tried a few times to start a conversation, but Richard's answers to her questions were short and often monosyllabic, so eventually she just gave up and enjoyed the scenery around her. She imagined he must be unused to talking to women. She knew he employed a number of ranch hands and he'd mentioned a man called Elijah Griffin who looked after the vegetable garden and the other animals they kept. Being around other men most of the time probably made Richard unsure as to how to converse with women. He had a housekeeper, Mrs. Lassiter, but he'd written that being out most days he didn't see her very much.

It didn't matter to Lizzy. Given enough time, she was

sure she could get anyone talking. She was looking forward to getting to know her husband, but there was no hurry. They had the rest of their lives together.

Eventually they crested a hill and Lizzy got her first sight of her new home. She put a hand to her mouth. "Oh!"

Richard glanced at her. "Something wrong?"

"Oh no. I just thought... well, I didn't think it would be so grand. Not that it's so big compared to some houses I've seen, but it's bigger than I was expecting." She winced. "I don't mean that to sound rude."

His mouth curled up in the first real smile she'd seen from him. It made him even more handsome. "I understand. It's certainly bigger than a lot of houses around here."

Studying the house as they drove down the hill towards it, she couldn't help feeling a little relieved. What she'd read about life out on the frontier made it sound rough and unforgiving, but so far everything she'd seen was positively civilized. Maybe those times were gone in California. Or the tales had been exaggerated for dramatic effect. Or maybe she'd been reading all the wrong books. She had come for the excitement and adventure, but a nice, comfy house was definitely going to be a good thing. In fact, the house looked bigger than the one in which she herself had grown up.

Richard circled around the house to the yard at the back and brought the wagon to a halt. "Well, welcome home, I guess."

Lizzy barely noticed the odd tone in his voice as she took in everything around her. A flower garden was immediately outside the back of the two storey house, a lawn surrounded by neat flowerbeds filled with color. A row of small rocks painted white separated the garden from the rest of the yard which, while functional, still managed to be attractive, surrounded as it was by several majestic oak trees. A collection of outbuildings stretched away to the left, including three huge barns and a long bunkhouse. Beyond them the top of a windmill peeked over the roofs. To the right an extensive pasture in which at least ten horses grazed stretched past a stable block to a line of trees in the distance. Straight ahead, on the far side of the yard from the house, a track disappeared into a stand of oak, aspen and sycamore.

Lizzy smiled at the thought of living there. There was so much to see and explore already and she'd only just arrived. She would have loved to grow up in a place just like the ranch. It was the perfect place to raise children.

Richard jumped from the wagon and walked around to help her down. As he took hold of her waist, her heart sped up a little. She would be raising children here. Richard's children.

She looked up into his eyes, wondering if he'd thought about their future family at all, hoping to see a hint of the excitement she felt reflected back at her. But he stepped back as soon as she was on the ground and looked away. She stifled a twinge of disappointment. They'd only just met, after all. She shouldn't expect any wild romance just yet. That would come later.

Across the yard a man emerged from the largest of the barns and walked towards them. He looked to be in his early twenties and was taller than Richard, with dark blond hair that grazed his shoulders and ruffled in the light breeze.

"Elizabeth, this is Elijah Griffin," Richard said. "He works with pretty much everything that isn't cattle around here and generally keeps it all running smooth. Elijah, this is my wife."

Elijah removed his hat. "P-p-pleasure to meet you, Mrs. Shand."

"It's a pleasure to meet you too, Mr. Griffin." Wanting to make a good impression, she held out her hand.

He looked down at it for a moment before wrapping it in

his own, his mouth turning up in a small smile that warmed his hazel eyes.

"Would you get the men out here to unload the wagon and then unhitch Jenny and Meg for me?" Richard said.

Elijah released Lizzy's hand and replaced his hat. "Y-yes, sir." With a final nod and smile to her, he turned and headed for the bunkhouse.

Lizzy had never met someone with a stutter before, although she'd read a book once where a character had one. Like every new experience she found it intriguing and a whole host of questions immediately presented themselves, none of which she'd ever be able to ask because it would sound rude. Not that she'd mean it as such.

Richard swept one hand towards the house. "Would you like to go inside?"

"Oh, yes please."

Her pondering on Elijah and his interesting stutter was eclipsed by enthusiasm to see the place that would be her home from now on as she walked up the path to the back door. The door itself was blue and matched the window frames, contrasting with the white of the outside walls. There was a large pink bougainvillea beside the door and window boxes on the windows to either side.

"Do you take care of the garden?" she said, admiring the flowers.

"Oh no, that's Mrs. Lassiter's doing. She only has a small garden of her own so she likes working on mine. And Elijah added the window boxes just last week. He thought you might like them."

"He did them especially for me?"

"Yup."

She loved the red painted boxes stuffed with blooming primroses. "I must remember to thank him."

Richard opened the door for her to enter and she

stepped into a large, well equipped kitchen. The center of the room was dissected by a long, sturdy-looking table that would comfortably accommodate at least twelve, more if they didn't mind knocking elbows. Benches along the sides and chairs at either end provided the seating. A free-standing range dominated one wall and a huge cabinet holding a profusion of shining copper pots and pans another. Twin sinks sat beneath the window and various other items of furniture provided storage and preparation surfaces. It was a kitchen clearly used to catering for large numbers of people.

A tall, thin woman wearing a dark blue dress, a white apron, and a severe bun in her graying hair looked up from where she stood at the range. Lizzy would have guessed her to be somewhere in her fifties, but it was hard to truly tell. She had a face that looked at once old and young.

"Mrs. Lassiter," Richard said, "I'd like you to meet Elizabeth. Elizabeth, this is Mrs. Lassiter. She looks after the house for me."

Lizzy approached with the friendliest smile she had. "Good afternoon, Mrs. Lassiter. I hope we can be great friends."

Mrs. Lassiter's eyes darted to her feet and back up again. Lizzy fought the urge to lift her hands to her hair to check it was in place. It almost certainly wasn't.

"Welcome to the ranch, Mrs. Shand," she said in a tone that held no hint of a welcome whatsoever. "Dinner will be ready at six." And then she turned back to the range.

Lizzy opened her mouth and closed it again. At a loss, she looked back at Richard. He shrugged, which was no help whatsoever.

At that moment a man appeared at the door, walking backwards. Lizzy decided to file Mrs. Lassiter away under problems she would deal with later and returned to Richard's side.

One of her travel trunks followed the man in through the door, with a second man carrying the other end.

"Where do you want these, Boss?" the first man said. He was young and taller than almost anyone Lizzy had ever met, with straight brown hair and a short, slightly scruffy beard. Seeing her, he nodded with a friendly smile. "Afternoon, ma'am. 'Scuse me not removing my hat."

"That's quite all right. I have an idea how heavy my luggage is."

"This is Anson Downs and Alonzo Salucci," Richard said.

"Pleasure to meet you, Mrs. Shand," Alonzo said from the other end of the trunk. He was typically Italian, with dark hair and eyes and a very slight accent.

Richard went to open a door that led into the rest of the house. "Put all of them in the first bedroom at the top of the stairs."

No sooner had they left the kitchen when another trunk entered, one end of this one carried by a red-headed man who was only a few inches taller than Lizzy but made up for his lack of height with bulging muscles that looked almost as big as those she'd seen on a strongman once at a fair. They were even larger than her brother, Freddie's. Richard introduced him as Herman Smith. Carrying the other end of the trunk was Elijah who smiled at her as they passed.

The next man through the door Richard introduced as Eugene Peck, who had dark brown hair and looked not even out of his teens.

"No wonder Mr. Shand chose you," he said, his grin revealing a missing tooth on the upper left side. "You're a real stunner."

"Please excuse him, Mrs. Shand," the older man on the other end of the trunk said. "We hope one day to be able to take him out in polite company, but he's got a ways to go yet.

I'm Amos Hopkins. Welcome to California."

"Thank you," she said, trying not to giggle. "To both of you."

"See, she didn't mind," she heard Eugene say when they were out in the hallway. "I was being complimentary."

"Someone's going to have to teach you how to speak to a lady," Amos replied, "but it ain't gonna be me. Get moving."

Next through the kitchen door was a tall Indian man with a long black braid that hung down his back almost to his waist. He was carrying two of Lizzy's valises. Richard introduced him as Kosumee.

"I'm very pleased to meet you, Mr. Kosumee," Lizzy said, thrilled she'd get to spend time around a real Indian. "May I ask what your name means? I read that Indian parents give their children names that mean something."

He smiled. "In the Miwok tongue Kosumee means one who fishes with a spear."

"Really? And do you? Fish with a spear, I mean?"

"Not if I want to catch a fish. Truth is, I'm much better at catching a steer with a rope than a fish with anything."

She laughed. "Well, it's a lovely name anyway."

"Thank you, ma'am."

Anson and Alonzo returned and headed out for another trunk and Kosumee continued on with her bags and barely five minutes later the wagon was unloaded and all her belongings were in her new home. The men left with wishes that she would be happy there and Mrs. Lassiter continued with her preparations for supper without even a glance at Lizzy. Richard followed Lizzy up the stairs and showed her into a bedroom at the top.

It was a large room with white painted walls, a small fireplace, a metal framed double bed, and various well made pieces of furniture - a wardrobe, chest of drawers, settee and two chairs, washstand, nightstand, a small desk. It was

31

functional rather than pretty, but she liked it anyway. But her favorite part was the large window that looked out over the yard and fields behind the house and across the valley with the mountains visible in the distance to the left.

"Is there anything else you'd like in here?" Richard said from where he stood in the doorway, his hands pushed into his pockets and one shoulder leaning against the frame. "If I don't already have it, I can get you whatever you need. Anything you want. I want you to be happy here so you just have to ask."

"Oh, no, thank you. This is perfect." There were no signs of any personal belongings and she wondered if he slept there too and how she could phrase the awkward question. "Um... do you, I mean, is this, um..." She puffed out a breath of frustration and decided to just come out with it. "Is this your bedroom?"

Eyes widening, he jerked up straight. "Oh no. No. My bedroom is along the hall, last door on the right." He stepped backwards into the hallway and pointed, somewhat unnecessarily. "This is all yours."

She nodded slowly. "All right. Thank you."

She wondered when she would be moving into his bedroom, when it would become *their* bedroom, but decided she definitely wasn't ready to ask that question. She'd need at least a few hours of being married before any topics like that arose.

"Well," he said, stepping back, "I'll leave you to settle in. Just come on down whenever you're ready."

She opened her mouth to invite him to stay, but he'd already turned away and started down the stairs. Releasing a quiet sigh, she walked to the window and opened it, letting in the warm, fresh air. She would have liked to talk with Richard some more, get to know him a little, but she supposed they'd have plenty of time for that later.

Gazing out over the beauty of the valley, she smiled. She was finally there after months of excited anticipation. She finally had her dream of coming to the west and marrying a handsome cowboy.

"Thank You, Lord," she whispered. "Thank You for keeping us safe on the journey, for bringing me here, for Richard and this lovely house and all my new friends. Thank You."

Movement caught her eye and she looked down to see Elijah walking across the yard. He glanced up and lifted his hand when he saw her. She waved back and watched him head along the track on the far side of the yard, disappearing into the trees. Wondering where he was going, she turned to her trunks and cases.

There was a lot to do in her new home. And that would include a lot of exploring.

CHAPTER 3

After unpacking a few essential items, changing from her travelling dress into something lighter, and washing off the grime of the train with the water and soap left on the washstand in her bedroom, Lizzy returned to the kitchen to what could only be called a tense standoff.

A short, plump, white-haired woman stood by the back door, a cloth-covered serving dish in her hands. Mrs. Lassiter was in the center of the room, wielding a wooden spoon in one hand and the other planted firmly on her waist. Richard stood by the sink, looking at a loss.

"And just why is *my* cooking not adequate?" Mrs. Lassiter demanded.

"I didn't say it wasn't," the other woman said, pulling herself up to her full height, such as it was. "In fact *adequate* is the perfect word for it. But on a wedding day, the bride and groom want something more than *adequate*."

Richard took a step forward. "Mrs. Goodwin..."

"You're just sore because Ma and Pa said my cinnamon cake was better than yours," Mrs. Lassiter said, waving her spoon.

Mrs. Goodwin rolled her eyes. "Sakes alive, Hester, that was almost fifty years ago!"

Richard tried again. "Mrs. Lassiter..."

She ignored him. "Jealousy, that's all it is. Kindly leave my kitchen, Harriet, and take that watery swill you pass off as beef stew with you."

Mrs. Goodwin gasped in a breath. *"What* did you call my stew?!"

Mrs. Lassiter took a step towards her, thrusting out the spoon. "You heard me."

Mrs. Goodwin started her own advance, brandishing the serving dish.

Richard rushed to place himself between the two. "Ladies, please. I'm sure we can work this out." Seeing Lizzy watching from the door, he gestured towards her in an apparent attempt at distraction. "Mrs. Goodwin, may I introduce my wife?"

Mrs. Goodwin's expression turned from animosity to cheer in an instant. She placed the dish onto the table, threw a warning glance at Mrs. Lassiter, and bustled over to Lizzy.

"It's such a pleasure to meet you, Mrs. Shand," she said, taking Lizzy's hand and beaming a warm smile.

"It's a pleasure to meet you too, Mrs. Goodwin," she replied, unsure exactly what was going on but entertained, nevertheless.

"I brought you beef stew and dumplings, my own recipe. Just something to welcome you to our little community."

Mrs. Lassiter harrumphed.

Mrs. Goodwin's smile didn't waver at the interruption. "I hope you will be very happy here." She patted Lizzy's hand and turned for the door, muttering, "Despite having to put up with my sister."

Not knowing what else to say, Lizzy went with a simple "Thank you."

"You're very welcome." Mrs. Goodwin glanced at Mrs. Lassiter. "Hester."

Mrs. Lassiter narrowed her eyes. "Harriet."

And with that, Mrs. Goodwin left. Outside in the yard, Lizzy glimpsed a wagon, an older man with a pipe sitting in the driver's seat. He removed the pipe to nod to her as Mrs. Goodwin climbed up beside him.

As they pulled away, Lizzy, Richard and Mrs. Lassiter all turned to look at the serving dish Mrs. Goodwin had left on the table. From beneath the red checked cloth emanated a smell so delicious Lizzy's stomach grumbled, even though she wasn't especially hungry. At least, she hadn't been. She very, very much wanted to try Mrs. Goodwin's beef stew and dumplings, however.

"If Elizabeth and I ate the stew, it would save you having to cook extra, Mrs. Lassiter," Richard said, a slight pleading note to his voice. "You already have so much to prepare for the men."

Lizzy held her breath.

"Well, it might as well not go to waste now it's here," Mrs. Lassiter said. "Can't say as I'd go anywhere near that slop, but you do what you want."

He visibly relaxed. "That's very gracious of you."

Lizzy's digestive system did a little leap for joy. Despite Mrs. Lassiter's denunciation of Mrs. Goodwin's cooking, surely nothing bad could produce such a wonderful aroma. It felt as if her nasal passages were being given a hug.

Mrs. Lassiter placed her hand onto the side of the dish. "Cold, unsurprisingly. I'll heat it up and bring it through to the dining room when it's ready."

"Much obliged." He walked towards Lizzy where she still stood in the doorway. "Would you like me to show you around?"

"Oh yes, please!"

Back out in the wood paneled hallway, he waved one hand around him. "Pick a door."

"That one," she said immediately, pointing to the first closed door she saw.

"That's a closet."

"Oh. Is it an interesting closet?"

A small smile crept onto his face. From what she'd seen so far he didn't seem to smile very often, so even that tiny display of amusement was a wonder to see. And she liked how it lit his eyes.

"Not really."

"But how do you know?" she said. "You're used to it. You see it every day. It could be the most fascinating closet in the world and you wouldn't realize it because to you, it's just mundane."

With a small shrug, he opened the door. Lizzy looked inside. There were shelves filled with candles and three lamps, a blanket, two flower vases, and a few other nondescript items.

"It's a closet," she said.

"Sure is."

"Nice blanket."

"Thanks."

She backed out and he closed the door. "What's in there?" she said, pointing to a door further along the hall.

Although the house was large, it didn't take long for her to inspect the parlor, the dining room, a living room, which Lizzy thought would make a wonderful play room for their future children, and Richard's office. There was one more room on the ground floor.

"That's Mrs. Lassiter's," he said when Lizzy asked about it. "She has her own house in town, but since she spends every day here and works so hard looking after us all, I thought it would be nice for her to have her own space. She's the only one who goes in there. Truth is, I haven't even seen inside in more than four years."

She stared at the door, burning with curiosity. She supposed it could be a perfectly ordinary room, with a chair and a table, maybe a few books on a shelf, but in her imagination it was a treasure-trove of weird and wonderful items that could only exist within a room into which she wasn't allowed.

"Dinner's ready."

She jumped at the voice, spinning around to see Mrs. Lassiter carrying Mrs. Goodwin's serving dish across the hall towards the dining room. Despite having done nothing wrong, she tried to not look guilty as she and Richard followed her.

Mrs. Lassiter placed the steaming dish into the center of the table, said, "Hope it doesn't poison you," and stalked back to the kitchen, closing the door behind her.

"Why doesn't she like her sister?" Lizzy said, keeping her voice down just in case Mrs. Lassiter could hear her.

Richard pulled a chair out for her. "It's only when there's food involved. The rest of the time they're friendly. I have no idea why and no inclination to ask. Those are two formidable women I don't want to come between. Whatever it was, it happened long before I met either of them and possibly before I was even born."

"If I had a sister, I'd want us to be best friends all the time," she said as she sat. "I love my brothers to bits, but having a sister would have been different."

"I have two sisters," he said as he took a plate and ladled out the thick, rich brown stew, topping it with two plump, creamy white dumplings. "They tormented me when I was little. Dressed me up like a girl when our parents weren't around. Put ribbons in my hair and everything."

Lizzy clamped her hand over her mouth, covering her snort of laughter.

He raised his eyebrows, no hint of mirth in his expression.

"Sorry," she said, choking back her giggles. "It just sounds funny."

38

He placed the plate in front of her and started work on his own. "Guess it does," he said without smiling.

When he'd finished filling his own plate he sat opposite her and she clasped her hands together, closing her eyes. There were a good ten seconds of silence before she opened them again. He was staring at her as if he didn't know what she was doing.

"Aren't you going to say the blessing?" she said.

He looked startled. "Oh. Yes. Of course."

Mentally shrugging, she closed her eyes again.

"Dear God," he said, "thank You for this food and for bringing Elizabeth safely here. And for all Your blessings. Amen."

Short and to the point. Just what grace should be when the most wonderful smelling food she'd ever come across was sitting right beneath her nose.

"Amen," she echoed, smiling.

~ ~ ~

Lizzy placed her knife and fork onto her sadly empty plate. There was still some of the stew and dumplings left in the dish, but she didn't want to look greedy by taking more. At least, not in front of Richard. Maybe she could sneak some extra up to her room later.

"That was wonderful," she said. "Mrs. Goodwin is an amazing cook." She leaned towards him and whispered, "Do you think Mrs. Lassiter is jealous?"

"Knowing Mrs. Lassiter, I doubt it," Richard replied, setting his cutlery down.

Her eyes lowered to his half full plate. "Aren't you hungry?"

He followed her gaze. "I guess not. I had a big lunch."

When he didn't elaborate further, she pushed her chair

39

back. "Well, I'll get this cleared..."

"Oh no," he said, leaping to his feet and grabbing her plate. "I'll do that. You've had a long journey, you go and relax. There are plenty of books in the living room, if you like to read."

Slightly taken aback, she smiled uncertainly. "Oh, um... all right. Thank you."

He added his plate to hers and strode from the room. Not knowing what else to do, she rose and made her way to the living room. In the hallway Richard appeared from the kitchen, heading back towards the dining room.

"Are you sure there's nothing I can..." she began.

He didn't even break stride. "No no, you just relax."

Sighing, she carried on into the living room.

Richard was right, there were lots of books. One corner was entirely taken up by floor to ceiling shelves packed with books of every color and size. In front of them were two green wingback chairs with a small table and reading lamp. The rest of the room was taken up by an assortment of settees and armchairs arranged around the ornate fireplace, a huge sideboard, and a games table surrounded by four chairs. One end of the room was dominated by a grand piano. Lizzy lifted the lid and ran her fingers over the keys. She didn't remember Richard mentioning that he played. She played a little. It would be nice to have something to practice on. Maybe he would teach her.

She wandered to the bookcases and scanned the titles. She doubted he would have any of the paperback books she enjoyed so much. They were looked down on in most circles and her mother had been mortified when she first found out Lizzy was reading them, calling them lurid filth. Lizzy hadn't read anything that could be classed as filth in any of them and challenged her mother to read one and point out the lurid parts. In an attempt to protect her daughter from such degeneration, she had. And then she'd read another. And another. Now her collection of paperbacks and story magazines was bigger than Lizzy's and they often discussed them with each other.

Lizzy swallowed a sudden lump in her throat. She missed her mama. And daddy. And her brothers and friends. Taking a deep breath in, she pushed her shoulders back and the feelings of sadness away. She had new friends and a new family in Richard and an exciting new life to live. It was what she'd always wanted. In many ways she was like the heroines in her books, braving the unknown to follow her dreams. She had no reason to be sad. This was the first day of her wonderful new life.

She was right, there weren't any paperbacks in Richard's collection, so she pulled a copy of Gulliver's Travels from the shelf. She hadn't read that one since she was fourteen.

She'd just settled into one of the wingback chairs when Richard walked into the room. Flipping the book cover closed, she started to stand, intending to join him on one of the settees.

"Don't get up," he said, raising a hand. "I'm really sorry for doing this on your first night here, but I have to go out. One of the men said there was a problem with one of the nursing cows and I need to go check on her."

Lizzy's heart sank. "Oh." Then she had an idea that perked her up. "Could I come with you? I can ride well, I won't have any trouble keeping up."

He shook his head. "I'm probably going to be a while and it's not safe out there for a woman after dark. I'm sorry. I'll introduce you to the herd another time, I promise."

She tried not to let her disappointment show too much, but she couldn't stop her shoulders slumping a little. "I understand."

"I'm really sorry. But you'll be all right here, won't you?

Mrs. Lassiter has gone home, but if you want anything just go to the bunkhouse and any one of the men will be happy to help you with whatever you need."

She nodded and tried to produce a convincing smile. "I'll be fine."

He returned her smile, although this time it didn't light up his eyes the way it had before. He left the room and a few seconds later she heard the back door open and close. Her shoulders slumped even lower. It wasn't how she'd imagined her first evening with her new husband to go. She'd thought they'd at least have some time to talk. He hadn't even introduced her to the milking cows like he said he would.

Sighing, she opened the book again. It looked like she would just have to make do with the company of Lemuel Gulliver for the evening.

CHAPTER 4

Twenty minutes later, Lizzy closed the book, bored.

She placed it onto the table beside her and sighed. It wasn't that Gulliver's Travels was boring, she just couldn't drum up any enthusiasm for reading. She wanted to be *doing* something.

She stood and walked to the window. The sun was heading for the horizon, but it was still light outside and the weather was warm and the sky clear. The perfect evening for a walk. Wondering if there were any wild animals around, she smiled. Perhaps she'd get to see some.

She ran up to her bedroom to fetch a shawl, returned to the kitchen, and was heading for the back door when a thought occurred to her. Taking a detour to the pantry, she found Mrs. Goodwin's dish on a shelf inside. She experienced a very small twinge of guilt at using her fingers to pick up one of the gravy-soaked leftover dumplings, but as there was no one to see she reasoned it couldn't really matter. Holding the dumpling over her left hand to catch any drips or crumbs, she returned to the back door and stepped out into the warm evening air.

Standing in the shadow of the house, she looked around as she ate. Birds settling in to roost in the trees around the yard filled the air with song. Hunting swallows zipped over and around the buildings and fields. High above her, groups of swifts screamed past. The low sun cast everything in a faint pinkish glow, giving the landscape around her a fairytale feel. It would have been romantic, if she hadn't been alone.

From the direction of the distant mountains she could hear the low murmur of mooing and she wondered if that was where Richard was.

Laughter emanated from the open windows of the bunkhouse away to her left and she briefly considered going over to ask if she could join them, but the evening was so beautiful that she decided she didn't want to spend any of it inside. If Richard hadn't returned by dark perhaps she'd go then.

Having finished the last bite of dumpling, she was about to begin her exploration when the bunkhouse door opened and Elijah Griffin stepped out. Without knowing why, Lizzy shrank back into the shadow of the bougainvillea and watched him walk across the yard. He passed forty feet in front of her without looking in her direction and she noticed a small, leather-bound portfolio in his hand. He was striding purposefully to his destination, wherever that was.

Lizzy's conscience had a brief but heated debate with her curiosity. As usual her curiosity won out and she slipped from behind the shrub.

Following Elijah without him noticing turned out to be easier than she'd thought it would. Although, to be fair, it wasn't the first time she'd clandestinely followed someone.

Back when she was fifteen, after reading about Kate Warne, the Pinkerton agency's first female detective, Lizzy decided that the job of detective would be perfect for her and had designed a program to train in all the skills she thought that would entail. Chief amongst those was trailing a person without them being any the wiser. Each of her family members became, at some point or other, unwitting subjects in her training, with varying degrees of success. Her three older brothers, once they realized what she was doing and

44

after she'd caught two of them in activities they would have preferred to keep secret, became especially vigilant. Not to mention annoyed to what she'd felt at the time was an unwarranted degree.

She darted from tree to bush to tree, her footsteps light, careful to avoid stepping on any branches that might snap or dried grass that might rustle. It wasn't easy to keep hidden at the speed Elijah was walking, but that just added to the fun.

Fun she shouldn't be having, her conscience informed her. She told it to be quiet.

They left the immediate area around the house and passed a large vegetable plot to join a path by the side of a stream. After following the stream for roughly half a mile, Elijah entered a wood of oak and alder, quickly disappearing into the gloom beneath the canopy.

Lizzy crept to the first oak tree, pressed herself against the trunk, and peered around it. There was no sign of her quarry. Frowning, she edged around the trunk and ran to the next, following the same procedure. Still no Elijah.

She almost stamped her foot in annoyance. How dare he disappear when she was trying to sneak after him?

Abandoning stealth, she walked deeper into the small forest, following a faint animal-worn path in the undergrowth.

A shape stepped from behind a tree directly into her path.

Lizzy collided with a chest.

She cried out in surprise, stumbling backwards, and would have fallen if Elijah hadn't grabbed her shoulders and kept her upright. Judging by his expression, he was as surprised as she was.

"Mrs. Shand? Why are you f-f-following me?"

She pulled away from his grasp and brushed off her skirt, attempting to regain her dignity. "I wasn't following you. I just happen to be going in the same direction."

"Where are you heading?"

"I..." She looked at the path ahead and then back in the direction she'd come. "I'm going... over there." She waved a hand vaguely to encompass every direction to her right.

He raised an eyebrow.

She puffed out a sigh. "Oh all right, I was following you. Richard went to tend to the cows and I'm bored."

"So y-you snuck after me?"

"I wasn't sneaking, I was walking after you. Clandestinely."

He clamped his lips together, his shoulders quivering.

"Which may be the definition of sneaking, I'll grant you." She couldn't help smiling at his obvious amusement. "Stop laughing at me."

"I'm not."

"Yes you are."

His silent laughter reduced to a smile.

Lizzy looked at the ground between them. "I'm sorry, I didn't mean to disturb you. I'll find somewhere else to walk." She turned to leave.

"W-w-would you like to join me?"

She whirled back and tried not to look too excited. "Where are you going?"

He flicked his head for her to follow, then turned and continued along the animal track. Lizzy hurried after him, intrigued.

After a hundred yards or so the path opened out into a wide clearing. A gentle breeze rustled the leaves overhead. Butterflies and bees flitted between wildflowers dotting the grassy ground in the dappled light from the lowering sun. Ahead, the stream pooled into a large pond created by a natural rock wall stretching across the far side of the clearing, before slipping between two boulders with a gentle burbling

46

sound to continue on its way. The occasional plop of a fish reaching for an insect was all that marred the crystal surface.

"It's beautiful," Lizzy breathed, taking in the whole scene. "It's like a painting."

"It is," Elijah replied with a smile.

She followed him to a wide, flat rock near the water's edge that formed a perfect seat and sat beside him. "Is that what's in there?" she said, indicating his portfolio. "Are you an artist?"

"Oh, no," he said, unwinding the leather thong that kept it closed. "I'm not artistic at all. I just like c-c-coming here to work."

He pushed back the cover of the portfolio and pulled out a sheet of paper on which was drawn what looked like a technical diagram of a machine or... something.

"What is it?" she said, trying unsuccessfully to work out what she was looking at.

"It's an irrrrr..." He puffed out a breath, closed his eyes, and said slowly, "Ir-ri-ga-tion system." He opened his eyes again. "For the vegetable garden. I'm having to redesign the p-pipework coming from the well." He took another piece of paper from inside the portfolio and handed it to her. "It'll look like this."

On the paper was a perfectly proportioned three dimensional drawing of the system of pipes on the graph paper, including plants. It looked so lifelike it could almost have been a photograph.

"I thought you said you weren't artistic," she said, gazing in awe at the sketch. "This is amazing. It looks so real."

He ducked his head and smiled. "Thanks."

"And you designed it?"

He nodded as she handed the drawing back to him. "I like to build things. Figure things out. Solve p-p-problems. I

47

design things for other people sometimes. Build them if I have the time after my work on the ranch."

She pointed to a set of pipes on his drawing that ran to a tiny rendition of the main house. "Are these for the house?"

"Yeah. Right now there's only running w-w-water in the kitchen, but I'm wondering if maybe I could put in a bathroom. I haven't ever tried that before. Although I haven't asked Mr. Shand about that yet." He glanced at her uncertainly, as if afraid she might tattle on him.

She leaned towards him and whispered, "Don't worry, I won't tell. I'd love a bathroom though."

His face relaxed into a smile. "I'll see what I can do."

She looked around at the clearing. "I can see why you come here to work. If I could do that I think I'd be inspired by a place like this." Her eyes moved back to the portfolio on his lap. "I guess I'm disturbing you being here. You probably just want to work. I should go."

Her statement was half-hearted and she knew it. What she really wanted to do was see more of his drawings and ask him all about them. They were fascinating.

By Elijah's smile, she could tell he knew what she really wanted too. "I d-don't mind if you stay, Mrs. Shand."

She didn't have to be told twice. "Thank you, Mr. Griffin." She eyed the stuffed portfolio. "I really was bored and your drawings are the most interesting thing I've seen since I got here. Could I see some more?"

~ ~ ~

The sun had just dipped below the horizon by the time Elijah walked her back to the house. With all the windows dark she knew Richard hadn't yet returned.

"How does he see at night out there?" she said. She knew he'd told her he'd be fine, but she couldn't help but be a little worried.

Elijah looked towards the mountains, now just a distant blue silhouette against the darkening sky with stars twinkling into life above. "I g-guess he took a lamp. He goes out there a lot at night. I don't rightly kn-kn-know why, but then I don't work with the cattle much, only if they're sick and need extra care here."

"Do you think he'll be all right?"

He gave her a reassuring smile. "Always is."

It was heartening to hear, but she still wished her new husband was home. "Well, thank you for allowing me to stay with you. I know I didn't let you get any work done."

"It was n-nice to have the company." He looked past her to the dark house. "Would you like me to go inside and light the lamps?"

She glanced back. The house did look forbidding with its windows all in gloom, but she didn't want him to think she was afraid of the dark. Even if she was, just a little. "No, thank you, I'll be fine. Oh, I almost forgot, thank you so much for the window boxes. They're beautiful. I adore them."

"I'm p-p-pleased you like them. I figured Mrs. L might not want you to change her garden, but the b-boxes are all yours so you can do whatever you like with them. You can change the flowers if you want."

"Oh no, I love primroses. They're perfect. It's one of the most thoughtful things anyone's ever done for me." She could have added that so far he'd been much more thoughtful than her own husband, but she didn't.

He stepped back. "Well, goodnight, Mrs. Shand."

"Please call me Lizzy," she said. She wasn't anywhere near used to being a Mrs. yet.

One corner of his mouth turned up. "Lizzy."

"Goodnight, Mr. Griffin."

The other corner joined it. "Elijah."

49

She smiled back. "Elijah."

He turned and headed towards the bunkhouse. Lizzy watched him for a few seconds before going inside, the smile still on her face.

She spent the next few minutes lighting every lamp she could find and then settled into the wingback chair with another cold dumpling and opened Gulliver's Travels again. It was a full ten minutes before her eyes drifted closed and the book slumped into her lap.

~ ~ ~

"Elizabeth?"

At the sound of her name and the touch on her shoulder, Lizzy opened her eyes, blinking sleepily at the face looking down at her. "Did I fall asleep?"

Richard straightened, his hand lifting away. "Looks like it."

She yawned and rubbed her knuckle into her right eye, which was itching. "What time is it?"

"Just after one. I'm sorry I'm so late getting back."

"How is the cow?"

He sat on a nearby settee. "The cow?"

"The one you had to go tend to. How is she?" She pushed herself upright in the chair.

"Oh, that cow. She's fine. It wasn't anything serious, but I had to stick around to make sure. Hope you weren't too lonely all by yourself."

She debated whether or not to tell him about her walk with Elijah. She didn't want him to think she'd done anything improper, but then again she did want him to know she'd been bored. Maybe he'd even be a little bit jealous.

"I went out for a walk and I met Elijah. Mr. Griffin. He showed me his drawings of all the things he's designed."

To her disappointment, the news that she'd spent the evening with another man didn't seem to faze her husband in the slightest.

"Elijah's very talented," he said with a smile. "He built the windmill that pumps the water from the well to the house and he's done work for a few other folks around here. Did he show you his plans for irrigating the vegetable garden?"

She nodded. "It was fascinating. I'm really looking forward to seeing it built."

"Well, I'm glad you weren't on your own." He placed his hands on his knees to stand. "You must be tired. Is there anything I can do for you before you go to bed?"

She wanted to say he could talk to her, but it sounded like she was being sent to bed. She couldn't deny she was exhausted from the trip. It was going to be nice to sleep in a bed that wasn't moving for a change. "No, thank you."

They walked out into the hallway and Richard turned in the direction of the kitchen.

"Well, goodnight, Elizabeth."

"Richard?"

He looked back at her. "Yes?"

"Will you be working tomorrow?"

An expression that might have been regret crossed his face. "I'm really sorry. But I'll try to get back before dark so I can show you around."

She stifled a sigh. She had imagined they would get more time together. "I'd like that."

Twenty minutes later she was lying in the exceptionally comfortable bed in her bedroom staring at the dim outlines of her unopened trunks.

She probably should have unpacked before getting into bed, but she hadn't been able to find any energy for the task. It could wait until tomorrow. She would evidently have plenty of time on her hands while Richard worked.

51

She listened to the sounds of him moving about beneath her and then climbing the stairs. A light appeared beneath her door briefly as he walked past and along the corridor his bedroom door opened and closed.

She sighed softly into the pillow. Of all the ways she'd imagined her first evening as a married woman would go, spending it with another man and barely having a chance to speak to her husband hadn't entered her mind at all.

Not that she hadn't enjoyed her time with Elijah. She could already tell they were going to be good friends. It was strange that Richard didn't seem at all bothered that she'd spent the evening with him. Maybe it was because he trusted Elijah. Lizzy trusted him and she'd only just met him. There was something about him, an appealing, easygoing nature.

Still, she longed to get to know her husband better. She would just have to be patient. They had the whole rest of their lives together, she didn't need to spend every second of the day with him right away. And he'd said he would show her around the ranch in the afternoon. There was that to look forward to.

She closed her eyes and opened her heart to God. "Thank you, Father, for bringing me and Amy and Sara and Louisa and Jo here safely. I hope each one of them has had a good evening in their new homes and that we'll all be happy here. Please bless Richard and help us to fall in love quickly. And also bless Elijah and thank You for the time I had with him today. I really enjoyed it. Please be with Mama and Daddy and Jack, Freddie and Nathaniel..." She stopped as a lump rose to her throat at the thought of her family. "I miss them. Help them not to miss me too much. In the name of Your Son, Jesus, Amen."

She sniffed and wiped at her eyes with the pillowcase. She wasn't going to be sad, not now she was on the verge of realizing her dreams.

Tomorrow would be a good day.
She just knew it.

CHAPTER 5

Lizzy intended to wake early so she could see Richard at breakfast before he left. After her long journey and staying up late the previous night, however, she didn't make it as early as she'd hoped. But she was still hopeful as she ran down the stairs, her hair loose around her shoulders and wearing the dress she'd worn the evening before because it was the quickest to grab.

She burst into the kitchen slightly out of breath. It was deserted. The smile she'd affected for Richard slid from her face, her heart sinking.

At a noise from the pantry she looked up hopefully, but it was Mrs. Lassiter who emerged, not her husband.

"Has Richard left already?" Lizzy said, hoping against hope that somehow she was actually too early.

"Everyone has," the housekeeper said, looking her up and down with an expression of disapproval. "It *is* after eight."

Lizzy smoothed her dress self-consciously and slid onto one of the benches at the table with a sigh. "I meant to wake earlier, but I must have been tired."

"I suppose you'll be wanting breakfast." Mrs. Lassiter's tone suggested wanting breakfast should be considered a criminal offence.

"Um... if it's not too much trouble?" Having been asleep only minutes before, Lizzy wasn't especially hungry, but if that was the reaction she got to wanting breakfast at breakfast time she didn't want to know what Mrs. Lassiter would say if she wanted it later. Better to have it now, while she had the chance. "But I can make my own. I don't want to be a bother."

She knew immediately it was the wrong thing to say.

Two deep furrows appeared in the center of Mrs. Lassiter's forehead. "No need. I'll do all the cooking in my kitchen."

Her kitchen? Lizzy almost said something before stopping herself. She was new there. It was natural that the woman who had been there for years would feel a little territorial. Lizzy was sure they could come to some arrangement where she could use the kitchen as well. She enjoyed cooking, especially baking cakes, and she was looking forward to preparing Richard some of her favorite recipes.

Taking a cloth from a hook on the wall beside the range, Mrs. Lassiter removed a full plate from one of the ovens and carried it to the table, placing it in front of Lizzy.

Lizzy opened her mouth and closed it again. She looked at the plate, then at the range, then at Mrs. Lassiter who was walking back towards the pantry. Finally she managed a mildly insincere "thank you" as Mrs. Lassiter disappeared again. The woman had acted as if making her breakfast was such a chore when she'd had it ready all along.

Trying hard not to be annoyed and praying for patience, Lizzy went in search of cutlery. She had to open three drawers before she found what she was looking for.

Back at the table, she stared at the food in front of her. There was a lot of it. She got the feeling Mrs. Lassiter was more used to catering for hard-working, six-foot-tall ranch hands than five-foot-two, twenty-year-old women with nothing more energetic than unpacking to do for the rest of the day. Sighing, she took her first bite of bacon and fried potato. At least it was tasty. Not Mrs. Goodwin's beef stew tasty, but certainly not unpleasant.

Fifteen minutes later she'd eaten half the food on the plate and was fairly certain she'd burst if she ate any more. Mrs. Lassiter had left the kitchen ten minutes before and was, presumably, somewhere in the house. Lizzy looked around, wondering what to do with the leftover food. She could leave it, but she didn't want to antagonize Mrs. Lassiter any more than she inadvertently already had.

Could she get it out of the house without being seen? She wandered over to the door and opened it to look outside. Beyond the bougainvillea next to the door there was no cover before the far side of the yard. If Mrs. Lassiter happened to be looking out a window as she made her escape, she'd be seen in an instant.

Heaving yet another sigh, she was about to close the door when Elijah appeared from behind one of the barns with a wheelbarrow, heading across the yard.

She glanced back into the kitchen to make sure she was still alone and then leaned out the door. "Psst!"

Elijah stopped and looked around him.

"Over here," Lizzy hissed.

He turned towards her and his eyebrows rose.

She beckoned to him, glancing behind her again.

Leaving the wheelbarrow, he jogged over to her. "Morning, Lizzy. Can I help you with something?"

"Are you hungry?"

"I beg your pardon?"

She suddenly felt very silly, but it was too late now. "Mrs. Lassiter gave me a huge breakfast," she whispered, "and I can only manage half of it, but I don't think she likes me very much and I don't want to just leave it like I'm ungrateful or don't like it."

He looked confused. "And you w-w-want me to eat it?"

"Well, not necessarily. But can you help me get it out of the house?"

His confusion vanished and he looked like he wanted to laugh. She should have been annoyed at him for thinking her funny when she was being perfectly serious, but his expression just made her want to giggle.

"Stop laughing at me," she said, fighting a smile.

"I'm not."

"But you want to."

He pressed his lips together and looked away for a moment, blowing out a breath. When he looked back at her his face was emphatically straight, which made her want to laugh even more.

"I'm not really hungry, b-but I can give it to the pigs."

She grinned up at him. "Thank you." She ran to fetch the plate from the table and brought it to the door. Looking down at it, she had a thought. "There's bacon. You can't give the pigs bacon. It would be like eating a family member."

When she looked up at him, he was smiling. "I think I can m-m-manage just the bacon." He took the plate from her hands, extricated the bacon rasher and handed it to her. "Wait here."

"Make sure you can't be seen from the windows," she hissed as he turned to go.

"I'll be careful."

She watched him walk away from the house, the plate shielded from view in front of him. Arriving at the wheelbarrow, he did something that she couldn't see, turned and moved the plate behind him all in one move, and returned to the house. In the wheelbarrow there was no sign of the remains of her breakfast amongst the pile of vegetables she assumed must be for the pigs.

He reached the door and handed her the empty plate, swapping it for the bacon she was still holding.

"Thank you," she whispered.

"You're welcome," he whispered back.

He gave her a conspiratorial wink, crumpled the bacon into his mouth, and headed back to the wheelbarrow.

Lizzy leaned against the doorframe as she watched him go, smiling to herself. She knew her behavior was a little strange and yet he hadn't made fun of her or told her she was being ridiculous. He'd simply helped. And tried not to laugh.

Maybe her new life so far wasn't exactly what she imagined it would be, but at least she had a friend.

~ ~ ~

After cleaning her breakfast things and putting them away, Lizzy went back upstairs.

She heard sounds coming from Richard's bedroom along the hall and crept in that direction, finding Mrs. Lassiter making his bed with her back to the door. Curious, Lizzy peered around the doorframe to take a look at the room she would soon be sharing with her husband. It was a little plain but not unpleasant. She tried to imagine how the walls would look painted blue, leaning forward to get a better look.

The floorboard beneath her foot creaked.

Lizzy froze.

Mrs. Lassiter looked round, her eyes narrowing when she saw her. "Something I can help you with, Mrs. Shand?"

"Uh... no. I was just... no. Can I help you with anything? Any housework?" It wasn't her favorite thing to do, but she wanted to be useful.

"No, thank you. Mr. Shand pays me to cook and look after the house and that's what I do. Don't need any help."

"Oh. Yes." She decided to see what a smile would do. "You could call me Lizzy."

"I've known Mr. Shand for close on five years and I've

only ever called him Mr. Shand. I've known you for less than a day so I'd rather keep calling you Mrs. Shand, if it's all the same to you."

Evidently, smiles had no effect. "If that's what you want."

Mrs. Lassiter gave a sharp nod and turned back to making the bed. Apparently that was Lizzy's cue to leave.

Sighing, she trudged back along the hall to her bedroom.

Having washed, changed, and pinned up her hair, she spent the next two hours unpacking her belongings and deciding what to do with them. The clothing wasn't a problem, there was a large wardrobe with plenty of room for everything she'd brought. But there were also many personal possessions, items that held sentimental value, and half of her wanted to put some of them in the rest of the house to somehow lay claim to this place that was now her home. The other half was afraid of how Mrs. Lassiter would feel about that. She had no idea how Richard would feel about it. She had no idea how Richard would feel about anything.

In the end she decided to arrange them as best she could in her bedroom. She could always move them later, perhaps when she moved into Richard's bedroom. Or when she worked up the courage to stand up to Mrs. Lassiter.

Finally, she sat on the bed, staring at a framed photo of her mother and father and brothers.

"Oh, Mama," she whispered, running her thumb over her mother's face, "I miss you so much."

Eleanor Cotton would know what Lizzy should do to make Mrs. Lassiter like her and get Richard's attention. She seemed to know everything. Even Lizzy's father said so and he was the smartest person she knew. She wished she could talk to her, just for half an hour, just long enough to ask her advice. And get a hug.

The sound of whistling drifted in through the open

window, a cheerful tune that cut through her melancholia. She placed the photo onto her nightstand and went to the window. On the far left edge of the yard Elijah emerged from the barn with a bucket in each hand and strolled towards the track that ran into the stand of trees opposite the house.

Homesickness forgotten, Lizzy whirled round and ran to her door, down the stairs, and out through the kitchen. Elijah had disappeared by the time she got outside, but she headed in the direction she'd seen him go and caught up with him quickly.

He smiled as she ran up to him, placing the buckets onto the ground. "M-Making your escape? Did Mrs. L find out?"

"What?" She looked back the way she'd come before realizing he meant her mad dash to catch up with him. She gave a breathy laugh. "Oh, no. She was none the wiser, thanks to you."

He nodded. "Glad to hear it." When she didn't say anything more, he said, "Can I help you w-with anything else? I'm guessing it's too early for you to be wanting to get rid of lunch?"

"Oh, no, ha!" She looked down at the buckets. One was full of dried corn, the other, smaller seeds. "So, um, you're working?"

"Yup."

"With the animals?"

"Yup."

She rocked from her heels to her toes and back again, biting her lip and trying to think of a way to phrase her question so it sounded like it would be a good thing.

"Would you l-l-like to help?" he said, before she could come up with anything.

She breathed out in relief. "I'd love to help. Mrs. Lassiter won't let me do anything inside."

He bent to pick up the buckets again, a smile in his eyes.

60

"Well, come on then."

As they continued along the track, she breathed in the scents of spring and listened to the hum of insects all around them.

"It's so beautiful here," she said. "I adore being outdoors."

"What's it like where you come from?"

"Oh, it's very pretty but different from here. This feels more..." she swept her hand towards the distant mountains, "open and untamed. The wild west, just like in the books."

He looked at the track ahead of them. "You mean cowboys and Indians and such?"

She nodded and then felt a little foolish. "Well, maybe not exactly like in the books. Although Richard's a cowboy, more or less, and Kosumee's an Indian, and there are others, aren't there?"

"There are. There's a reservation not far away."

"There you go then, cowboys and Indians." It made sense to her.

"I g-guess you're right," he said, smiling. He turned off the track onto a worn path that led to a gate. The gate opened into a large, grassy enclosure surrounded by sturdy wire fencing at least a foot taller than Elijah, who was in turn nearly a foot taller than Lizzy.

She looked up at the top of the fence as she followed him through the gate. "Why's it so high?"

"So foxes can't get in," he replied, placing the buckets on the ground and securing the gate behind them.

"They can jump that high?"

"If they're m-motivated enough." He pointed to the far side of the enclosure.

At the sight of a whole flock of chickens pecking at the dirt, her eyes widened. "There are so many different colors."

He picked up one of the buckets. "Watch this." He gave

it a small shake, sending a few pieces of corn rattling against the sides.

Every last chicken raised its head and looked in their direction. Under a second later the whole flock was sprinting towards them.

"It's like my brothers when my mama makes blackberry pie!" Lizzy said, laughing.

Elijah scooped a handful of corn from the bucket and scattered it in a wide circle then held it out for her to do the same. The chickens rushed to gobble up the corn as soon as it hit the ground.

They made their way across the enclosure, scattering corn as they went, until the bucket was empty and they'd reached the large henhouse in the middle.

"We'll go and c-collect the eggs in there when we're done with this," he said, setting the empty bucket by the door and holding up the second bucket.

"Who's that for?"

He gave her a mysterious smile. "Follow me."

He led the way around the henhouse to another gate which opened into another, smaller, enclosure. There were more trees, bushes and undergrowth here and at first she couldn't see what it was for.

Elijah gave a shake of the bucket and waited. After a few seconds a brown and white chicken emerged from beneath a bush, having to duck to escape the dense foliage. First one, then two, then a whole cloud of tiny baby chickens followed, their long legs pumping to catch up with their mother. Further away another chicken came into view trailing more of the yellow bundles of fluff.

Lizzy hadn't seen anything so enchanting in her entire life. She raised a hand to her mouth. "Oh!"

"I thought y-y-you might like them," Elijah said, sprinkling a handful of the contents of the bucket over the ground.

"They're the most adorable things I've ever seen," she replied, looking around her as more chickens with offspring of varying ages joined the growing crowd around them.

"Hold your hands together, like this." He formed his hands into a cup.

When she'd done the same, he placed the bucket onto the ground, bent to scoop two young chicks into his hand, and placed them onto her cupped palms along with a pinch of the food from the bucket. They immediately set about picking the tiny pieces from her skin.

"They're so light! I can barely feel them." Gently, she stroked a thumb over their tiny backs. "And they're so soft!" She raised her eyes to find him watching her, a small smile on his lips. "Thank you for letting me come with you."

"Oh, I d-didn't do it for you," he said, his smile becoming a grin. He picked up the bucket again and waved it at her. "You have work to do."

Laughing, she carefully placed the two chicks onto the ground and dusted off her hands. "I'm ready."

They spent some time in with the young chickens, more time than Elijah would normally have taken to feed them, Lizzy suspected, but he didn't complain. When they left the nursery enclosure they returned to the henhouse to collect the morning's eggs.

"What do you do with all of these?" she said as she carefully placed two brown eggs into the bucket she held.

"A lot of them are for Mrs. L to feed all of us," he said from the other end of the wooden building where he was filling his own bucket. "Between all of us we g-get through quite a few every day. The rest I take into town to sell at the market."

She spun round to look at him. "There's a market?"

He was facing away from her, expertly scooping up

several eggs with one hand and apparently oblivious to her excitement at this news. "Every Wednesday."

She tried to sound casual, but it wasn't in her nature and instead she was sure she sounded slightly breathless. "Could I come?"

He glanced back at her. Even in the gloomy interior of the henhouse she could tell he was fighting a smile. "I was just about to suggest you might like to."

"Oh I would, very much. Like to."

"All right then." He went back to collecting eggs.

Lizzy moved to the next nest along, a huge smile stretching her face.

Having collected two buckets' worth of eggs, they returned to the house and carried them into the kitchen. Mrs. Lassiter was by the sink, peeling potatoes. Her eyebrows shot up when they entered together. For some reason she didn't quite understand, Lizzy felt guilty.

"We brought eggs," she said, holding the heavy bucket she was carrying forward as evidence and internally wincing at her need to prove what she'd been doing.

"They go in the pantry," Mrs. Lassiter said and returned to her peeling.

Elijah gave Lizzy a small shrug and followed her to the pantry where they unloaded the eggs into a large wooden box in silence. When they walked back into the kitchen Mrs. Lassiter was still peeling. Lizzy briefly considered offering to help, but then she remembered how the older woman had reacted to the suggestion she could make her own breakfast.

"Lunch is at one," Mrs. Lassiter said without turning as they walked to the door.

"Yes, ma'am," Elijah said, opening the door for Lizzy.

"So what's next?" she said once they were back outside.

He seemed to study her, a speculative look on his face. "You truly want to help me?"

"Oh I do. If I'm not being too much trouble. I don't want to slow you down or anything." She meant what she said, but she desperately hoped he'd say yes. She was having fun.

"You're no trouble. It's nice having the c-c-c-company. I'm usually alone more or less all day."

She bounced a little on her toes. "Thank you. I'll do everything you say, I promise. I really want to be a help."

He nodded, pursing his lips. "Well, what do you say to helping me feed the pigs?"

She tried not to bounce again because it was childish to bounce. "I'd love to."

He started in the direction of the barn, Lizzy following. "There are piglets too."

She gasped in a thrilled breath. "Piglets?!"

CHAPTER 6

Lizzy blew out a sigh and watched it fog in a brief cloud on the window. She would have drawn a smiling face into it, but it faded too quickly.

On second thought, the way she was feeling it would more probably have been a sad face.

She lowered her chin onto her hands resting on the windowsill and focused through the glass at the dim outlines of the trees across the yard. There was no getting past the fact that it was now thoroughly dark and Richard wasn't back yet. He'd said he was going to be back before it got dark to show her around the ranch. She'd come inside sooner than she wanted so she could wash up and change into a clean dress and tidy her hair, just so she'd be ready when he returned. But he hadn't.

She'd been waiting for two hours now. Mrs. Lassiter had left more than an hour before. And still no Richard.

She sighed again and closed her eyes.

She was trying not to be angry, but it wasn't easy when she was this confused and upset. So she'd only arrived the day before, but was it too much to ask that he should at least make some effort to spend some time with her? Or at the very least talk to her. It felt as if he didn't want to be around her at all. In the admittedly short time she'd been at the ranch she'd spent far more time with Elijah than she had with her own husband.

At the thought of Elijah, her anger faded and a small

smile crept onto her face. It had been the most fun day she'd had in ages, what with the chickens and piglets and working on the vegetable garden. She'd even milked a cow. Well, under his guidance she'd *tried* to milk one of their four dairy cows. It hadn't gone particularly well and now her arms ached, but she'd enjoyed it anyway. Though she wasn't sure the cow would agree. Lizzy could have sworn that at one point the huge beast had rolled its eyes at her. When she told Elijah he'd burst into laughter. He seemed to laugh often, which made her laugh often.

She'd had a wonderful day.

But she'd left Elijah early to get ready. Tired as she was from everything they'd done, she'd wanted to stay with him. Maybe she could have gone to the pond again. She didn't know how often he went, but he may have been there.

But now it was too late and here she was, sitting at the living room window with her head on her hands, waiting for Richard like a dog waiting for its master.

Huffing out an irritated breath, she sat up. Why was she even waiting? It was too dark for him to show her any of the ranch now anyway. She might as well do something else.

Standing, she looked around the room, as much as she could in the gloom. She hadn't lit any lamps and it was now more or less completely dark inside. A shiver ran down her spine. Logic told her there was nothing to fear, but she'd never been good at being alone.

She glanced back outside, her eyes drawn to the light of the bunkhouse windows. Elijah was probably there. It wouldn't be proper for her to be in there with him alone, but maybe one or two of the other men were there too. They'd seemed very nice when she met them the day before. Surely they wouldn't mind her intruding, just for a little while until Richard got home.

Her decision made, she wrapped her shawl around her

shoulders and headed for the kitchen, only hitting her shin on the furniture once in the relatively unfamiliar room, which she regarded as a victory. She managed to make it through the kitchen to the back door without any more mishaps and stepped out into the chilly evening air, pulling her shawl more tightly around her.

Outside, the night was alive with sound. Lizzy had never noticed how loud the darkness could be, never having been in it alone, but now she found herself surrounded by crickets and rustles and hoots and snuffling and even a distant howl that made the hairs on the back of her neck shiver. It was at once both fascinating and terrifying and she was torn between lingering to hear the peculiar song of the night and running as fast as she could to the safety of the bunkhouse.

A high pitched *yip yip* sound and the rapid beating of wings nearby made the decision for her and she took off across the yard, only slowing when she reached the bunkhouse door. She gulped in some air, smoothed her skirt, waited ten seconds for her heart to slow, and raised her hand to knock.

The door opened and Amos Hopkins looked down at her in surprise. Her nerves calmed a little. She hadn't spoken to him any more than the others, but he seemed nice, and he was around her father's age which somehow made him more comforting.

"Mrs. Shand, come in. Is everything all right?"

"Oh, yes, I just wondered if..." The first thing she saw on stepping inside was Elijah lounging on a bed in the far corner of the room, a black, leather-bound Bible open on his chest. Relief washed through her. "I wondered if I could join you for a while, if I'm not intruding? It's kind of lonely over in the house all by myself."

He shut the book and sat up. "Isn't M-Mr. Shand back

yet?"

"No."

"Well you can stay just as long as you want," Amos said. "Come and take a seat. Would you like some coffee?"

She took the seat at the table he indicated. "Only if you have some around. Don't make any just on my account."

"Mrs. Shand," Amos said, walking to a small stove against one wall, "this here is a bunkhouse. You may not know much about bunkhouses, you being a refined lady and all, but the one thing you can always count on there being in a bunkhouse is a pot of coffee. And you're in luck because this particular one was made by me and I officially make the best coffee."

Elijah stood and placed his Bible down on the bed. There were ten beds arranged around the walls, but his corner was by far the tidiest in the general mess of the all male domicile. It was like a little oasis amidst the clutter, bed made neatly, clothes hung on pegs on the wall. There was even a shelf above the bed filled with books and she saw titles on engineering, mathematics and physics. There was no doubt it was Elijah's space.

"Where is everyone else?" she said as he slid into a chair opposite her.

"Either with their families or girls or... other p-p-people," he said. "What with Sunday being our day off, they mostly go out Saturday nights."

"And you don't have anyone to visit?" Was that prying? She didn't want to seem nosey.

"All my family's back in Idaho."

"You don't have a sweetheart to go see?" Even though there was a shortage of women, she was sure a handsome man like Elijah must have had his pick of those there were.

He dropped his gaze to the table top. "No, not m-me."

"Unattached ladies out here tend to not remain

unattached for too long, and there's fierce competition," Amos said. "Sugar?"

"Three, please. I suppose that is why I'm here."

"Remember about Carl and Ethan Lawson, Elijah?"

He chuckled, shaking his head. "Yeah."

"Who are Carl and Ethan Lawson?" she asked, intrigued.

Amos returned to the table, placing steaming cups in front of her and Elijah. "Twins, live on the other side of town," he said as he sat. "A closer pair of brothers you would never have found."

"Until C-Cornelia," Elijah said.

"Cornelia?"

"Her family moved here from somewhere around Sacramento 'bout two years ago," Amos said. "She was nineteen and both Carl and Ethan were besotted the moment they laid eyes on her. You'd never believe two young men could go from friends to enemies so quick."

"They had a f-fist fight in church over who got to fetch her a hymnal," Elijah said, laughing. "Mrs. Jones just waded in between them, grabbed an ear in each hand, and marched them outside."

Amos grinned. "Can't say that wasn't fun to watch."

"So what happened?" Lizzy said. "Which one of them won her heart?"

"Neither," Elijah said. "While they were b-b-busy fighting over her, Sam Emerson, who was visiting his brother, he met Cornelia and they f-fell in love."

"Emerson," she said. "Is he Adam's brother?"

"That's him," Amos said. "Sam and Cornelia were married not a month later. Last I heard, they had a baby boy and were happy as anything. They have a house on Adam's parents' farm."

"So what happened to Carl and Ethan?"

"They spent about a month not speaking and blaming each other until they finally realized they were both in the same boat and forgave each other. But that was an entertaining couple of months. Barely a day went by when they didn't get into some kind of trouble. Marshal Cade even had to step in a couple of times." Amos shook his head, chuckling. "Not much can make a young man lose his senses more than a girl."

She couldn't help but wonder when that theory would pan out with Richard. So far he seemed to be holding onto his senses without any trouble at all.

"I imagine you had quite a few suitors before you decided to come out here," Amos said. "Pretty girl like you."

From any other man it would have sounded highly improper, like a compliment designed to get her attention, but in addition to his age Amos had a fatherly air. She guessed he needed it, surrounded by much younger, unmarried men as he always was.

"A few from the university where my father teaches," she said, shrugging. "Nothing serious. I always wanted more than to just marry and settle down and have babies."

"Adventure in the w-wild west," Elijah said with a smile.

She grinned back, gave him a solid nod, and said, "Yup."

~ ~ ~

By the time the knock sounded on the bunkhouse door, it was close to nine.

She probably should have returned to the house earlier, but she was having too much fun listening to Amos and Elijah's stories of life on the ranch.

She couldn't help but notice, though, that Amos did

most of the talking. During their time at the pond the previous night and today as they worked together, Elijah hadn't seemed to hold back on speaking to her. It was true he didn't talk as much as she did, but then most people didn't talk as much as she did. But with another person around he seemed content to let Amos be the one to speak, for the most part. She wondered if it was due to his stutter and she longed to ask but didn't want to appear rude. She hoped one day he'd tell her about it. He also didn't talk at all about his life before coming to the ranch. She longed to know about that too.

Amos talked about Richard as a child, however, which was endlessly entertaining. Her husband had got into more than his fair share of scrapes growing up, it seemed.

So although a little voice in the back of her mind suggested she might be outstaying her welcome, she'd remained despite the late hour. Right now, to Elijah's good natured exasperation, Amos was telling her about the time Elijah had been cornered by an angry mother cow who objected to his treating her injured calf, and she wanted to know how it ended.

"So what did he do then?" she said as Amos rose to answer the knock at the door.

"He leaped athletically over the f-f-fence to safety," Elijah said.

"That's exactly what he did," Amos said with a smirk, "if athletically means he panicked, fell over, scrambled for the fence, missed being kicked by an inch, and landed in a puddle of mud on the other side."

"You poor thing," she said, struggling to contain a giggle.

"It was a very deep, very m-muddy puddle," Elijah said solemnly.

She nodded, attempting to appear sympathetic, and

clamped her mouth shut when a squeak of laughter escaped.

His solemn expression turned to a smile as they looked at each other.

"Elizabeth?"

She jumped at the sound of her name and looked round at Richard standing in the doorway. She was surprised to see him, having enjoyed her evening so much she'd forgotten she'd been waiting for him.

"Evening, Richard," Amos said. "While you were out, your lovely wife has been delighting us with her company."

He was smiling, but Lizzy didn't miss the edge in his tone, as if he was scolding the younger man. She wondered if Richard would be angry at such insubordination, but instead he managed to look chastised.

"Sorry about that."

"Well, I suppose I'd better be going," she said, wrapping her shawl around her shoulders.

Elijah stood and moved to pull out her chair.

"Thank you for letting me stay," she said. "I had a wonderful time."

"You're welcome to c-come round any time." Elijah said with a smile that told her he meant it.

"You sure are, Mrs. Shand," Amos added. "You'll always be welcome here."

His words gave her a warm sense of belonging she had yet to experience in the main house. "Thank you. I appreciate that very much."

Richard hadn't moved from the door and after bidding Elijah and Amos a good night she walked over to him as he stepped outside.

She followed Richard towards the house, looking back at the bunkhouse when they'd gone a little way. Elijah stood in the open doorway, waving when she saw him. She waved back and looked at her husband. He didn't seem to have noticed.

When they got inside, he lit the lamps and Lizzy walked into the living room. Seeing the chair by the window where she'd waited for him to return for two hours reminded her that she was angry at him.

"I waited for you," she said as he replaced a lamp cover and a warm glow spread through the room. "You said you'd be back before dark."

"I'm really sorry," he replied, not looking at her. "I promise we'll do something together tomorrow."

She swallowed a sigh. It was clear he wasn't going to tell her where he'd been and, much as she wanted to, she wasn't going to become one of those wives who needed to know where her husband was every second of every day. If he kept his promise, things would be better tomorrow.

Besides, she'd enjoyed her evening. When she really thought about it, she didn't feel at all disappointed he hadn't come home. It made her sad to feel that way, but she was too tired to want to talk about it.

"Well, I'm going to bed," she said, picking up a lamp and walking to the door. "Goodnight."

"Elizabeth?"

She looked back at him.

He rubbed one hand across his face. "I truly am sorry. I didn't mean to leave you alone." At least he sounded sincere.

She nodded and gave him a small smile. "It's all right."

And it was, she thought as she walked up the stairs to her bedroom. They'd spend time together tomorrow and things would get better.

CHAPTER 7

Lizzy arrived downstairs to the sounds of breakfast - men's voices, cutlery clinking on dishes, Mrs. Lassiter's occasional exhortation to "Close your mouth while you're chewing. Were you raised in a barn?"

Even though she'd been introduced to the ranch hands two days before, she felt a little intimidated by the prospect of being in a more social setting with all of them at once. But she was a rancher's wife now so she'd better get used to it. And Richard would look after her, she was certain.

Pushing her shoulders back, she reached for the kitchen door handle.

"Well, they *are* newlyweds." She recognized Eugene's voice. "It ain't a surprise they're late for breakfast, if you know what I mean!"

Lizzy froze as raucous laughter erupted beyond the door.

"Hey! Show s-s-some respect."

She breathed out at the sound of Elijah coming to her defense. Evidently Richard wasn't in there, but she had someone who was on her side.

Eugene yelped. "Ouch!"

"Elijah's right," Mrs. Lassiter's voice said. "I'll have no talk like that in my kitchen. Apologize."

"To who?"

"To us decent folk. And to God."

"But... all right, all right. Just don't hit me again. I'm

sorry."

"And the rest of you who laughed," Mrs. Lassiter said.

There were a few mumbled apologies.

Lizzy decided this was the best time to enter if she was going to make their embarrassment as acute as possible, which was what she very much wanted to do. She squared her shoulders again, grasped the handle, and swept into the kitchen.

Seven pairs of eyes looked up at her. She suddenly and inexplicably wished she hadn't worn the brightest, most yellow dress she owned.

"Good morning," she said, attempting to exude an air of confidence.

There was a smattering of muted replies.

No one seemed to want to meet her gaze, except for Elijah who said, "Good morning, Mrs. Shand."

She felt instantly more at peace for seeing his smiling face.

"Have a seat, Mrs. Shand," Mrs. Lassiter said without turning from the range.

Lizzy started towards her. "I can help..."

"No need. I got everything under control. You just sit yourself down and have some breakfast before church."

Lizzy came to a halt halfway across the kitchen. She looked at Mrs. Lassiter at the range and then at the table surrounded by men, feeling her shoulders slump a little. There didn't seem to be anywhere she belonged.

And then Elijah stood from his seat at the end of the table. "W-would you like to sit here?"

She wanted to hug him. "Thank you."

She hurried over to the table where he stood behind the chair and he pushed it in behind her as she sat. Then he took his plate and looked pointedly at Anson next to him. It took Anson a couple of seconds to grasp what Elijah was wordlessly telling him to do and he shuffled along the bench, forcing Alonzo and Herman to move to make room for him. Everyone moved their plates along and Elijah sat closest to Lizzy.

The eating resumed. In silence.

Mrs. Lassiter placed a full plate on the table in front of Lizzy and returned to the range.

She stared down at the pile of bacon, biscuits, eggs and gravy. Like the morning before, it looked enough to feed her plus two other people. Two other very large people. She couldn't help wondering how Mrs. Lassiter would react if she didn't eat it all. There wasn't much chance of her being able to get rid of it this time, surrounded by people.

Elijah leaned towards her. "Something wrong?" he whispered.

"I don't think I can eat all this," she whispered back, glancing at Mrs. Lassiter to make sure she wasn't watching.

He followed her gaze and nodded in understanding. Quietly, he slid his plate next to hers and motioned with his fork between the two. Smiling gratefully, she transferred more than half of the food from her plate onto his.

He pulled the plate back in front of him and nudged Anson next to him. When he looked at him, Elijah nodded at his plate and pointed to his. Again it took him a few seconds to understand, then he pushed his plate next to Elijah's and Elijah moved the majority of the food Lizzy had given him over.

As she watched, her breakfast silently made its way around the whole table until the excess was distributed between all seven men. Each one of them glanced at her with a smile or a nod and went back to eating.

She covered her own smile with her fingers and gave Elijah a look of gratitude. He winked back.

"This is delicious, Mrs. Lassiter," she said after her first mouthful of what remained on her plate. She had to try something to get on the woman's good side, wherever that was. And the food was tasty.

Mrs. Lassiter glanced back at her, nodded her acknowledgement, and went back to moving the cooking pans to the sink.

Lizzy sighed and returned her attention to her food. Clearly compliments weren't going to be enough.

The door to the hallway opened and Richard walked in. Her heart gave a little excited jump at the sight of him.

The men around the table paused in their chewing to greet him with "Morning, Boss," or "Mr. Shand," or "Sir," before returning to the important task of eating.

"Morning," he said as he walked over to the range where Mrs. Lassiter was removing a loaded plate from the oven. "Good morning, Mrs. Lassiter. Breakfast smells good as always."

For the first time since Lizzy had entered the room, the older woman's face stretched into a smile as she looked up at him. The smile immediately vanished. "You look tired. Are you getting enough sleep?"

Eugene sniggered softly. Elijah gave him a warning look.

"I'm just fine," Richard said, taking the dish from her hands. "You don't need to worry about me."

She gave his cheek a motherly pat. "Yes, I do."

He carried his food to the table. If everyone moved along there would be plenty of room on the bench opposite Elijah for him to sit by her and she looked up at him expectantly as he approached the table.

He nodded to her. "Good morning, Elizabeth."

"Good morning, Richard," she replied, giving him her best smile to let him know she was pleased to see him.

Her smile faded as he walked past her to the far end of the table and sat.

He asked Amos a question and conversation began around the table. She swallowed and looked down at her food. She was being silly, she told herself. He'd only sat away from her at the table. It wasn't like he'd yelled at her or anything.

And yet it somehow felt worse. At least if he yelled he'd be showing some kind of emotion towards her.

From the corner of her eye she noticed Elijah watching her and when she glanced up at him she saw sympathy in his eyes. She hadn't said anything to him about Richard's lack of attention, in fact Richard hadn't come up at all in any of their conversations, but somehow Elijah knew there was something wrong.

She gave him a small smile to reassure him that she was fine.

Even though, deep down, she didn't feel that way.

~ ~ ~

Lizzy and Richard took the buggy into town for church, with Amos driving the wagon, Mrs. Lassiter at his side, and Elijah and the rest of the men in the back.

Lizzy had made up her mind that she was going to get Richard talking if it was the last thing she did, so she was glad of the time alone with him. In fact, other than the journey from the station to the house two days previously, it was the longest time they'd spent together since she'd arrived.

The trouble was, once they got going she couldn't think of anything to say. It was a problem she was completely unaccustomed to.

After ten minutes or so of awkward silence, Richard cleared his throat. It made her jump.

"I thought we could, I mean I planned to go and visit my

79

folks after church, spend the afternoon with them," he said.

She wasn't sure how to respond, or even what that meant. Would she be going with him? "Oh?"

He glanced at her for a moment before looking back at the road ahead of them. "They'll be pleased to meet you."

She breathed out in relief and smiled. "Oh. Yes. I'm looking forward to meeting them too." Taking her to meet his parents had to be a good sign. "Do they live far?"

"About an hour's ride in the buggy."

Unreasoning panic gripped her. If she couldn't even fill ten minutes with conversation, how was she going to cope with two hours?

She shook her head in annoyance. This was ridiculous. She'd been wanting to spend time with her new husband, this was the perfect opportunity.

She was married to Richard. It was about time she started acting like it.

"So what's their ranch like?"

~ ~ ~

There was a crowd of people in front of the church when they arrived.

For a few seconds Lizzy thought something unusual must have happened, until she realized they were simply socializing, the adults gathered into chatting groups while laughing children ran and played in between. It was very different at her church in Ithaca; when you arrived you went straight in and found your seat, which was usually the seat you sat in every week and had done since you were born. Here you seemed to arrive and greet all your friends. Lizzy liked it. Having experienced less than forty-eight hours on a ranch far away from town, she could understand why. It got lonely away from other people. Without Elijah she'd have been losing her mind already.

Mrs. Lassiter and the men piled out of the wagon while Richard helped Lizzy from the buggy, then Amos and Alonzo drove the carriages round to the back of the church where the horses would be left for the service.

Lizzy looked around for any of her friends but couldn't see Sara, Amy, Jo or Louisa. Richard introduced her to a few people and she happily joined in the conversations, but her eyes were drawn to Elijah. He, Anson and Eugene had joined a group of young men whose primary occupations seemed to be laughing and exchanging glances with a nearby gathering of young women. Elijah stood on the periphery, hands in his pockets and only speaking occasionally. She wondered if his stutter made him uncomfortable speaking in large groups. The thought made her want to go over and talk to him, just so he wouldn't feel alone.

He turned his gaze to her and, seeing her watching him, smiled and raised his hand.

"Elizabeth?"

She looked round at Richard. "Hmm?"

"I said, would you like to go in now?"

She hadn't heard him. "Oh, yes, sorry." She waved to Elijah and then followed Richard to the church entrance.

Just inside the door, welcoming the congregants, she was glad to see Mr. and Mrs. Goodwin. "Mrs. Goodwin, I wanted to thank you so much for your beef stew and dumplings on Friday. It was just about the most delicious thing I've ever tasted."

At a *harrumph* behind her, Lizzy turned and was horrified to see Mrs. Lassiter just outside the door. Her heart sank. She was certain Richard's housekeeper hadn't been anywhere near when she'd stepped inside.

"I-I mean..." She looked between the two sisters.

"Don't you mind that old woman," Mrs. Goodwin said.

"She's been jealous of me our entire lives. And you're a dear for saying how *delicious* my cooking is." She gave Mrs. Lassiter a pointed look.

Narrowing her eyes, Mrs. Lassiter stalked forward. "Harriet."

"Hester," Mrs. Goodwin replied.

Lizzy and Richard stepped back to allow Mrs. Lassiter past. When she was out of earshot, Lizzy leaned towards Mrs. Goodwin and lowered her voice. "I'm not sure your sister likes me very much and I think I just made it worse, but I meant it about your stew. It was wonderful."

Mrs. Goodwin laughed and gave her hand a pat. "It's true Hester can be a mite abrasive, but don't take it personally. She likes you just fine. She's like that to just about everyone, especially any woman in her kitchen. Believe me, I know that all too well."

"I'll try to remember that."

Mr. Goodwin removed his pipe from his mouth just long enough to say, "Ma'am, Richard," and handed them each a hymnal.

~ ~ ~

Lizzy was thrilled to see her friends again, apart from Jo who hadn't come due to being unwell, her husband told them.

She spoke to Amy and Sara before the service and Louisa joined them afterwards. It felt like she hadn't seen them for ages, despite it being less than forty-eight hours. So much had happened since they arrived that she almost felt like a different person. She also got to properly meet Adam, Daniel and Jesse, all of whom were wonderful and exactly the men she would have chosen for her friends. Even though Amy and Louisa weren't yet married, Lizzy felt sure they would be soon. She could easily see their lives ahead of them, families, children, grandchildren, and it filled her with joy. She knew it would happen for all of them, including her. It might take a little time for Richard to warm to her, but it would happen.

When the crowd of churchgoers finally began to dissipate almost an hour after the close of the service, she said goodbye to her friends and looked around for Richard. Sara and Daniel passed in their wagon and she sighed happily as she waved to them. It was wonderful to see Sara so delighted with her new husband.

Having seen her and Daniel together, the way Sara wrapped her arm around his whenever they were side by side and the way his eyes lit up when he smiled at her, gave Lizzy hope for her own marriage. She and Richard could be like that one day. Maybe this trip to see his parents would be the start of their relationship blossoming into something beautiful like Sara had.

No, not maybe. It definitely would be. She'd prayed for them to become closer, all she needed was faith as small as a mustard seed. Richard would surely be easier to move than a mountain.

An image came to her of a giant hand pushing a mountain into the sea and then flicking Richard in after it and she raised a hand to her mouth to cover her giggle.

"Are you ready to leave?" Richard said behind her.

Startled, she spun to face him. "Nothing."

A faint line appeared between his brows. "I'm sorry?"

Clearing her throat, she lowered her hand. "Uh... nothing stopping us from leaving now. No. I mean yes, I'm ready."

"Right. Well, I'll bring the buggy round." He looked beyond her. "Elijah, will you look after her till I get back?"

Elijah stepped up beside her. "Sure will, Mr. Shand."

Richard nodded and headed for the rear of the church.

"So, you're g-going to meet his folks," Elijah said.

"Mm hmm."

"Nervous?"

"Of course not. Why would I be nervous?"

He raised one eyebrow in the way that always seemed to make her tell the truth, whether she intended to or not.

"Maybe a little. But that's natural, isn't it?"

He pushed his hands into his pockets. "I reckon. It's n-n-not something I've ever had to do."

She sighed and bit her lip. "Have you met them? Richard's parents?"

"A few times. They come to the ranch every now and then."

"Are they nice?"

He paused, looking to one side and frowning in a way that filled her with trepidation.

"What's that look for?" she gasped. "Are they awful? Are they judgmental and mean? They're going to hate me, aren't they."

He shook his head, a smile replacing his frown. "They're not awful and they'll love you. They just c-come across as a mite..." He looked up as if searching for the right word.

She tried not to sound too panicked, but she wasn't at all sure she succeeded. "A mite *what*?"

"They just like things done their way, is all."

She considered his words. That didn't sound so bad, as long as they were living an hour away and wouldn't come to visit too often. "I think I can probably deal with that." A thought occurred to her. "How does that work with Mrs. Lassiter?"

The corner of his mouth twitched. "I've never dared stick around long enough to find out."

She gasped in feigned shock, pressing a hand to her chest. "Why, Elijah, I never took you for a coward."

"I kn-know when to make a strategic retreat," he said.

She burst into laughter as he grinned, her nerves forgotten.

Richard arrived in the buggy at that moment, pulling alongside them. "What's funny?"

Elijah's eyes widened ever so slightly and he looked at the ground.

"The, um, sermon," Lizzy said. "What the pastor said about being wise. I thought it was very astute. It made me laugh."

Richard looked between the two of them and shrugged, apparently unconcerned.

Elijah shot her a small, grateful smile and she pressed her lips together to stop herself from giggling, feeling as if they were two naughty children who'd just got away with some nefarious deed.

"Well, I'm ready to go if you are," Richard said.

When he didn't make any move to help her into the buggy, Elijah offered her his hand, placing his other hand onto her back to steady her as she climbed up into the seat beside Richard.

She smiled down at him. "Thank you."

"Have a good afternoon," he said, glancing at Richard before giving her a covert wink.

She bit back another laugh, waving to him as the buggy started off.

As they turned a corner and she lost sight of him, she couldn't help wishing Elijah was going with her.

CHAPTER 8

"You and Elijah seem to be getting along well."

Lizzy tore her gaze from the beautiful scenery through which they were driving and looked at Richard beside her, unsure if he was accusing her of something. But his expression held no anger as he watched the road ahead.

"He's been teaching me about the animals and the garden," she said. "I'm enjoying helping him, although I'm not sure how much help I actually am. I have a lot to learn, but he's very patient. I like working with the animals."

He glanced at her briefly before returning his attention to the road. "You don't have to work. I'll give you anything you need."

Other than your attention, she thought but didn't say. "I enjoy it. Besides, I need something to do. Mrs. Lassiter won't let me do any cooking or cleaning or anything in the house."

He chuckled, the first time she'd heard him laugh. "She's like a force of nature, the way she looks after everything and cooks for me and the men. Works harder than any of us, I'd say."

Lizzy considered asking him to tell the force of nature to let her do something in the house but decided against it. She really did like working with Elijah and the animals and if she started doing more inside the house, she might never get out of it. Perhaps she'd be able to get Mrs. Lassiter to let her at least cook the odd cake here and there on her own. There had to be some way to get through to her.

"How long has she been working for you?"

"Over four years, almost since I bought the ranch. I needed someone to cook and clean, she needed a job after her husband died. It just fit. She's been taking care of us and bossing us around ever since."

That sounded like the Mrs. Lassiter Lizzy knew. "I didn't know her husband was gone. Did they have any children?"

"No. They were married more than twenty years, but young 'uns just never came along. I sometimes think me and the men are a bit like substitute children for her."

Lizzy felt awful for thinking badly of her. She could be trying harder to get to know her. "It's nice she has you."

He nodded slowly, his attention fixed on something in the distance, and murmured, "It goes both ways."

She followed his gaze and her eyes widened at what she saw ahead of them. On the crest of a hill to the left of the road three men sat on horses, unmoving. They were still a way away and she couldn't see their faces clearly, but she knew they were watching them. And she couldn't miss their long, black hair blowing in the wind and the rich sepia tone of their skin.

"Indians," she breathed with a mixture of fear and excitement.

"Yes."

"Are we in danger?"

"Probably not."

She'd met some Indians on the journey. Not the type she'd read about who would scalp her or shoot her with an arrow or abduct her so much as look at her. These ones were very nice, women mostly, who sold items they'd made to the passengers on the train during one of their stops. Lizzy had been fascinated and asked them question after question. She'd also bought a bracelet and a beautiful knitted shawl.

And then of course there was Kosumee who was lovely and not frightening in the least.

But the ones up ahead looked like proud warriors, sitting tall and imposing on their horses, the sun shimmering on their bare chests. She desperately wanted to see them up close, maybe even talk to them. So she hoped they weren't the scalping type.

They kept going until they were closer and he pulled to the side of the road and stopped, setting the brake on the buggy and reaching behind him. Her stomach clenched when he pulled forward a rifle, suddenly less concerned with meeting her first Indian warriors and more concerned with getting away with her life.

"Richard...?"

"It's all right," he said, his eyes on the men up ahead. "Just stay here. I'll find out what they want."

"You're *leaving* me?!"

"Just for a minute or two. You'll be safe, I promise." He jumped to the ground.

"What about you?"

He looked up at her and smiled. "I'll be safe too. Don't worry, I wouldn't put you in any danger."

She nodded, even though she was far from reassured. Although it did feel good to know he cared about her, even just a little.

He made his way through the long grass towards the hill and she looked around, searching for any others who might be sneaking up on them. The terrain was fairly open, but a suspicious looking bush caught her attention. She kept one eye on it and the other on Richard as he climbed to where the three men still sat motionless on their horses, ready to shout a warning if the bush made any sudden movements.

When he reached the Indians, one of them slid to the ground and spoke, gesticulating towards the buggy. Lizzy's heart leaped into her throat. They didn't want her, did they? She'd heard stories of how Indians prized white women's hair and thought it would give them magical powers if they took them as a wife. Although she'd also heard that was only blonde hair. Her hair was almost as dark as any Indian woman's, but maybe it was the curls they were after.

The Indian man's gestures became more agitated as the conversation, or possibly argument, progressed. She could hear Richard's voice raised in anger but couldn't make out the words from where she was. He looked up at one of the two on horseback and pointed at him. He raised his hands, palms out, looking for all the world like he was trying to avoid getting involved. Richard moved his attention back to the man standing who was again motioning at Lizzy.

Eventually, Richard's hands went to his waist and he looked down at the ground between them. The voices went silent. For a few seconds nothing happened. Then Richard shook his head, said something, and turned away, heading back down the hill.

The Indian warrior watched him for a while before climbing back onto his horse and speaking to the other two.

"Is everything all right?" she said as soon as Richard reached the buggy.

He replaced the rifle behind the seat and climbed up beside her. "We're fine. I know them. They live on the reservation, not far from the ranch."

She looked up at the three men. "They didn't seem very happy to see you."

He smiled a little and shook his head. "It was an old argument, about where my cattle are ranging. We worked it out. Everything's fine, you don't have to worry."

He seemed more relaxed than he'd been before he spoke to them so she assumed it was true. "Could I meet them?"

He stared at her, his eyebrows raised in surprise.

"I've never met a real life Indian warrior before," she said, shrugging.

He chuckled. "Maybe next time."

He urged the horses on again and she gave a small sigh of disappointment. Noticing the Indians watching them pass, she raised her hand in a wave.

None of them waved back.

~ ~ ~

They arrived at Richard's parents' ranch half an hour later.

At least, he told Lizzy they'd reached their land. It took another half an hour to get to the house. The place was huge.

The home was as sprawling as the property and immaculate gardens and a small city of outbuildings surrounded the house. It was set over only one storey which probably made it appear larger than it was, but Lizzy nevertheless thought she might get lost in it.

"It's so big," she said as they approached along a tree-lined drive between fenced pastures where horses lifted their heads from the grass to watch them pass.

"Yeah," was all he said in response.

She didn't miss the hint of tension in his voice. "Is something wrong?"

"No, I'm fine. I just don't come back here very often."

She thought about her own family. "Don't you miss your mother and father and your brother and sisters?"

He drew in a deep breath before answering. "Yes and no. I grew up here and I love the ranch. All I ever wanted to do from when I was small was have my own ranch. Spent every moment I could with the hands and the cattle, learned everything there was to know about running a place like this."

"Mr. Hopkins said he worked for your parents for a long

time."

The tension faded from his expression and he smiled. "Amos was here from before I was born. It was almost like having another father, I spent so much time with him. I learned all the business side of things from my father, but Amos taught me about the cattle."

"So you asked him to work for you?"

"Not exactly," he said, smiling. "I was planning on it, but before I could he just said to me one day, 'I'm coming with you. No way I'm letting you go off by yourself to mess things up.' And that was that."

After spending time with Amos the evening before, Lizzy could believe that of him. "I like Mr. Hopkins."

"So do I."

He brought the buggy to a halt at the end of a path leading to the front porch of the house, set the brake and jumped to the ground. He stood for a few moments looking off into the distance. Watching his back, she saw his shoulders rise and fall with a deep breath. If she hadn't known better, she would have thought he was afraid to be home.

But then he turned and smiled up at her. "Well, are you ready to meet my parents?"

Her stomach curled in on itself. "Yes. No. I don't know. I'm afraid they won't like me."

He walked around the buggy and reached up to help her down. "Oh, they'll like you. You don't have to worry about that."

A strange, almost bitter expression flashed across his face as he spoke and she would have asked him about it, but at that moment the door to the house opened and her nerves wiped the thought from her mind. In fact, they seemed to wipe every thought from her mind as a slender, elegant blonde woman emerged from the house and walked towards them, smiling.

Lizzy was suddenly conscious of the dust she'd accumulated during the journey. And her clothing. And her hair. And her... everything. She brushed at her skirt, wishing she'd had the chance to check her appearance in a mirror before they arrived.

"Richard, this is a surprise," the woman said, giving him a fleeting and somewhat lukewarm hug and then settling her gaze on Lizzy.

"Good afternoon, Mother," he said. "Is Father in?"

"He's in his office, as usual. Are you going to introduce us?"

Richard looked at Lizzy. "Uh, yes. Elizabeth, this is my mother, Florence Shand. Mother, this is Elizabeth, my wife."

Lizzy didn't expect him to gush over her introduction to her new mother-in-law, but the way he said 'my wife', his tone flat, caught her off guard.

Mrs. Shand's mouth dropped open. "Your *wife*? When did you get married?"

Lizzy glanced at him in confusion. Surely he'd told his parents she was coming? He'd proposed weeks ago. They'd been corresponding for months before that.

He met her eyes for a brief moment before looking at the ground. "Friday."

Although she had not the slightest idea what was going on, Lizzy decided she needed to rescue the situation if she was going to gain any kind of approval at all from Richard's family. And since he didn't seem inclined to help her.

She stepped forward, smiling and holding out her hand. "Good afternoon, Mrs. Shand. It's a pleasure to meet you. You have a beautiful home."

Mrs. Shand seemed to collect herself and a smile spread over her face. She took Lizzy's hand in both of hers. "Forgive me, my son neglected to mention he was getting married. But

I am very pleased to meet you."

Lizzy patted at her hair self-consciously. "I'm sorry, I must look a fright. It was a long, dusty journey."

"Oh no, not at all," she said warmly. "And you are lovely. My son is a lucky man. Don't you agree, Richard?" She raised her eyebrows in his direction.

"Yes, Mother." He gave Lizzy a small smile that didn't reach his eyes.

"Take the buggy around to the barn. John should be in there. He'll take care of your horses." Mrs. Shand turned her back on her son and placed her arm around Lizzy's shoulders. "I'm sure you must be thirsty. I believe our cook, Maisie, made a fresh batch of lemonade this morning. And you must meet my husband. He'll be thrilled to hear Richard has finally decided to settle down..."

She continued to talk as she guided Lizzy in the direction of the house. Lizzy glanced back at Richard to see him watching them, a frown on his face. She couldn't help but feel confused and a little apprehensive. It wasn't exactly how she'd pictured meeting her husband's parents.

The inside of the house was as immaculate as the outside. They entered into a large central foyer with half wood paneling and printed wallpaper, a style that wouldn't have been out of place in any house in the city.

A young woman dressed in a maid's uniform emerged from a door ahead of them.

"Mary," Mrs. Shand said, "would you tell Maisie we have two more for dinner and fetch us three glasses of lemonade? Thank you."

"Yes, ma'am." The woman bobbed a curtsy and hurried back through the door.

The formality took Lizzy by surprise. She hadn't expected to encounter such behavior in the west, especially on a cattle ranch, although on reflection she realized there was no real reason to her thinking She'd just had an idea that everything would be more... uncivilized. She'd been looking forward to it.

Leaving Lizzy by the front door, Mrs. Shand walked to a door part-glazed with stained glass to their right and knocked.

From inside, a deep male voice answered, "Yes?"

"Please excuse me, I'll be right back." With a smile at Lizzy, Mrs. Shand slipped inside, closing the door behind her.

For half a minute all she could hear were muffled voices, too low for her to make out. She was dying to creep to the door and listen, but she didn't want to be caught eavesdropping.

The front door opened behind her and she turned to see Richard step inside.

His eyes darted around the room before settling on her. "Where...?"

She pointed to the door Mrs. Shand had gone through.

He nodded. "Father's office. She just left you here alone?"

"I think she's warning him," she whispered. "Why didn't you tell them about me?"

He sighed and pushed his hands into his pockets. "I'm sorry. Can we talk about it later?"

She wanted to know *now* why her husband had kept her a secret, but at that moment the door to the office opened and Mrs. Shand walked out. Lizzy clamped her mouth shut.

Behind Mrs. Shand emerged a man with light brown hair and a neatly trimmed beard and moustache. Even though he must have been in his fifties, he was still handsome, with piercing blue eyes and a strong posture. Richard clearly took after his father.

Mr. Shand approached and held out his hand. "Elizabeth, it's a pleasure to meet you, even if I wasn't aware

94

of your existence until my wife informed me just now." He cast a remonstrating look at Richard and then smiled as Lizzy took his hand. "Welcome to our family."

"Thank you, sir."

Releasing her hand, Mr. Shand moved his gaze to his son. Richard stared back at him. Lizzy, feeling a little like she was caught in between two bulls facing off, dropped her eyes to the floor and wondered if anyone would notice if she sidled away.

"Elizabeth," Mrs. Shand said, walking up to her, "would you like to freshen up after your journey? Dinner won't be served for another hour or so."

She breathed a silent *thank you* for the opportunity to escape. "I would like that very much, thank you."

As Mrs. Shand led her away, Lizzy didn't miss the look she threw her husband and son.

She was taken, wonder of wonders, to a bathroom, complete with a bathtub and basin with running water. As she washed her face and hands and re-pinned her hair, she wondered if this was what Elijah had in mind when he talked about a bathroom for the house at Richard's ranch. A bathtub with running water, even better, *heated* running water, would be a wonderful addition to her new home. She decided to ask him more about it when they were next at the pond.

Staring at herself in the mirror, she paused. She hadn't realized it, but she'd been hoping to go back ever since Friday. Would Elijah mind her intruding on his time again? She hoped not. She wasn't the kind of person who was happy with her own company and with Richard working so much and Mrs. Lassiter apparently hating her, her options were limited. She'd just try to be sensitive to any clues that he didn't want her around.

She shook her head and rolled her eyes at herself. Here she was in Richard's childhood home and she was thinking about spending time with Elijah. If things went well here maybe Richard would take the time to be with her more and she wouldn't have to pester Elijah for company.

She dried her hands on the towel Mrs. Shand had given her and headed back out into the hallway. Her hostess was nowhere to be seen, but she could hear voices so she headed in that direction and quickly found herself back in the central hall.

The voices were coming from Mr. Shand's office and this time she didn't have to eavesdrop to hear what they were saying.

"...without any warning! You could have at least told us you had placed an advertisement for a bride," Mr. Shand almost shouted.

"What must she have thought of us not having any notion you were even considering getting married?" Mrs. Shand said.

"What are you complaining about?" Richard sounded angry. "You told me to get married, I got married! She's exactly what you wanted. I don't know why you're surprised, since you pretty much forced me into it."

Lizzy gasped, her hand flying to her mouth.

"We just want to know why you didn't tell us," Mrs. Shand said.

"He didn't tell us because he's trying to punish us for looking after his best interests."

There was a long pause before Richard answered his father. When he did, his voice was filled with bitterness. "Well that's the joke, isn't it? The thought that you care about my best interests, much less know what they are."

Hearing footsteps, Lizzy darted back into the corridor, out of sight of the door to the office. She heard it open moments later and the front door after that. Not wanting to chance anyone finding her, she fled back to the bathroom and locked the door behind her.

She pressed both hands to her chest and slumped against the wall, her breath coming in short, shallow gasps.

Richard hadn't married her because he wanted her; he'd married her because his parents told him to find a wife. She'd come all the way across the country to marry a man who probably couldn't stand the sight of her. No wonder he didn't want to spend any time with her. All he felt towards her was resentment, she'd heard it in his voice as clear as day.

All her dreams of a life of love and excitement were crushed with just a few overheard words.

What would she do now?

Tears burned at her eyes and she pushed away from the wall and went to the basin to splash cold water onto her face. Her hands were shaking and she clenched them into fists. She couldn't fall apart, not here.

A knock on the door startled her. She swallowed and called out, "Yes?"

"Are you all right, Elizabeth?" It was Mrs. Shand.

Lizzy grabbed the towel and rapidly dabbed at her eyes. "Yes, I'm... one moment."

Checking her face in the mirror, she was relieved to at least see no telltale trace of redness around her eyes.

She stared at her reflection and whispered, "You can do this." Then she drew in a deep breath, gave mirror image Lizzy a determined nod, and reached for the door handle.

Mrs. Shand was waiting for her when she opened it.

"I'm sorry," Lizzy said. "That took me a bit longer than I thought it would."

"That's quite all right, Elizabeth." She linked their arms and guided her along the corridor. "How would you like a tour of the gardens before we eat? They're so beautiful this time of year."

"That sounds lovely."

Lizzy dredged up what she hoped was a fairly convincing smile and tried to ignore her breaking heart.

~ ~ ~

Lizzy didn't see Richard again until he joined them for dinner an hour later. He greeted her with a friendly smile, something she would have been pleased to see just an hour before. Now she couldn't help thinking how insincere it was.

Did he hate her, she wondered. Did he regret ever placing the advertisement for a bride and answering the letter she'd taken so long to craft? Did he resent the time it took to write each reply? Did he wish he'd never asked her to be his wife? Did he dislike her so much that he dreaded even the thought of spending the rest of his life with her?

Logic told her he couldn't find her completely repulsive. She knew she was pretty, if not beautiful, and not awful to be around. It shouldn't be impossible for a man to at least consider her for marriage. And yet obviously that wasn't enough for Richard.

You pretty much forced me into it.

Somehow she managed to get through the meal, although afterwards she couldn't remember eating one single bite. She smiled, participated in the conversation, told Mr. and Mrs. Shand about her family and life back home. She avoided looking at Richard as far as she could, however. It hurt too much when she did and she was afraid they'd be able to see the pain in her eyes.

They stayed for another hour or so after the meal before Richard announced that they should leave if they wanted to get home before dark. Lizzy knew that wasn't strictly true, but she wasn't about to object. The whole charade was exhausting. She imagined it was doing the same to Richard, although she couldn't quite bring herself to feel any sympathy for him. Not now.

"You must come again soon," Mrs. Shand said as Richard helped Lizzy into the buggy and she settled onto her seat. "I know it wasn't the best of starts, but we truly are thrilled that you've married Richard. We know the two of you will be very happy."

Mr. Shand put his arm around his wife's waist. "We couldn't have chosen better for him ourselves."

Now she knew to look for it, Lizzy could see the tightening of Richard's mouth as his father spoke. Mr. and Mrs. Shand genuinely seemed to be pleased at their marriage. They were probably the only ones who were.

"Thank you for the lovely welcome," she replied, smiling. "It was so good to meet you. I've had a very interesting afternoon." If she looked at that statement from a certain angle, she could believe it.

Richard urged the horses into motion and Lizzy waved goodbye as they began the long drive home.

And it was indeed a long, long drive home. If she hadn't known any better, Lizzy would have guessed it was twice as far as the journey there, even though they took the same route. She and Richard barely spoke to each other which gave her time to think. Much of that time was spent debating whether or not she should tell Richard what she'd overheard.

Part of her wanted to confront him, to ask why he'd proposed to her and how his parents could have forced him to wed when they didn't even know he was doing so. She wanted to ask him if in the whole thing he'd thought about her feelings at all. She also wanted to know what he intended for their future. Was this a marriage of convenience? Did he intend to try to make it work? Would he give love between them any thought at all? Did he really think so little of her?

She wanted to ask all of those things, but she didn't. And the reason she didn't, she suspected, was because she didn't really want to know the answers. She didn't want to sit there hearing how she would either be trapped in a marriage to a man who would never love her or have to endure the humiliation and shame of divorce followed by a life alone.

There was, of course, a chance she was wrong. Maybe he would come to love her in time. Maybe he just needed to let go of his resentment and once he did he would see that being married to her wasn't the worst thing in the world. Maybe she could still hang onto hope.

As long as she didn't give him the chance to tell her no.

So she sat silent as the horses plodded towards the place she'd thought would be a happy home and tried very hard not to cry.

CHAPTER 9

It was well past four by the time they arrived back at the ranch.

Richard brought the buggy to a halt in the yard and turned to Lizzy. "Are you all right? You've been so quiet."

She gave him a small smile. "Not like usual, you mean?"

The smile he gave her back could have been real. "That wasn't what I meant but... yes."

"It's just been a long day, I suppose."

For a moment he looked like he wanted to say something else, but he turned away and climbed from the buggy.

"It's Mrs. Lassiter's day off," he said as he helped Lizzy to the ground, "but she always leaves us something to eat."

"Mrs. Lassiter isn't here?" Despite her mood, she couldn't help feeling a frisson of excitement at the idea. "Does that mean I can bake?"

He blinked, looking confused. "You can bake whenever you want to."

"Tell Mrs. Lassiter that," she muttered under her breath.

"Pardon?"

"Nothing. It's just... nothing." At least for now, she had to live with Mrs. Lassiter. Tattling on her probably wasn't the way to get on her good side. "Will the men be coming for supper?"

"I don't know. It's their day off too so they don't always stay around. They usually tend to drift in and serve themselves whenever they feel like it. Mealtimes aren't at a set time like other days."

Not like when the dragon lady is here to keep them in line, she thought, then immediately felt guilty. *Sorry, Lord.* "Will you be eating here?"

He looked awkward, his gaze going past her. "I don't rightly know. With it being my ranch I don't get a day off. I have to check on the herd and..." He trailed off, still not looking at her.

She'd held out a little hope that something would be different, although why it would she didn't know.

"I understand." Not entirely the truth, but she wasn't about to beg him to stay.

He nodded and stepped towards the horses. "I'll get the buggy unhitched. Just ask if you need anything."

Lizzy wandered towards the house as he led the horses in the direction of the stables. Her eyes were drawn to the bunkhouse and she wondered if Elijah was there or if he had somewhere else to go on a Sunday. Surely he did something for fun other than go to the pond.

After changing out of her church clothes and washing off the dust from the journey, she went downstairs to the kitchen, coming to a halt in the center and turning in a slow circle. If only for today it was hers. All hers.

A smile spread across her face. She might be trapped in a loveless marriage to a man who couldn't stand to be around her, and she might be barred from doing anything in her own home for the rest of the week, but right now, at this moment, she could do whatever she wanted.

And what she wanted to do was bake.

Richard came in after fifteen minutes, went to change his clothes, and left again. Lizzy did her best to not let it spoil the fun she was having.

An hour and a half later she opened the oven door,

breathed in the combined aroma of apple sponge, ginger cake, and flannel cake, and smiled. Nothing could make her feel better like the scent of freshly baked cakes.

"I think that may be the most delicious smell that's ever graced my nostrils."

She straightened and looked round at Amos silhouetted in the doorway she'd left open to let out the heat of the oven. "Come on in. You have perfect timing, they're just ready."

He grinned and walked in, going to sit at the table. "My ma always used to say I could tell when food was ready from over a mile away."

She laughed as she pulled out the apple sponge with a dishcloth and placed it on the top of the range. "That must be a very useful skill to have."

"It's served me very well over the years."

She slid a fork into the center of the sponge and when it came out clean removed the ginger cake and flannel cakes as well. She transferred them onto cooling racks and picked up a knife.

"Would you like gingerbread, flannel cake, or apple sponge?"

He affected a hurt look. "You're gonna make me choose?"

"I don't know what I was thinking," she said, cutting a slice from each and arranging them together on a plate.

She took a slice of ginger cake for herself and carried the two plates to the table.

"Much obliged." He took a bite of the apple sponge, closing his eyes as he chewed. "Mrs. Shand, if you weren't already married, I'd marry you myself." He leaned forward and lowered his voice as if he might be overheard. "Don't tell Mrs. Lassiter, but this is even better than her molasses cake."

Grinning, Lizzy whispered, "My lips are sealed. And thank you."

They ate in silence for the time it took her to formulate the question she wanted to ask him. "Mr. Hopkins, Richard said you worked for his parents on their ranch before you came here with him."

"Sure did. Right from when their oldest, Mark, was still in diapers."

"So you know them pretty well?"

He shrugged one shoulder. "I reckon."

She took another bite of ginger cake and chewed for a few seconds. "Richard told me his brother and sisters are all happily married."

"Yup. Mark, Felicity and Helen are all real happy."

She nodded casually. "So... I suppose Mr. and Mrs. Shand were eager for Richard to marry too. What with him being twenty-eight already."

The slice of flannel cake paused for a split second in its journey to Amos' mouth. "I think they want what they think is best for him."

What *they think* is best for him. Not what *is* best for him, but what *they think* is best for him. Was his choice of words deliberate, she wondered, or simply a casual statement?

"Is anything wrong?"

Her eyes snapped to Amos' face and she realized she'd been staring at her half-empty plate for some time. "Wrong? Uh..."

She wanted to ask him about it, but he and Richard were close. She didn't want what she knew getting back to her husband, and she also didn't want to put Amos, who she liked a lot, in the position of having to lie for her.

"No, nothing's wrong. I was just wondering how they felt about him getting married is all."

"They do something to make you think you weren't welcome?" He was watching her now, the hand holding the flannel cake lying unmoving on his plate.

104

"Oh no, they were charming. Very friendly." She smiled. "It's a beautiful ranch."

His cake-holding hand resumed its work. "That it is."

"You ever think of having your own place?" she said, wanting to know more about him. "Richard said you taught him everything he knows about cattle. You must have more than enough experience to have your own."

"No doubt about that," he said. "But I never did have any ambition to have more than what the good Lord has given me. I'm content to be who I am. I ain't got no family to take care of so I don't need any more."

"Haven't you ever wanted a family? A wife and children to love?"

His gaze moved to the range although his eyes were unfocused, as if he was seeing something else. "There was a girl once. For her I wanted everything." He lowered his gaze and started eating again. "But it didn't work out and that was a very long time ago, before you were born I reckon. I don't think I was meant for love. But I don't mind. I'm happy with my life as it is."

Lizzy finished her last bite of ginger cake and rested her chin on her hand, gazing at the blue sky beyond the window. "I can't imagine going the rest of my life without having someone to love and who will love me. I've always dreamed of falling madly in love."

It was a few long seconds before he answered. "You're a good person, Mrs. Shand. I'm sure God has good things in store for you."

She didn't know whether it was because of his words or just the kindness with which he said them, or because of the afternoon as a whole, but she found herself feeling teary. She grabbed her plate and stood, turning away to hide her emotion.

"Would you like some more cake, Mr. Hopkins?"

"I'd be lying if I said no, but I think it's best if I stop at three slices." He pushed his chair back and stood.

"Um... is there anyone else around who might like some?" She tried to make the question sound nonchalant, but she really wanted to know if Elijah was home.

Amos stopped at the back door. "Most of the men are out, but Elijah's usually around someplace. I'm sure he'd appreciate a slice or three. If I see him, I'll tell him."

"Thank you, Mr. Hopkins."

He grinned and patted his stomach. "No ma'am, thank *you*."

She watched him stroll back to the bunkhouse and go inside, and then she waited. When after five minutes Elijah hadn't emerged, she guessed he wasn't there, so she hurried to cut three more slices of cake, wrapped them in a napkin, and stepped outside.

If he wasn't in the bunkhouse, she knew where he might be.

~ ~ ~

It was as if a huge weight lifted from Lizzy's shoulders the moment she reached the wood. Even though it was only the second time she'd been there, it felt safe, comforting. After the day she'd had, it was just where she needed to be.

A little of her usual mischievous nature returning, she crept up to the clearing, hiding herself behind a huge oak when she came in sight of Elijah where he sat on the rock by the pond. From where she stood she could see his profile, the light from the low sun filtering through the leaves of the surrounding trees enough to highlight the waves in his hair and glow over his cheekbones. His gaze was fixed on the paper on his lap, but then he raised his face to stare across the water and the light sparkled in his hazel eyes.

Lizzy imagined his mind working, thinking through some problem. She wished she could see it, watch the process like some giant three dimensional diagram displayed above his head, connecting ideas and theories and formulas with brightly colored lines and circles and arrows and images of machines with moving cogs and rods.

Becoming so engrossed in the idea, she failed to check the ground in front of her when she took a step forward to see him better.

A twig snapped beneath her foot.

Elijah's head whipped round, his startled gaze coming to rest where she stood. When he saw it was her, his face relaxed, a slow smile curling his lips.

Feeling a blush heating her cheeks, she stepped into the open, her eyes on the ground as she made her way over to him. Where they should have been before she carelessly stepped on a stick.

"Sneaking up on m-me again?" he said.

She looked up to see his eyes crinkling in amusement and she couldn't help smiling. "Maybe. I didn't want to disturb you."

He slid across the rock to make space for her and she took a seat next to him.

"How'd it go today?"

She considered telling him what she'd heard Richard say about her to his parents, but the last thing she wanted to do was cry in front of Elijah. Right now her friendship with him was the best thing that had happened to her since she'd arrived in Green Hill Creek and she didn't want to do anything to jeopardize it.

So she simply shrugged, staring at the pond. "It was okay. The Shands were very nice. Oh, we saw three Indian men on the way. Richard spoke to them. He said they were from the reservation and there was an old argument about the cattle. I would have liked to have met them, but he said I could next time."

"Next time? He's expecting to m-meet them again?"

She frowned as she thought about that. It hadn't occurred to her at the time, but it had been an odd thing for Richard to say. "I don't know. I didn't think about it. Do any Indians come onto the ranch?"

"Other than Kosumee, not that I've noticed. The reservation land butts up against the north eastern corner of the ranch though, so maybe the others see them m-m-more than I do." His eyes lowered to the napkin-wrapped bundle she held on her lap. "What's that?"

"Oh!" She'd almost forgotten the cake she'd brought with her. "Mrs. Lassiter wasn't there when we got back so I got to use the kitchen." She unfolded the napkin. "I didn't know which you'd like, so I brought all three."

His face lit up in a smile. "They look delicious. Which would you like?"

"I've had some." She handed him the bundle. "They're all yours."

"Th-th-thank you." He chose the ginger cake and took a bite. "Good," he said around the mouthful. "So, so good."

She laughed at his expression of bliss. "I'm glad you like it."

He nodded vehemently and took a bite of the apple sponge.

Her eyes were drawn to the paper on his lap and she recognized the irrigation system he was designing for the vegetable garden.

"How's it coming?" she said, indicating the paper.

He finished his mouthful of sponge. "I've hit a problem. Because the g-g-garden is quite a bit higher than the well, I'm having to use the windmill to move the water. But there's a place where the gradient is too steep and the pressure won't

108

be enough. I'd like to try building a holding tank, but that's a b-big expense. Although in the long run it would mean better irrigation and better plumbing for the house."

"I could speak to Richard about it," she said. "I'm sure he'd agree to spending the extra money."

It was more hope than certainty, but it was her house too now, in theory. Surely he wouldn't object. He was her husband, after all. In name, if nothing else.

She tried not to think about how often she was having to remind herself of that fact.

He smiled at her, his skin once again forming into tiny wrinkles that warmed his eyes. "Thank you."

She found herself wondering what he'd look like when he was older, in twenty years or so when the laughter lines were etched permanently onto his face, showing the world that he was a man who loved to smile.

Realizing she'd been staring at him for longer than was proper, she dropped her gaze to the paper. "How do you know how to do all this? Did you go to university?"

A moment of sadness flickered across his face. "N-No. I wanted to, but there wasn't the money."

"So how do you know all about physics and math and how to make these things? They never taught us this advanced in school, not even the boys."

"Books, mostly. My teacher knew how much I enjoyed it and he had a f-f-friend who was a civil engineer in Boston. He would send books for me to borrow and I'd copy them out and send them back."

She gaped at him in astonishment. "You copied out entire books? That must have taken forever."

He shrugged. "I enjoyed it. It helped me l-l-learn."

She couldn't imagine loving something so much that she'd spend hours and days and weeks just copying out whole books about it. "I think you're amazing."

His eyes widened and she felt another blush coming on. She really needed to learn to think before she spoke.

"I mean, you're so dedicated," she elaborated. "And talented. One day you'll be building tall buildings and huge bridges and... and..." She tried to think of other big things that needed engineers to design them. "And railroads!"

He looked at the paper. "You're really k-kind to say so."

"Not kind, truthful. You'll do great things, I just know it."

This time she thought she detected a hint of a blush on *his* cheeks as he smiled.

Not wanting to embarrass him, she changed the subject. "So do you come out here every evening?"

"Most evenings. It can get a b-bit rowdy in the bunkhouse some evenings, especially during poker games. I come here so I have quiet to think. Although today I just came here because it's such a nice afternoon."

Her heart sank. She had wanted to stay, but she was obviously disturbing him. Her disappointment must have shown on her face because his smile disappeared.

"I-I-I didn't mean I want you to go," he said quickly. "I like the company."

"I'm not disturbing you?" She couldn't keep the hope from her voice. She very much wanted to stay.

"Not a bit."

"I'll just watch you then," she said, relieved she didn't have to go back to the big, empty house.

He nodded and returned his attention to his design.

Lizzy watched him for a while, but it was a slow process that seemed to take place more in his head than on the page. After a few minutes she couldn't help looking around for something to occupy her attention.

A piece of paper was held out above her lap. She took it and looked up at Elijah. He dug into his portfolio, withdrew a pencil, and offered it to her with an understanding smile.

They spent the rest of their time there in companionable silence, Elijah designing and Lizzy sketching the plants around them. Until the sun went down and they made their way back to the ranch.

And even though Richard wasn't yet home and the house was empty, Lizzy didn't feel so alone any more.

CHAPTER 10

Following breakfast the next morning, Lizzy asked Richard if she could speak with him.

She'd been in bed by the time he returned to the house the night before, and even though she'd heard him come in, by that time she hadn't been in any mood to get up and greet him. Or offer him cake.

So that morning was the first opportunity she'd had to talk to him.

"What is it?" he said as soon as he closed the living room door. "The men will be ready to head out soon."

Her resolution to be extra nice to him suddenly became very difficult to keep. "Well I would have spoken to you about this last night, but you weren't here."

He sighed, his shoulders slumping. "I know, I'm sorry. I didn't mean that to sound like it did. I'm just tired." He indicated a chair and took one across from her as she sat. "What can I do for you?"

Words came unbidden to her mind - *You can tell me why I'm here and why you married me if you never wanted me.* But this wasn't the time for that conversation. And besides, she wasn't the slightest bit ready for it.

"You know the irrigation system Elijah's designing for the vegetable plot?" she said.

"Yes."

"Well, for it to work he needs to build a tank to store the water so there's enough pressure, especially when it's not windy enough for the windmill to do it. He also said there'd be enough pressure then for a bathroom in the house, if you ever want one. I told him I'd ask you about it since I thought I'd see you first. Although I didn't."

She wondered if he'd ask when she and Elijah had been discussing it all, but it turned out she should have known better.

"Sure," he said. "Tell him to draw up the costs for me and if it's not too much it won't be a problem. Ask him to work out the cost of having that bathroom too."

She stared at him for a few seconds, somewhat surprised it had been so easy. "Oh. Um. Thank you. I will."

He nodded. "Is there anything else?"

"Uh, no. That was all."

"Okay then. Well, have a good day."

When he'd left, Lizzy sat back and stared at the chair where he'd been sitting. After a while, she sighed. She'd been prepared to convince him of the merits of Elijah's plan, to expound on the wonders of an indoor bathroom, even to argue if it came to that. The ease with which he'd agreed was disappointing. Even an argument would have been better than the apathy she always seemed to receive.

Through the window, she heard the familiar sound of Elijah's whistling. She leaped to her feet and ran to meet him.

Outside, she fell into step beside him as he pushed the wheelbarrow along the track, heading for the pig enclosure.

"I asked Richard about the water tank," she said, excited to tell him the news. So Richard didn't care about her. She had other people who did, and chief among those was Elijah. She could still have a happy life on the ranch with him there.

"W-what did he say?"

"He said to draw up the costs for everything, including the bathroom, and if it isn't too much we can do it." She gave a small laugh. "You can do it."

He looked sideways at her. "You're not going to help me?"

She grinned. "Until you tell me to go away because I'm slowing you down too much."

He looked forward at the track and shook his head. "Never happen."

Her heart gave a little leap of joy.

"So," he said, "you given any thought to what you want your new b-bathroom to look like?"

"Maybe."

He glanced at her and raised an eyebrow.

"There's a possibility I might have done a few drawings. And notes. And scouted the house for locations to put it."

The sound of his laughter chased away all her sadness.

Just like it always did.

~ ~ ~

Later that afternoon, Lizzy closed her book and peered through the rain-spattered window at the gray sky.

It was still an hour until sunset. The weather had been lovely all day, but for the past hour or so a steady drizzle had been falling. It was disappointing. She had hoped to join Elijah at the pond again, but he wouldn't be going in this weather.

Richard was still out, as usual. She did wonder that he hadn't come back, given how unpleasant it must have been in the rain, and it occurred to her that was probably an indicator of how much he wanted to avoid her. He would rather be soaked and uncomfortable with his cows than dry and warm with her.

She huffed out a breath and dropped the book onto the table next to her, making the lamp wobble beside it. It had possibly been more of a throw than a drop.

She leaned her head onto the back of the chair and stared up at the ceiling.

"Please tell me what to do, Lord," she said. "I know I'm impatient, Mama and Daddy always tell me so and I can't deny they're right. But I thought... I thought..." She stopped and wiped her sleeve across the tears that were suddenly pooling in her eyes. "I thought that he would want me here, that we would fall in love and be happy. I thought he would at least give me a chance. I know he didn't want to marry me, but that could still change, couldn't it? Couldn't you just give him a nudge, make him see that being married to me isn't such a bad thing?"

Distant laughter drifted through the glass and she lowered her eyes to look at the bunkhouse with its windows lit from within. It sounded like they were having fun over there. All the ranch hands had already returned for the evening, of course. They'd told her at supper Richard said he'd be back soon. That had been an hour ago.

She frowned as more laughter emanated from the bunkhouse. This was ridiculous. Why was she sitting there in a dark, lonely house, waiting for someone who didn't even want to spend time with her, when she could go and see if the men who *were* around would let her join them for a little while?

Having made her decision, she pushed herself from the seat, picked up the lamp, and made her way upstairs to fetch her coat.

CHAPTER 11

"Forgive me, gentlemen, but it looks like I will be taking your m-money. As usual."

Elijah placed his cards down, leaned back in his chair and smiled at the other four men, probably with a little more smugness than was necessary.

Eugene dropped his cards onto the table in front of him and threw his hands into the air. "I'd be broke if we were playing for real money. It's not fair. He's cheating."

"It's not cheating to be smarter than you," Alonzo said.

"Actually I win around f-f-forty percent of the time," Elijah said, reaching out to draw the pile of pennies in the center of the table towards him.

Eugene scrunched up his forehead. "How much is that?"

"And that's why you don't win," Amos said. "Try reading a book once in a while."

"Elijah reads enough for all of us."

Elijah merely smiled as he arranged his haul into a neat row of piles of ten. There were twelve in total. Not a huge amount, but it all helped.

Anson stood and stretched his long arms over his head, his fingers brushing one of the rafters as he wandered over to the small stove. "Anyone want some more coffee?"

"I'd rather be able to sleep later," Amos said, gathering the cards from around the table. He pushed them together and shuffled the deck. "You get to my age, you need to watch what you drink this close to bedtime."

"When I get to your age I'll be living in one of those grand houses in Sacramento with servants to see to my every whim," Anson replied, filling his cup from the battered metal pot sitting on the stove. It was the third refill Elijah had seen him pour in the last hour. He had no idea how he could drink so much of it.

"Not if you keep losing to Elijah," Eugene said.

"It's not..." Anson was interrupted by a knock on the door.

Amos went to open it and a chilly breeze wafted into the comfortable warmth of the bunkhouse.

"Mrs. Shand, come on in out of that rain."

Elijah looked at the door in surprise as Lizzy, her coat pulled around her, stepped over the threshold and squinted up at Amos.

"Mr. Hopkins. Um... I was just wondering..."

Elijah leaped to his feet and raced over to her. "Li... Mrs. Shand, is Mr. Shand not home yet?"

She gave him a relieved smile. "No, not yet. I wondered if I could join you for a while?"

"Of c-c-course you can." Elijah wanted to kick himself for not inviting her to stay immediately. "Uh, can I take your c-c-coat?"

He thrust the damp garment at Amos when she'd shrugged it off and rushed to the table ahead of her to pull out a chair. He glanced around the room as she sat and winced. He always kept his corner in order, but the rest of the place was about as tidy as could be expected for the home of seven unattached males. It had been better on Saturday when most of them had been out for the evening. At least the windows had been open all day so the general odor was at a mostly acceptable level.

"Would you like some coffee?" Anson said, holding up the pot.

117

"That would be lovely, thank you," she replied, before Elijah could do anything to warn her. She smiled at Eugene and Alonzo. "Thank you for letting me stay. Where are Mr. Smith and Mr. Kosumee?"

"Kosumee is with his folks on the reservation," Amos said. "His ma's not feeling well so he's gone to help them. As for Herman, let's just say he likes to spend his evenings enjoying some... entertainment in town."

"Entertainment?" She frowned in confusion.

Elijah waited for the penny to drop.

Her eyes widened. "Oh, you mean...? Oh. I see. Well, I'm sorry to interrupt your evening. It's just..." She glanced at Elijah. "I was bored on my own and you sound like you're having so much fun here."

Amos took his seat on the other side of her. "We're glad to have you here. Just like I said Saturday, you're welcome to come over anytime."

Being the oldest by far in their group, Amos often took on an almost fatherly role. As Lizzy smiled, Elijah had never been more grateful for it than he was at that moment.

Anson placed a steaming cup onto the table in front of her. At least he'd used one of the better ones, with only one small dent.

She looked up at him and smiled. "Thank you."

He nodded and returned for his own cup.

Elijah wondered if he should say something to her. In the end, he left it too late.

She took a sip of the coffee.

Her eyes widened a little.

She swallowed.

And coughed a few times.

Leaning towards Elijah, she lowered her voice to a whisper. "It's a bit strong."

"I know, I'm sorry," he whispered back. "I should have

said something."

"Anson!" Amos snapped. "Are you trying to kill the poor woman? She's probably used to more refined beverages. Your coffee could take down a charging buffalo."

Lizzy raised a hand to cover her mouth and Elijah could see she was trying not to laugh.

Anson's eyes widened. "I'm real sorry, Mrs. Shand. I'm so used to making coffee for just us, I didn't think." He hurried over and took her cup. "I'll water it down and add some milk and sugar."

"That would be lovely, thank you."

She glanced at Elijah briefly as Anson returned to the stove, her eyes sparkling with amusement. Fortunately she looked away again or he would have burst into laughter himself.

"Are you playing cards?" she said, looking at the deck on the table.

"Uh, yes, ma'am," Amos said, "but just for fun."

Her eyes went to the piles of pennies in front of each chair.

"M-mostly for fun," Elijah said, embarrassed.

"We can't afford anything more than that when Elijah's playing," Eugene said, apparently having no concept of the fact that gambling, however small, was frowned upon in certain circles.

She looked at Elijah's neat columns of pennies which were significantly higher than anyone else's. "You must be very good."

"It's like any machine, if you kn-know how it works, you can make it work for you."

Alonzo retook his seat. "Meaning he's very good."

"I used to play cards with three of my friends at home," she said. "But we didn't play for money. Even so, we never told anyone. Some of the ladies at church would have

119

thought us very wicked."

By her not entirely innocent smile, Elijah got the feeling she would have done it for that very reason.

"May I join in? What are you playing?"

"We were playing p-p-poker," he said, panicking slightly, "but we could switch to something you're more familiar with."

"Oh no, poker sounds like fun. I'm sure I'll pick it up if you could just remind me of the rules."

She was so honest and trusting, completely the opposite of what playing poker demanded. The last thing he wanted was for her to feel humiliated when she lost badly. Maybe he could somehow work the game so she could win one or two hands. Or maybe the others would be kind and go easy on her. He glanced at Eugene. Well, three of them at least.

After a brief lesson in the rules of poker and a fresh cup of coffee that didn't make her eyes water, Lizzy was all set. Elijah, however, was becoming increasingly nervous at the thought of being in some way responsible for the loss of her wonderfully sunny disposition.

"That seems simple enough," she said.

"You d-don't want me to go over it again?"

"Oh, no, I don't want to hold up your game. May I borrow some of your pennies? I'll pay them back."

"Of course." He pushed a few columns of coins over to her as Amos began to deal.

This wasn't going to be easy.

~ ~ ~

"I call," Eugene said, sitting back with a self-satisfied smirk.

Elijah wanted to punch him.

Lizzy looked up from her cards. "Does that mean I have to show you my cards? I mean my hand?"

"Sure does."

She looked down again, biting her lip. Elijah had noticed she often did that when she was feeling uncertain, like on Saturday morning when she'd wanted to ask him if she could go with him to feed the chickens. It was sweet, only now it made him nervous.

If only she hadn't stayed in the hand. Over and over he'd silently urged her to fold, but she just kept on going until Eugene was the only one left in with her, and of course Eugene wasn't going to give her any kind of break. But there was nothing Elijah could do about it now.

He hoped she wouldn't cry. She didn't seem like the type to cry easily, but she did seem very emotional. He didn't know what he'd do if she cried. The thought terrified him more than just about anything on earth.

"All right," she said. "I did my best." She placed her cards onto the table and folded her hands in her lap.

Elijah's mouth dropped open. So that was where all the tens had gone.

Eugene was doing a fair impression of a fish on dry land gasping for air. "How... I don't... but... but you did that thing."

She raised her eyes and blinked. "Thing?"

"Yeah, when you did that..." He waved vaguely at his mouth. "That thing where your lip shook. When you looked at your hand. Just after Amos dealt. You... you looked sad."

"I did?"

Eugene's other arm joined in the gesticulation as his voice rose. "Yes, you... you know. You were sad. You had a bad hand, I know you did."

Amos cleared his throat in the way he had when one of them was getting out of line. "Just show us your hand, Gene."

Eugene looked at him. "You saw it, right? She did that thing."

Amos raised his eyebrows.

Eugene huffed out a breath and slapped his full house, jacks over threes, onto the table.

Lizzy looked between his cards and her own four tens and a queen. "Do I win?"

She raised her eyes to Elijah's and he saw something flicker in her expression, just for an instant.

He began to smile. "Yup."

She looked at the sizeable pile of pennies in the center of the table. "So all these are mine?"

"Yup."

"How did you do that?" Eugene said, watching her gather the money to her section of the table.

"Well," she said as she arranged the coins into columns as Elijah had done with his, "I may have forgotten to mention those friends I play with are my three older brothers who taught me to play poker and several other card games when I was eleven and have spent every game since regretting it. We use buttons instead of money, well, since our parents caught us gambling we do, but it all works the same."

Amos and Anson began to chuckle. Alonzo snorted into his fist.

Lizzy looked at Elijah and a slow smile crept onto her face. He burst into laughter.

Eugene was frowning. "I don't understand."

"Gene," Amos said, clapping him on the back. "I do believe you've been flimflammed." He winked at Lizzy. "And very well too, if I may say so Mrs. Shand."

"Why thank you, Mr. Hopkins."

Eugene finally caught on. "You were bluffing?"

She smiled and nodded.

He looked around at the rest of them. "And the rest of you knew?"

"I didn't know," Anson said. "I just had a rotten hand."

"Not me," Amos said.

"Me neither," added Alonzo. "She's very good."

"Well, Elijah must have known," Eugene said, pointing an accusing finger at him, "or he wouldn't have folded so early. He can make any hand work."

That wasn't quite true, but Elijah didn't correct him. Instead, he looked at Lizzy. "No, I didn't know. I just thought she d-d-didn't know how to play poker."

Her large, gray eyes widened a little and he hoped she understood what he was saying, not that he thought less of her, but that he had been trying to help her. Then she gave him a small smile and he knew that she did.

"Now that we do know," he said, "and that she has a large p-part of our money, shall we play some more?"

Her smile grew. "I'd love to."

"Deal 'em, Amos," Eugene said, rolling up his sleeves. "And this time, I'm not going to believe anything she does."

Lizzy lifted her fingertips to cover her mouth and Elijah could see she was trying not to laugh again. He was having a hard time with that himself.

As Amos shuffled the deck, she separated out the money Elijah had lent her and slid it over to him and he carefully arranged his neat columns again. Having things in order helped him concentrate and he could tell he was going to need every bit of his focus to not lose to her this time. He was pretty sure he would never underestimate Lizzy again.

This was going to be very, very interesting. And no doubt a lot of fun.

~ ~ ~

Two hours later, Lizzy stood as Elijah pulled her chair out for her.

She smiled at the others around the table who were

already on their feet, most from good manners. "This has been fun!"

"For you, maybe," Eugene grouched, plodding across the room and dropping onto his back on his bed.

Elijah opened his mouth to reprimand him, but Amos beat him to it.

"Eugene! You don't behave like that in front of a lady. Get up and apologize to Mrs. Shand."

"But she took my money!"

"She won your money fair and square."

Heaving a sigh, he hauled himself up. "Sorry, Mrs. Shand," he said to the floor.

Embarrassed, Elijah was getting ready to apologize for the apology when he saw Lizzy smiling.

"If you like, next time I'll teach you how to play better," she said. "If you wouldn't mind me coming back."

Eugene raised his head, his eyes lighting up. "You will? Can you teach me how to beat Elijah?"

She glanced at Elijah. He rolled his eyes and mouthed, *Sorry*.

"I don't know about that," she said to Eugene. "*I'm* not even sure how to beat Elijah."

He was sure that wasn't true. The pile of coins on the table in front of her was bigger than his. And he'd loved every second of the competition. He didn't know whether it was because she was a woman or because she was Lizzy, but he couldn't read her at all. It was at once frustrating and exhilarating.

Eugene shrugged. "Well, don't matter. I'd be happy to learn anything."

Fetching their coats from the pegs by the door, Elijah saw the windows of the house across the yard lit up. He returned to the table and held Lizzy's out for her to put on. "I'll w-walk you back. Looks like Mr. Shand's home, but it's dark out there."

He pulled on his own coat and began sliding her winnings off the edge of the table into his upturned hat.

"You don't have any pockets," he said when she looked at him, indicating her coat. He never did understand why women's coats were so impractical, but it did give him an opportunity to be chivalrous.

"You come over here any time you want," Amos said. "I mean it. Don't even think of staying all alone in that big, empty house."

"And you got Anson to make some drinkable coffee," Alonzo added. "That's barely short of a miracle."

"I heard that," Anson said from the stove where he was pouring himself another cup.

Elijah had never felt as much appreciation for his bunk mates as he did at that moment. He desperately wanted her to come again, but he'd been trying to work out how to word the invitation.

She looked around at all of them, smiling. "Thank you. I enjoyed myself very much."

Elijah wasn't certain, but he thought he saw a faint shimmer of tears in her eyes. As he ushered her out into the night, he desperately hoped that meant she was happy.

He carried his hat of pennies in one hand and a lantern in the other. The clouds were beginning to clear and the air carried a fresh, clean, after-rain smell. The moonlight created diamonds on the wet grass and bushes.

Lizzy looked into the sky and drew in a deep breath of the cool air. "I enjoyed tonight so much."

He followed her gaze. "So did I."

She bit her lower lip. "Do you think the others meant it when they said I could come back? I was afraid I would be intruding."

"Oh no, n-n-not at all." It was extremely important he

convince her they wanted her to return. "Did you notice how much they were talking? They don't normally do that when it's just us. After being together all day, there's not much they have to say to each other at night. Well, n-not me, but I'm not a woman so I'm nothing exciting. You being there made everything more fun." He cringed at how eager he was sounding.

Thankfully, she didn't seem to notice.

"Maybe not for Mr. Peck."

He waved the hand holding his hat. "He's always like that. D-don't mind him."

She smiled and looked at the ground ahead of her. "So, as you and I spend all day together, does that mean you'll get tired of my company?"

"Never," he said quickly. Then he looked up, pretending to think about it. "Although we have only known each other for four days. I might be s-s-sick of you by next week."

She laughed and pushed his shoulder, making him stumble a little to his side where his foot landed in a puddle.

"Oh!" She lifted her hand to her mouth, looking mortified. "I'm so sorry!"

He lifted his dripping foot from the water. "It's fine. I like having a wet foot." Smiling, he very deliberately placed his other foot into the puddle and waggled it around, flinching slightly as the cold water sloshed into his shoe. "See? Now they b-both squelch." He stamped both feet to demonstrate.

She shook her head slowly, laughing again. "You are so strange."

"Got you to laugh though."

Her laughter faded to a smile. "Yes."

After a few more yards they'd reached the back door to the kitchen, to his disappointment. He would have happily walked with her for another mile or two, even in soggy shoes.

He held out his hat. "Don't forget your huge riches."

She took the hat and he opened the door for her.

"Thank you for walking me back," she said, stepping inside.

"Good night, Lizzy."

"Good night, Elijah."

He turned and made his way back down the garden path, looking back when he reached the yard. He fully expected to see a closed door, but instead she was standing in the open doorway, watching him. She waved and he raised his hand in return, then she closed the door.

Elijah stared at the place where she'd been for a few seconds before starting the walk back to the bunkhouse.

And because he was soaked anyway, he jumped in a few more puddles on the way, grinning the entire time.

~ ~ ~

Lizzy closed the door and wandered through the kitchen, smiling to herself.

Elijah had stuck his perfectly dry foot into a puddle, just to make her feel better after she'd pushed him in. She was certain she couldn't have asked for a better friend. Her first few days in California would have been so much less pleasant without him.

Thank You for Elijah, Father, she prayed, not for the first time. She knew God had sent him to her.

Richard's coat was hanging on the coat rack by the front door in the hallway and she was about to walk past when something occurred to her. Stopping, she took hold of a sleeve and ran her hand up to the shoulders and down to the hem. The material was perfectly dry.

A lamp was lit in the living room so she headed in that direction. Finding it empty, she tried Richard's office. He was sitting at his desk, a leather-bound ledger open in front of him. When he didn't look up at her approach she knocked softly on the open door.

He glanced up at her with something that wasn't quite a smile. "Oh, you're home."

A flash of annoyance coursed through her at the ridiculously obvious statement. Had he even known where she was? Did he care?

"I was at the bunkhouse."

He lowered his eyes to the ledger again. "I figured you were."

He *figured*? She wanted to ask him why he hadn't bothered to at least make sure that his wife was safe and not off lying hurt somewhere or abducted by bandits, but she didn't. She also wanted to ask how the coat she knew he'd been wearing was bone dry when he'd been out in the rain all evening, but she didn't do that either. She wasn't sure she would like the answer to either question and she didn't want to dampen her good mood any further.

"We were playing poker."

At least that got his attention.

He looked up, raising his eyebrows. "Poker?"

"Yes, and I won. A lot." She held up Elijah's hat and shook it, causing the coins inside to jingle.

His eyes bored into the hat. "Is that Elijah's?"

So maybe there was another way to get his attention. "Yes. I didn't have any way to carry the pennies so he lent it to me. He walked me back here."

There were a few moments of silence.

Richard rubbed one hand across his face. "Elizabeth, I know I haven't been around much and I'm sorry for that. And I know you want the company, and that's fine. And they're good men over there, they'll look after you, and I guess they like you enough to let you win at poker..."

She took a step back, her jaw dropping in disbelief and what was left of her good mood evaporating instantly. "Let me win at poker? *Let* me win?!" She could tell by his horrified expression that he knew he'd made a mistake, but she was too angry to care. "For your information, no one *let* me win at anything. I'm a very good poker player and I can beat just about anyone, which you might know if you spent any time with me or bothered to get to know me at all. Every single one of those men in there knows more about me than my own husband! And right now it feels like they care more about me than you do too."

She whirled around and strode into the hallway, hurrying for the stairs.

"Wait, Elizabeth!"

She ignored his call, picking up speed until running footsteps caught up with her and he stepped into her path. Unable to stop her forward momentum in time, they collided and Elijah's hat fell from her hands. Small copper coins scattered over the tiled floor, rolling into dark corners and glinting in the light of the lamp Richard held.

Emotional as she already was, the sight of the pennies Elijah had so thoughtfully gathered for her strewn all over the floor with his hat listing on its side in the midst of the mess made her want to burst into tears.

Richard exhaled a long sigh, placed the lamp on a nearby table, and lowered to the floor. "I'm sorry."

She watched him pick up the hat and begin to painstakingly retrieve each coin. Remorse crept up on her uninvited. It wasn't that she didn't think her anger had been justified, but watching him on his knees, casting around in the semi-darkness to find every penny, made her sorry she'd shouted at him. She didn't regret it, but she was sorry.

Taking the lamp from where he'd left it on the hall table, she lowered beside him, placed it on the floor where it would cast more light for the search, and began to collect the gleaming coins with him.

"You don't have to do that," he said. "It was my fault they fell."

"I don't mind. It'll be quicker with both of us."

They worked in silence until all the coins they could find were back in the hat.

He sat back on his heels and looked at her. "I'm sorry, Elizabeth, I truly am."

"They're only pennies."

"That's not what I meant." He stood with the hat of coins and offered her his hand. "What I said about the poker, it was stupid," he said as he helped her to her feet. "You're right, I don't know you, and that's my fault. I hope I can change that. It's still calving season now, but I'll have more time soon, I promise."

Looking into his blue eyes, the eyes she'd dreamed of for so long before coming, she wanted to believe him. But there was still the matter of what she'd overheard the day before at his parents' house. He didn't want her, had never wanted her. Was there really any way he could come to actually be glad she was there? To love her?

"I hope so too," she replied.

He handed her the hat. "That's an impressive take. I've played poker with them and they're good, especially Elijah."

She couldn't help smiling at that. "He was my main competition, I can't deny that. He plays like he's designing one of his projects, like he can see all the pieces fitting together. But they can all play." She thought for a moment. "Except Eugene."

He chuckled softly. "Except Eugene. Fortunately, he's better with cattle than he is with cards."

His smile was genuine. It looked good on him.

"Well, I'm going to go to bed," she said.

He nodded and stepped away from her. "Goodnight, Elizabeth."

"Goodnight."

As she readied herself for bed, Lizzy wondered if this was the turning point she'd been waiting for the past few days. Would Richard keep to his promise to spend more time with her?

Then a question popped into her mind that shocked her - did she really want him to?

She frowned at her reflection as she brushed her hair at the dressing table. "Of course I want him to," she replied quietly to herself. "Why wouldn't I? He's my husband. I want us to fall madly in love."

But as she slipped under the covers, she was bothered by three things.

First, what Richard had said to his parents.

Second, the dry coat hanging downstairs by the door, a coat that should have been at least a little wet from the rain if he'd been with the cattle all evening.

And third, try as she might, she still couldn't find the enthusiasm for being with her husband that she'd had when she arrived.

And for the life of her, she didn't understand why.

CHAPTER 12

Lizzy's yawn was so wide she felt as if her face might split in half. She placed the basket of eggs onto the wagon bed and belatedly slapped a hand over her mouth.

"I'm so sorry," she said. "I'm truly excited to be going to the market, I promise."

Elijah smiled at her from the other side of the wagon where he was arranging the boxes of onions they'd harvested the day before. "I know it's a mite early. Especially after your busy night yesterday winning all our m-money again."

"I didn't win much of *your* money." The previous evening she'd spent time with Elijah at the pond *and* gone to the bunkhouse to play poker. Despite her tiredness now, she'd loved every second.

"But I had to be really careful to make sure of that."

She grinned. "Don't get comfortable. Everyone has some sign that they're bluffing, and when I work out yours, watch out."

He shook his head, picking up a box of garlic bulbs and situating it next to the onions. "Won't happen."

She carefully tucked in a cloth around the eggs. "I will bet you two dollars I'll know when you're bluffing within two weeks."

"Two weeks, huh?" He walked around to where she was placing a second egg basket and held out his hand, grinning. "I could use an extra t-two dollars. You're on."

She took his hand. "You won't be so sure of yourself in

two weeks."

"We'll see."

He looked down at her, his eyes dancing with amusement, and it was a few seconds before she noticed that, even though the handshake had come to an end, his hand was still wrapped around hers. It felt warm and slightly tingly and she found that she didn't want him to let go. She also noticed there were the most beautiful flecks of green in his hazel eyes.

He suddenly released her hand, looking away and clearing his throat, and she realized she must have been staring. Embarrassed, she grasped the handle of the basket and pushed it over to the other one.

"B-b-better get finished loading," he said, not looking at her. "The earlier we get there, the better space we'll get for our stall."

She nodded and grabbed another cloth, hoping he wouldn't see her reddening cheeks.

~ ~ ~

"I wonder if Sara and Jo will come into town to the market," Lizzy said as she fussed with the onions in the box on the table in front of her.

"Daniel Raine usually has a stall for his honey and fruit, so Mrs. Raine might come with him," Elijah replied, watching her hands. "I haven't seen him yet though. W-what are you doing?"

She looked up at him then down at the onions. "I'm turning them so they all face the same direction."

He nodded slowly. "Why?"

"It looks neater." She took a step back and assessed the stall. "You know, if I brought a tablecloth next week it would make it look much prettier."

133

He looked at the table. "I... guess." It hadn't ever occurred to him to try to make it look pretty, but now she'd mentioned it he could see how it might work. Most of his customers were women, after all. "That's actually a really good idea."

"I wonder if I'd be able to sneak a tablecloth past Mrs. Lassiter," she said with a smile.

"I c-could just ask her if we could borrow one."

Her smile turned mischievous. "But that wouldn't be nearly as much fun."

"I g-get the feeling you have a long history of sneaking."

She moved on to rearranging the garlic bulbs. "I can neither confirm nor deny that."

It was all he could do to keep from laughing. He didn't think he'd laughed so much in his entire life as he had since she'd arrived.

"Oh, bueno, you have your wonderful onions." Mrs. Sanchez bustled up to them. She was almost always the first to the stall. "Buenos dias, Mr. Griffin."

"I have some s-saved just for you, Mrs. Sanchez," he said, retrieving the box he'd kept aside for her. "Mrs. Shand, this is Mrs. Sanchez. She's the head cook in the hotel."

"And Mr. Griffin here grows the most delicioso vegetables to cook with," she said. "It's a pleasure to meet you, Mrs. Shand. I hope you and Mr. Shand are enjoying married life?"

"I, er, yes, thank you. It's certainly... an experience."

It seemed to him that Lizzy's smile slipped a little as she answered, but Elijah had no idea what that could mean. He was probably just seeing things.

"I hope one day to see the two of you in the hotel," Mrs. Sanchez went on, oblivious to the subtle nuances he was no doubt imagining. "You let me know when you come in and I'll make you my famous strawberry shortcake with cream.

Ask Mr. Griffin how good it is, he has it every time he comes in when the strawberries are in season."

Lizzy's smile returned as she looked up at him. "In that case I'll definitely have to try it sometime."

He suddenly had an intense desire to be the one who took her for her first strawberry shortcake. He didn't know if it was wrong to want to take another man's wife to eat strawberry shortcake, but he asked God's forgiveness anyway, just in case.

"I'll take ten of the garlic as well," Mrs. Sanchez said, interrupting his silent confession. She turned and looked around the stalls for a moment then raised her hand and shouted in a voice that probably carried all the way to San Francisco, "Javier!"

A lanky young man with wild hair and limbs that seemed too long for his body jogged over to them. "Sí, Mamá? Morning, Elijah." His gaze moved to Lizzy. "Ma'am."

"Take the onions to the kitchen," Mrs. Sanchez told her son. "And no eating any!"

"Sí, Mamá." He took the onions from Elijah and jogged off in the direction of the hotel.

"No eating any?" Lizzy said.

"He eats them raw, like apples," Mrs. Sanchez replied. "Gets it from his papá. I don't know how they do it, but..." She shrugged. "Gracias for the onions. Don't forget to come for that shortcake whenever you like."

"I wonder what it's like to eat a raw onion," Lizzy said, watching Mrs. Sanchez head for another stall. "Does he peel them first, do you think?"

"We have plenty, if you'd like to try," Elijah said, waving at the box of neatly arranged vegetables in front of her.

She stared at them for a few seconds as if seriously considering the idea then shook her head. "Maybe another

135

time. When there's a lot of water to drink if it's not as much fun as it sounds."

Over the next hour Green Hill Creek's weekly market filled with people as the town woke up for the day. It was as much a social occasion as anything and Elijah always enjoyed chatting to the patrons of the stall.

There was a time when he avoided talking as much as possible, when he was young and all he wanted was to be able to speak smoothly like everyone else. Then in his late teens the embarrassment had turned to antagonism and often he would speak for no reason other than in the hope of getting a reaction to justify the anger he carried with him. Now, he was finally coming to accept his stutter as part of who he was, and he knew he had God to thank for that. He still wasn't what anyone would call loquacious, but at least he didn't intentionally go out of his way to avoid speaking.

The truth was, he'd spoken more to Lizzy than anyone he could remember, apart from his family. There was something about her that made him want to be open and honest, an innocence and brightness and joy that radiated to those around her. And watching her with their customers, he could see he wasn't the only one who felt it. She greeted everyone with a radiant, beautiful smile that seemed to infect each person she spoke to and had them smiling in return. He couldn't be completely sure, but he suspected it was helping their sales too. Throughout most of the morning he simply stood back and happily watched her charm everyone she met.

Before eleven most of what they'd brought was gone, a full hour before that usually happened. He'd have to try to bring more for the next market day.

"Mornin', miss. What's a pretty little thing like you doing selling vegetables? If you was mine, you wouldn't want for nothin'."

Elijah whirled from where he was loading an empty

136

onion box into the wagon to see Lizzy's smile melt from her face. A rough-looking man with greasy, scraggly brown hair and a patchy beard stood on the other side of the stall, his eyes travelling disgustingly down her body and back up again.

She took a step back. Elijah was at her side in a flash.

She looked up at him, her expression uncertain. "Um..."

"You her husband?" the man said.

Elijah fixed him with a warning stare. He'd met men like him, in all the most unpleasant places. He didn't belong anywhere near someone like Lizzy. "S-something I can help you w-w-with?"

The man stared at him for a second and then erupted into laughter. "Well, will you listen to that? That's just the dumbest, funniest talkin' I ever heard."

Elijah gritted his teeth. God may have helped him overcome his constant anger, but that didn't mean it never reappeared. "I think you should l-l-leave."

The man was still laughing, clutching at his gut. "Oh, you think I should l-l-l-l-leave, do you? Should I l-l-l-l-l-leave? Is that what you w-w-w-w-w-want?"

Elijah's hands were balling into fists almost of their own accord. If it had been two years ago, the man would have already been laid out on the ground. He opened his mouth to give him the only warning he would get.

"What is *wrong* with you?!"

He looked down at Lizzy in surprise.

She stepped up to the stall, her fisted hands on her waist and a look of utter fury on her face. "Are you mean or just stupid? Because you look like both."

Around them people stopped what they were doing to look at the commotion.

"Well, are you going to answer?" Lizzy demanded.

The man was staring at her as if he didn't know quite

what to do. "I... uh..."

"How would you like it if I started laughing at you?" she said, her voice rising further. "And believe me, there is plenty to laugh at."

He looked down at himself. "There ain't."

Elijah realized his mouth was still hanging open. He closed it.

"Oh really?" she said. "So I shouldn't point out that your clothes look like they haven't been washed since 1865? Or that you have sweat stains on your sweat stains? Or that your sense of humor is so pitiful you think mocking people is funny? Or that your hair looks like a mouse tried to nest in it but couldn't bring itself to lower its standards? Or that you smell so bad even the flies are avoiding you?"

"Hey, there ain't no call for..."

"Oh, but I think there is. I think that anyone whose behavior is as rude and nasty as yours deserves to get a taste of their own medicine." She pointed towards Elijah. "This man is one of the smartest, kindest, nicest people I know and you have no right to laugh at him. In fact, you should apologize, right now."

Compared to the man she was tiny, and yet she stood, hands on her hips, staring him down as if she was eight feet tall.

And she was doing it all for Elijah.

The man swallowed and his gaze darted around their audience. It seemed like the entire market had stopped to watch them.

"Well?" Lizzy snapped.

He glanced back at her, flashed a glare at Elijah, and turned and walked quickly away through the crowd.

For a few seconds there was complete silence, and then someone began to clap. Elijah didn't know who started it, but within moments everyone around them was applauding

Lizzy. He joined in wholeheartedly, a grin stretching his face and pride filling his heart.

Her cheeks flushed red as she smiled her radiant, beautiful smile.

Several people came up to them as the crowd dissipated, saying things along the lines of "well done" to Lizzy or expressing how appalling the man's behavior had been to Elijah. But eventually they were alone again.

"That was a-m-mazing," he said.

"I just got so mad! He had no right to do that to you." She looked around them and lowered her voice. "If the table hadn't been between us I do believe I would have slapped him. Hard."

His heart was pounding in his chest. He so badly wanted to tell her how proud of her he was, how honored that she would defend him as she had, how much he valued their friendship, how she was the most incredible woman he'd ever met. But all he seemed to be able to do was smile.

She looked up at him. "You're laughing at me."

"Oh, no," he said. "Believe me, I am m-most definitely not laughing at you."

Judging by the slow smile that spread across her face, something in his words must have convinced her he was being truthful.

He pushed his hands into his pockets. "Thank you for sticking up for me."

"You would have done the same for me."

She was right.

The truth was, at that moment he would have fought fire-breathing dragons for her.

~ ~ ~

Elijah held out a sheet of paper. Instead of taking it, Lizzy

139

opened the bag she'd brought with her to the pond and took out a few sheets of paper.

"I bought it today in town," she said. "I didn't want to use up all of your paper."

"I have plenty. I don't mind, I promise."

"I know you don't. I do have a favor to ask though." She gave him a sheepish smile. "I forgot to bring a pencil."

He handed over the pencil he'd brought for her, returning her smile.

"Thank you." She stared at the pond for a while, then at the blank page on her lap for another while.

"Is something wrong?" he said after the two whiles had gone on longer than it usually took her to find inspiration.

"No. Everything's fine." She bit her lip for a few seconds.

Elijah waited.

"Um... would you mind if I ask you something?"

He'd wondered when she would get around to it. "About my stutter?"

She nodded, her eyes fixed on the ground in front of her.

"You can ask me anything. You d-don't have to be embarrassed. I don't mind at all."

She finally looked up. "Really?"

If there was anyone he wouldn't mind talking about his stutter with, it was her. "I p-promise."

She nodded and looked away, thinking. "Have you always had it?"

"As long as I can remember. My ma said she and my pa hoped I'd g-g-grow out of it when I got older, but I never did."

"Couldn't the doctors help?"

"We didn't have much money for doctors. I remember when I was ten or so I was told to do th-things like holding the tip of my tongue against the top of my mouth when I

140

spoke, but n-n-nothing worked."

"Does it hurt?"

He smiled. "No, it never hurts."

"Good. I'd hate to think it caused you pain to talk to me. I talk too much anyway."

His smile disappeared. "Who t-told you that you talk too much?"

She shrugged. "My teachers, mostly. And my mama, although she doesn't mean it in a mean way. She just says I should let other people talk too, especially men. She said men like to talk about themselves and that a woman should try to look interested, even if she's not." She gasped and covered her mouth with her fingertips as if to take what she'd said back. "I'm sorry, I didn't mean at all that you're like that. I'm *always* interested in what you have to say."

"I'm really glad to hear that." He was. Very, very glad. "And I think your mother's right about some men l-l-liking to talk about themselves. I've met them. But I respectfully have to disagree that you should stop talking for any man. I l-love listening to you talk."

Her eyes widened. "Truly?"

"Truly." He wanted to tell her she was delightful and he could have listened to her all day, but he didn't think that would be appropriate. It was true though.

She smiled and lowered her eyes again, a hint of pink staining her cheeks. That often happened when she received a compliment and he couldn't help thinking, inappropriately or not, that it made her even prettier.

"I suppose it was hard growing up with a stutter," she said.

This time it was him who looked away. "Yeah."

He was quiet for a while, gathering his thoughts. The way his stutter had affected his life wasn't something he ever talked about, with anyone. Truth was, when she'd started

141

asking questions he intended to just gloss over the details, make light of it. But for reasons he didn't understand, he found himself wanting to tell her when he would have run a mile to not have to tell anyone else.

"I had the usual problems, what you'd expect from being different f-f-from everyone else. Other children picked on me. I was an easy target for b-bullies, although not so much once I grew. From when I was young, I avoided speaking to people I didn't know unless I had to. I was very self-conscious. It wasn't until I w-was sixteen, when I had Mr. Evans, that teacher I told you about, that anyone thought I'd amount to anything. He helped me so much. He even got me an interview for a scholarship to study at c-c-college."

Lizzy's face lit up. "You went to college? Which one?"

"I d-d-didn't get the scholarship." He couldn't keep the bitterness from his voice. "They said they didn't feel I would be able to c-cope with the academic demands. Their words."

"That's ludicrous!" she exclaimed. "Why in the world would they think that?"

He wondered that anyone could be so naive, but then he looked into her wide, innocent eyes and realized it wasn't naïveté. It was simply that she was such a good person that she couldn't conceive of anyone not seeing the world the same way she did. He had a sudden, overpowering urge to wrap her in his arms and protect her from all the evil in the world, all the unkindness and cruelty he'd endured his entire life.

"They thought I must be slow, like my speech. I was n-nervous and my stutter got really bad, then I got frustrated which made it even worse. It was a disaster."

It had been one of the worst experiences of his life. All his dreams of becoming an engineer dashed in one humiliating, stutter-filled interview. His teacher had offered to explain and persuade them to give him another chance, but he hadn't wanted to go through the whole thing again. So he'd given up.

Not long after, he'd left home and things went downhill from there. But that was another story and one he wasn't ready to tell, not even to Lizzy. Maybe he never would be.

"I'm so sorry," she said quietly. She wiped at one eye with the back of her hand.

He immediately felt terrible. "P-p-please don't cry. I'm all right." He dug into his pocket and pulled out a handkerchief, handing it to her. "It's clean."

She dabbed at her eyes. "Can I ask you one last question?"

"Of course."

"If you could, would you want to go to college now?"

He looked down at the portfolio on his lap, its bulging interior filled with the designs and ideas he couldn't stop dreaming up. "More than almost anything."

"Then I shall pray hard that you get the chance."

~ ~ ~

As was usual when Lizzy got home from the pond, the house was empty, but she was glad Richard wasn't home tonight. She went straight to her bedroom and sat at her tiny desk with a pen and writing paper.

The thought of Elijah leaving the ranch, leaving her alone, was almost more than she could bear and just the possibility made her chest ache. But he deserved the opportunity to fulfill his dreams and if there was a chance she could do something to help him, she had to try.

So she pushed her own desires aside and began to write.

Dearest Daddy,
I hope you and Mama and the boys are well. I have arrived

safely and I'll tell you all about my new life later, but first, I have something to ask of you...

CHAPTER 13

Elijah whistled as he strolled along the track towards the yard, carrying the two dead chickens by their legs at his side.

He liked having chicken for Sunday dinner; it reminded him of home and his mother's cooking. He briefly wondered if she and his father still had chicken and roast potatoes every Sunday like they used to. It had been over three years since he'd been home, but surely that wouldn't have changed. There would be honey-glazed parsnips and carrots, and rich gravy that he would lick from his plate when his ma wasn't looking.

He wondered how Lizzy would prepare the chickens if she had the opportunity. If her cake was anything to go by, whatever she did would be delicious. Not that Mrs. Lassiter's cooking wasn't good, but Lizzy would add something extra, something uniquely her, something wonderful. It was the same with everything she did; she simply made it all better, whether she was feeding pigs or weeding rows of vegetables or holding clouds of chicks in her hands and laughing. He wasn't sure how she did it, but it always gave him a feeling of warmth. She had a magic about her that spread to everything around her and he felt blessed to know her.

How Richard could spend all his time with the cattle when Lizzy was waiting for him at home, Elijah had no idea. If she'd been *his* wife...

He stopped abruptly, closing his eyes. He wasn't going to think like that. Wanting another man's wife was about as wrong as things got. There was even a specific commandment about it - *thou shalt not covet thy neighbor's wife.* It couldn't get plainer than that. He might only have been a Christian for barely more than three years and he knew he was still learning, but there was no room for misinterpretation there.

"Help me to just look at Lizzy as a friend," he whispered heavenward. "I don't want to break any of Your commands and I know You don't want that either. So if You could just help me out on that one, I'd be grateful. In the Name of Your Son, Jesus. Amen."

Reassured that God would keep him from sinning, he continued on across the yard to the house. He began whistling again, this time a hymn they'd sung on Sunday, *Shall We Gather at the River.* He couldn't remember all the words, but he liked the tune.

"Afternoon, Mrs. Lassiter," he said as he stepped into the kitchen.

He walked over to where she stood at the sink and placed the two chickens onto the draining board next to her. "Looking forward to seeing what you do with these tomorrow." He didn't add he'd actually been musing mostly on what someone else would have done with them.

There was a sharp intake of breath behind him. He turned to see Lizzy standing in the doorway to the hall, her wide eyes on the chickens.

The chickens she'd been looking after for the past week.

The chickens who had eaten from her hand as she'd stroked them gently, soothing them with her soft voice.

The chickens he'd just slaughtered.

His heart dropped to his feet.

"Lizzy, I'm so s-s-sorry. I d-didn't think."

She moved her eyes to him and he was horrified to see them glistening with tears.

146

She swallowed and lowered her gaze to the floor. "I... it's all right. I... um... just wasn't expecting..." And then she fled through the back door.

Elijah looked at Mrs. Lassiter for help, not sure what to do.

"Reckon you'd better go explain to her where chicken meat comes from," she said, turning back to the sink.

He looked at the chickens once more and hurried outside. Lizzy was already halfway across the yard and he ran after her.

How could he have been so stupid? He should have at least prepared her for what would happen. He'd just assumed she knew that the birds weren't there only for laying, but she came from the city. He didn't know what she was used to, but he imagined it wasn't suddenly being confronted with the corpses of her feathered friends.

He caught up to her in the stand of trees that marked where the track left the yard. "Lizzy, p-please."

She stopped but didn't turn to face him.

"I'm s-s-sorry." He reached out to touch her arm and then thought better of it. "I didn't kn-know you were there and I didn't think that... I just didn't think."

Her sad sniff went a long way to convincing him that he was, in fact, the worst person on earth.

"It's not your fault," she said. "I knew some of them would be for the table. It was just a shock to see them like that, that's all. This morning Emily was eating from my hand."

"Emily?" he said, confused.

"The ginger one."

His shoulders slumped. She'd given them names. And he'd killed Emily. He felt like a monster.

"You must think I'm such a foolish girl, getting upset over a chicken."

147

He moved to stand in front of her and she raised her red-rimmed eyes to his.

I think you're perfect.

The thought was so unexpected that for a moment he couldn't speak. He swallowed and made an effort to pull himself together. It wasn't easy. "I-I-I think you are one of the most c-caring people I've ever met and there's n-nothing foolish about that."

A small, rueful smile touched her lips. "I suppose I shouldn't have named them."

"P-probably not." He just knew the next time he had to kill one he was going to be wondering what its name was. He hated the task at the best of times, now it was going to feel like he was killing one of Lizzy's friends. "If you don't want to keep working with them..."

"Oh, no, I do," she said quickly. "I just have to start thinking of them as farm animals, not as pets." She looked along the track in the direction of the chicken pen. "Could we go up there, just to see them?"

"Sure."

They started walking and Elijah felt somewhat relieved. She didn't seem to be taking it too badly.

"Do you think the others notice that two of their friends are gone?"

His shoulders slumped even lower. Did they? Lizzy may have been taking it well, but he was turning into a wreck. "I sure hope not."

They walked a few more paces before he spoke again. "Um... you do realize that one day... the pigs..."

"Yes, I do."

He nodded and kept walking. "Just checking."

~ ~ ~

148

Later that evening, when he and Lizzy were at the pond, Elijah finally put down his pencil, having unsuccessfully been trying to work on a design for ten minutes.

"I have to know," he said, "did you n-n-name all of them?"

She looked up from her drawing. "Did I name all of what?"

"The chickens."

"Oh no, just my favorites. The prettiest ones." She frowned. "Does that make me shallow?"

He had no idea. He hadn't even been aware there was a scale of attractiveness among chickens. "I... no. So how many did you name?"

"I'm not sure. Fifteen, maybe?"

Fifteen chickens had names. That gave a roughly twelve percent chance that each time he selected a chicken for the table, it would be one of them. "You're going to have to point out which ones they are."

"Okay. But why?"

"So I don't k-kill any of them."

She laid her hand on his arm. "That's sweet of you, but I was just being silly. I understand they're for eating sometimes. You don't have to avoid taking them just because I gave them names."

He sighed and gave her a resigned smile. "I really do."

CHAPTER 14

The next morning after the service finished Lizzy went to talk to Jo. She'd arrived late to church and without her husband and Lizzy was worried about her.

"You're sure you're all right now?" Lizzy said, moving back to allow a little girl and her mother past in the aisle.

"I'm completely fine," Jo replied. "It was likely just something I ate."

"Did Gabriel cook it?"

She snorted a laugh. "No chance of that. If it's more complicated than heating up a can of beans, he can't do it. If I had money I'd pay Mrs. Goodwin to bring us food every day." She gazed across the church and sighed. "What must that be like, having someone to cook and clean for you every day?"

"I do have someone cooking and cleaning for me every day," Lizzy said with a grimace, "and it's not as much fun as it sounds. If it wasn't for helping Elijah with the farming, I'd die of boredom."

"Wanna swap places?" Jo said. "You can cook and clean to your heart's content in Gabriel's shack and I'll help your good-looking ranch hand with his farm work." A wicked smile curved her lips as she looked at Elijah where he stood talking to Mrs. Jones on the far side of the building.

Lizzy smacked her arm with the back of her hand. "You are terrible. What would your husband think if he knew you were looking at another man like that?" She tried to ignore the discomfort she felt at the fact it was *Elijah* who Jo was admiring.

"Don't know, don't care. He's not here anyway."

Lizzy knew Jo had a habit of being flippant, but she got the feeling there was more truth to her words than she probably wanted Lizzy to know. "Is it really a shack?"

"No, not really. Not quite. It's just in need of a woman's touch. A lot of woman's touch. Several women's touches. I'm working on it. Gives me something to do. I've lived in worse, that's for sure."

She moved closer and took Jo's hand. "Where is Gabriel today? Are you all right with him? Is he treating you well?"

There was a hint of sadness to Jo's smile. "He's away at his placer claim for a few days and he's treating me just fine. I get a bit lonely being so far away from town, that's all. I'm used to being surrounded by people. I'll get used to it."

Guilt tugged at Lizzy. She'd been so taken up with everything she did with Elijah that she hadn't been to visit Jo once. In fact, she hadn't actively been to see any of her friends. She'd seen Amy, Jo and Louisa at the market on Wednesday, and Sara paid her a visit on Friday after an argument with Daniel, but Lizzy hadn't made any effort at all. She felt like a terrible friend.

"Well, I'm going to come and visit this week. I'll talk to the others too. I'm sure they'd like to see your new home. We can help with all those women's touches your home needs. Just wait, you'll have so many visitors you'll be glad to get rid of us."

Jo laughed and patted her hand. "Never happen."

Louisa walked towards them along the aisle. "How would you two like to join me for lunch? Pastor and Mrs. Jones are going to be out all afternoon and they said I could invite you all over. I know it's short notice, as in no notice, but Jesse said he'd drive everyone home afterwards."

"Perfect timing," Lizzy said. "Jo was just saying how desperately she misses all of us."

Jo raised an eyebrow. "I don't recall saying that."

Lizzy squeezed her hand and grinned. "Not in so many words, but I could tell you were implying it."

"I also thought it would be good for Sara," Louisa said, lowering her voice. "She looks so sad today and Daniel didn't come to church with her. I think it's hard for her, with his accident and all."

Lizzy looked at where Sara and Amy sat together in the back row, talking. "I'll get her to come."

"Don't tell her what I said," Louisa said quickly. "I don't want her to feel like we're all here feeling sorry for her."

"Don't worry," she said with a wink, "I'll be the soul of discretion." Leaving Jo and Louisa in the aisle, she edged along the row in front of Amy and Sara and sat, twisting around in the seat to face them. "I would like to formally invite you two to lunch."

~ ~ ~

There was something about being among friends they knew they could trust that made it easier to admit when their new lives weren't living up to expectations.

Amy and her confusion about her feelings towards Adam, Sara and how difficult it was with Daniel following his accident, Louisa and her fears of disappointing her parents, Jo and... well, Jo didn't give much away, but they could all tell she wasn't happy. And then there was Lizzy.

When it came time for her to tell her story, she didn't know what to say. Her instinct was to tell them everything was fine between her and Richard, but that wasn't true and she didn't want to lie to her friends. But admitting to them what was happening meant she would have to admit it fully to herself - her marriage was an empty failure and she was rapidly losing hope for her future with Richard.

When she didn't immediately speak, Amy took her hand. "Whatever you want to tell us is all right. Or you don't have to tell us anything. It's entirely up to you. We're all too nosey anyway."

Lizzy smiled and leaned against her shoulder. "You're all so wonderful. I thought I was coming here just to marry Richard. I didn't think I'd find such good friends too." She drew in a deep breath and let it out slowly. "I don't think Richard wants me. I don't think he ever wanted me."

Blinking back the tears even saying those two simple sentences brought, she told them how Richard seemed to be actively avoiding her, about the journey to see his parents the previous Sunday and what she'd overheard him say about his parents being the ones who wanted him to marry, about her suspicions that he wasn't with the cattle when he said he was.

She gave up trying to hold in her tears around halfway through and when it was over the others gathered around her, just as they had for Sara when she'd wept, and engulfed her in a group hug that made her feel incredibly warm and loved.

"You know," Jo's voice said from somewhere in the huddle, "I know a recipe for rice pudding that wouldn't let Richard get more than twenty feet from an outhouse for days. That would keep him around."

Someone started to giggle. Someone else joined in. Within moments the hug had morphed into so much laughter they were holding onto each other for support as they gasped for breath.

"We should do this every week," Sara said when they were finally able to speak again.

"I second that," Amy said.

Louisa raised her hand. "All in favor?"

Four more hands joined hers in the air as everyone cried, "Aye!"

"Just to clarify," Jo said, "were we voting on meeting for lunch or poisoning Lizzy's husband?"

And they all dissolved into giggles again.

CHAPTER 15

Lizzy was the last of the group to be taken home, although it turned out that only she and Sara needed the ride from Jesse and Louisa. Amy simply walked back to her home in the post office in town and Jo had brought a buggy.

Their time together had lasted far beyond lunch and by the time they parted it was almost five. Lizzy had loved every second. Meeting Amy, Sara, Louisa and Jo was undoubtedly the best thing that had happened to her since leaving home, along with meeting Elijah and the other ranch hands of course. But especially Elijah.

Elijah. It hadn't occurred to her at the time, but as they drove towards the ranch and she reflected on what she'd told her friends about her life there, she realized she had barely mentioned Elijah. It wasn't that he was unimportant, completely the opposite, in fact. Yet she had, for some reason, treated her friendship with him almost as a secret. And she had no idea why.

"Where should I go?" Jesse said from the driver's seat, interrupting her thoughts.

"Around to the back is good," Lizzy replied and he followed her directions, bringing the wagon to a halt in the yard and setting the brake.

"This is very nice," Louisa said, gazing up at the house.

Lizzy rose up onto her knees on the blanket she'd been sitting on and leaned her arms on the back of the seat between the two of them. "It's lovely inside, not that I've had

155

anything to do with that. Mrs. Lassiter takes care of everything, but it's her day off today. Would you like to come in and look around? I could make us something. Last week when I got the kitchen to myself I baked three different types of cake."

Louisa and Jesse shared a look and suddenly Lizzy realized she had become a third wheel.

"Or the two of you could leave now," she said, "which would give you a good two hours before dark for you to take a ride, see the countryside, talk." She looked down, tracing a knot in the wood of the seat between them with her fingertip. "Kiss."

Louisa gasped, her cheeks turning red. "Lizzy!"

She raised her eyes, affecting a look of innocence. "Yes?"

Jesse snorted, clearly trying not to laugh. Louisa gave him a reproachful look, the severity of which was utterly ruined by the sparkle in her eyes. By the way he'd been looking at Louisa, Lizzy had no doubt he would have no objection to the kissing part. And if she was any judge of her friend, neither would Louisa.

"Well," Lizzy said, pushing herself to her feet, "my work here is done." She climbed down from the back of the wagon and walked around to the front. "Have a good afternoon. Don't do anything I wouldn't do."

"What wouldn't you do?" Jesse said.

Louisa nudged his shoulder with hers. "Don't encourage her."

"But I need to know where the boundaries are," he replied, smiling.

A mischievous, most un-Louisa-like expression slid onto her face. "I'll let you know."

His smile faded, his eyes widening.

Lizzy exclaimed a loud "Ha!" which had the horses looking at her sideways. She reached out to pat the nearest one. "Sorry."

She waved as they left, sighing happily. Even though her own love story wasn't going so well with Richard at least her friends were finding the romance they'd come for, and she was thrilled for each one of them.

She looked at the bunkhouse and wondered if Elijah was inside or if he was already at their pond, deciding to freshen up first then go and find out. She could take advantage of Mrs. Lassiter's absence and bake something later. She didn't want to miss seeing him.

Once in the house, she walked through the kitchen and headed for the stairs.

"Elizabeth?"

She gasped in a startled breath, spinning to face the living room. "Richard?"

He stepped through the door, his eyes widening at the sight of her hand on her chest. "Are you all right?"

She willed her heartbeat to slow. "You just startled me. I thought no one was home."

"Sorry. I was waiting for you."

She stared at him. "You... were?"

He glanced away, running a hand over his hair. "Uh, yes. I wondered if you'd like to go for a walk."

She didn't try to hide her shock. "With you?"

"Yes, with me. If you're not too tired after your afternoon with your friends."

A week ago she would have leaped at the chance. She tried to find the enthusiasm she would have felt then. "No, I'd like that. I'll just go and freshen up and I'll be right back."

He nodded, moving back towards the living room. "Whenever you're ready."

Once upstairs, Lizzy sank onto her bed and stared out the window.

Why on earth did he want to go for a walk now? She

realized how ridiculous thinking that seemed, but after ten days of barely seeing him she'd become used to the lack of attention from her husband. Now he had not only waited for her to get home, he also wanted to spend time with her. Alone.

It was... suspicious.

Several different explanations for his sudden desire for her company suggested themselves, all of which she discarded immediately. Nothing made sense... and then it came to her. What if he was taking her out to tell her he'd made a mistake bringing her here and he was divorcing her and sending her back home?

Her heart constricted. He couldn't do that after barely a week. He hadn't given her any chance at all. She didn't want to leave. She'd been planting blueberry bushes on the edge of the vegetable garden and the young plants needed extra care. And she was helping Elijah lay the pipes for the new irrigation system. Since Richard agreed to the cost of building a cistern Elijah had been working on getting the area ready and with all the extra work he needed her. A few more games of poker and she knew she'd be able to read him better. And she would miss their evenings at the pond desperately.

Richard couldn't send her away, he just couldn't.

Taking a deep breath, she stood. She was getting too far ahead of herself. It might be nothing. He may simply want to go for a walk with her. It was a pleasant afternoon and the sun was shining. It was just a walk, that was all.

Just a normal, harmless, not at all foreboding walk.

When she got back downstairs, Richard was waiting for her in the kitchen.

He smiled as she walked in. "You look pretty."

A compliment, that was a good start. Granted, it was the first compliment he'd ever paid her which in itself was suspicious, but it didn't indicate he was about to divorce her.

Or maybe he was just trying to soften the coming blow.

Her brief spark of optimism snuffed out.

"Thank you."

He ushered her through the back door and offered his arm. That was unusual too and she had no idea if it was good or bad, but she had no option but to slip her hand around his elbow and hope for the former.

She cast a longing glance at the path that led to the pond as they passed, wondering if Elijah was there waiting for her. Would he miss her when she didn't go? Would he wonder why, think she no longer wanted to spend the time with him?

Would she never get the chance to meet with him again before Richard sent her home?

"Did you have a good time with your friends?"

Richard's question startled her. Even though he was walking right beside her, she'd almost forgotten he was there.

"Very good. It was nice to spend time with all five of us together. I've missed them."

"You can go and visit any of them whenever you like," he said. "Take the buggy anytime. Elijah can hook it up for you."

She didn't say one of the reasons she hadn't been leaving the ranch often was because she was helping Elijah. She wondered if Richard even knew how much she'd been working with him.

"Thank you. I would like to go and visit Jo sometime this week."

"How's Mrs. Raine?"

She thought of Sara and the way she'd burst into tears the moment they'd asked how she was. "It's hard for her. Daniel's having a difficult time adjusting since the accident and she doesn't know how to help him."

He frowned. "How are they coping on the farm? Maybe I should go over there and ask if they need some help. I could spare one or two of the men for a while."

Lizzy didn't know why, but his concern surprised her somewhat. She had to remind herself that he was still the good man she'd corresponded with for months. "She said Will is keeping it all going so far, but I'm sure they'd appreciate the offer. Well, Sara would. Daniel is having trouble coming to terms with being unable to do things like he could before."

"I can understand that. I'd probably feel the same way in his place. I'll give it a couple of days and then go over. You could come if you want."

So he wasn't planning on sending her away in the next couple of days. That was a relief, at least. "I'd like that."

Richard took them along the track that led to the chicken and pig enclosures and she found herself looking forward to the next day when she'd be coming this way with Elijah to feed the animals. Often, that was her favorite part of the working day.

"How are you getting along here?" Richard said after a while. "Mrs. Lassiter said you've been spending a lot of your time outside, helping Elijah."

"I enjoy it. She doesn't let me do anything in the house, but I like being outdoors more anyway. I love working with the animals." She was suddenly afraid he'd tell her to stop. "That's all right, isn't it?"

"You can do whatever you want. I don't mind. I wouldn't want you to be bored and I'm sure Elijah is glad of the help."

She breathed out the air she didn't realize she'd been holding in. "Thank you."

"How are the plans for the water tank coming along?"

She smiled. "If we come back that way I can show you where it will be. Elijah has ordered the parts. He says that once they arrive..."

Forgetting her fears about why he'd asked her to go for a walk with him, she spent the next ten minutes telling him all about Elijah's plans for the irrigation system and the plumbing for inside the house. They left the animal enclosures, pasture and vegetable garden behind and headed out onto the cattle ranch proper, with its rolling pastures and scattered clumps of trees, the mountains rising ahead of them.

A lone rider on horseback approached and Lizzy recognized Eugene when he got closer. He tipped his hat to Lizzy when he reached them, bringing his chestnut gelding to a halt.

"Everything all right, Gene?" Richard said.

"Yes, boss. Cattle are all grazing, no sign of any of the cows getting ready to give birth. I was just heading back in, thought I'd see if you needed anything."

"We're just out for a stroll. You can go on back."

Eugene nodded and looked at Lizzy. "Coming round for a game tonight, ma'am?"

Richard raised his eyebrows but didn't say anything.

"No gambling on the Lord's day, Mr. Peck," she said with a smile.

"Oh yeah, sorry. Does that mean no lessons about how to gamble better either?"

She shielded her eyes with her free hand to look up at him. "I don't think there's anything in the Bible about that, but better not, just in case."

He gave a shrug. "You'd know better about what's in the Bible than I would, Mrs. Shand."

"Well then, there's something you can do tonight. Read the Bible."

"Will it help me play poker better?"

She couldn't help but laugh. "You never know."

"Then I'll give it some serious thought," he said with a

161

grin that said he would do nothing of the sort. He tipped his hat again before turning his horse in the direction of the house. "Ma'am. Boss."

"Lessons on how to gamble better?" Richard said as they watched him ride away.

"I felt sorry for him. He was just so bad at it. But he's getting a bit better now."

"With your help?"

She couldn't tell by his tone if he disapproved or not, but there was no way to sugar-coat it. "Yes."

They started walking again.

"Well, I guess if I get in on one of those games again I'd better watch out for Eugene."

"Truth be told, he's still not that good," she replied, smiling in relief, "but he's better than he was."

He seemed to sigh as he looked ahead of them. "You're quite a woman, Elizabeth."

She wasn't sure what to say to that, so she didn't say anything. She still had no idea why they were out there, even though it was pleasant, and the uncertainty kept her from truly enjoying the walk.

They reached a massive, ancient oak and stopped in the shade beneath its spreading branches. Hidden somewhere in the canopy above them, a bird sang. A huge fallen branch lay on the ground, large enough to provide an impromptu seat, and they sat side by side.

"It's so beautiful here," Lizzy said, looking towards the distant mountains. "I think this must be the most perfect spot to have a ranch."

"I thought the same thing when I chose it." He let out a long sigh. "You know, I don't own this ranch."

This was news to her. "You don't?"

"I wanted this place so much that I would have done just about anything to get it, but the bank wouldn't give me a loan. They said my track record was unproven for such a large amount of money."

"So how were you able to buy it?"

He sighed again. "I asked my parents for help."

His parents. Was that how they had made him marry her? She wondered if she should reveal what she'd overheard him say at their house a week before. *You told me to get married, I got married! She's just what you wanted! I don't know why you're surprised, since you pretty much forced me into it.* At the time, she'd felt terribly hurt, but now the memory of his words didn't even bring a twinge of sadness. Maybe she'd already given up on her marriage.

But if that was the case, why was she so afraid that he would send her home?

Her worry that his reason for bringing her out here was to give her that bad news returned in force. She had to know, one way or the other.

"Are you going to divorce me and send me home?"

His jaw dropped open. "Am I what?"

Fear pushed the words out all in a rush. "You barely speak to me or spend any time with me and you haven't even touched me. I've been around every other man on this ranch far more than I've been around you. You act like you can't stand to be around me. I know you don't want me here."

He puffed out a breath and stared at the ground for a few seconds before raising his eyes to hers. "Elizabeth, your presence here is making all this possible, in ways you can't even imagine."

She could imagine, but she didn't say so.

"Can I ask you something?" he said.

She nodded.

"Why did you want to come here and marry me?"

His question threw her. "I... I..." She looked away, embarrassed. Her reasons had seemed so logical and

163

reasonable at the time, but now she wasn't so sure. "I wanted to see new places and come to the wild west and have adventure and excitement and... I wanted to fall madly in love."

There were a few seconds of silence, then he murmured, "Madly in love," as if to himself. He leaned forward, resting his elbows on his knees and clutching his hands together as he stared out across the grass and trees to the mountains.

There was a full half a minute of silence before he spoke again and Lizzy found she was practically holding her breath.

"I know it hasn't been easy for you so far," he said, "but I want you to know I appreciate that you've come all this way to marry me. And I do want you here."

Relief flooded through her. "I want to be here."

There were another few seconds of silence during which he darted a glance at her and she was certain he wanted to say something more. But then he drew a deep breath in and stood, holding his hand out to her.

"Let's go back and you can show me where that water tank will be."

She nodded and stood with him, linking her arm through his again.

They chatted as they returned to the house, small talk mostly, but her mind was on other things.

Relieved as she was that he wasn't about to send her home, the whole exchange had left her more than a little confused. Why, of all her reasons for coming, was it the part about falling in love that had caught his attention? Wasn't that what husbands and wives were supposed to do? Was there a chance that Richard was coming around to the idea of having a wife, even if it hadn't been his choice?

And, most confusing of all, why did that thought not make her even a little bit happy?

CHAPTER 16

Lizzy leaned on the windowsill of her bedroom and rested her chin on her arms, staring out into the dark night.

The light of the moon shimmered silver on the barns and fences and trees. And on the bunkhouse, which was the real focus of her gaze.

It was ironic that in all the days she'd longed for Richard to pay her attention and stay with her, he never had. Today he had and all she'd wanted was for him to make an excuse and leave like he usually did. But he hadn't. He'd stayed while she baked, complimented her on her flapjacks, and ate the supper Mrs. Lassiter had left for them. He really seemed to be making an effort.

She wished he wouldn't.

She hadn't been able to go to the pond and it broke her heart that Elijah might have been there waiting for her. Even though she'd seen him that morning, she missed being with him there. She missed his laughter and the way his eyes crinkled at the corners when he was not quite smiling. She missed how he always seemed interested when she talked and paid attention to what she was doing, even if it was just drawing a flower. She missed how he would animatedly explain to her how his designs worked, his face lighting up as he spoke. She missed the way the sun filtered through the branches in the clearing and shone in his gently curling blond hair and hazel eyes. She missed his stutter, how it became more pronounced when he was excited and almost disappeared sometimes when he was relaxed.

Abruptly, Lizzy sat up, gasping in a breath of realization. She'd been with her husband, but all she'd wanted was to be with Elijah. And it wasn't just because they were friends.

It was because she wanted them to be more.

"Oh no," she whispered. "No, no, no."

She pressed a hand over her mouth as if she could stifle the feelings she now recognized she had for a man who wasn't her husband.

"Please, Lord, no."

She stood and looked around the dark room as if she would find the answer there. When nothing presented itself, she began to pace back and forth, her fear growing.

"This can't be happening. I can't be falling for Elijah, I just can't." She stopped and looked up at the ceiling, pressing her hands together over her heart. "Father, please take these feelings away from me. I want to feel like this for Richard, not Elijah. Please, You have to do something. It isn't right."

A floorboard creaked in the hallway outside her bedroom. She froze, staring at the door in horror. Was Richard out there? Had he heard her begging God to take away her feelings for another man?

She waited for what seemed like an age before she heard the squeak of one of the stairs and then a door downstairs opening and closing. Going to the window, she watched Richard stride across the yard towards the stables. A few minutes later he emerged with his horse, mounted, and rode out towards the road.

A flash of anger momentarily eclipsed her confusion and anguish. Here she was, devastated over her developing feelings for Elijah and pleading with God to take them away, and Richard was again doing what had driven her to seek out company elsewhere in the first place.

"Why are you doing this?" she shouted at the window, even though he was long out of sight.

Shaking her head in frustration, she threw herself onto the bed and burst into tears.

CHAPTER 17

Elijah pushed the wheelbarrow out into the sunshine. As he turned to close the barn door a sound caught his attention, a sound he'd never heard on the ranch before – singing.

He looked around, trying to pinpoint the source of the faint but beautiful melody. To his astonishment, it seemed to be coming from the direction of the pig enclosure.

It wasn't entirely accurate that he'd never heard singing on the ranch. There was the occasional drunken, and usually filthy, ditty from one or more of his bunkmates when they returned from the saloon late at night. And Mrs. Lassiter sometimes hummed or sang as she worked when she was in a particularly cheerful mood, although calling her tuneless would have been a generous description. Elijah hesitated to call either of those singing, however. Certainly not compared to what he was hearing now.

When he reached the field his pigs called home, all he could do was stop and stare.

A little way inside the gate was a chair that must have been brought from the house. It wasn't one of the ornate, expensive ones from the dining room, this one looked more like one of the plain chairs that sat around the kitchen table, but he couldn't help wondering what Mrs. Lassiter would say if she knew it was now sitting in a field.

But even more surprising than the chair was that on it sat Lizzy, facing away from him.

And she was singing *In Heavenly Love Abiding*.

To the pigs.

But even more astonishing than all that was that they appeared to be listening to her.

At least thirty adult pigs and countless piglets were gathered around her, sitting, lying and standing, and Elijah could swear they were enjoying what they were hearing. He couldn't blame them. She had a beautiful, clear voice that could have been an angel singing, or what he imagined an angel would sound like. Nestled on her lap was one of the piglets, eyes closed and snout resting on her arm.

For a moment, Elijah had a deep desire to be that piglet, to be resting in her embrace, her arms cradling him and her voice soothing his cares away.

She hadn't come to the pond the previous evening. He'd waited for her until it was almost dark and he had to pick his way back by the light of the moon. When he'd got back to the bunkhouse Eugene mentioned seeing her with Mr. Shand. And Elijah's heart had sunk.

He hadn't intended any of it to happen. All he'd wanted to do was help. Since the day she arrived he'd seen how lonely and unhappy she was and he couldn't very well turn her away when she wanted to help him. They'd become friends, which was fine, there was nothing wrong with that.

And then, over the past few days, he'd come to realize that his feelings were creeping dangerously beyond mere friendship. And despite repeated prayers that God would take them away, they were only growing. It scared him. He didn't want to give up being Lizzy's friend. Just being around her made him happy. It was like stepping into the sun every time she was near and if that was all there was it was enough.

But as he watched her singing to a crowd of pigs, he couldn't escape the knowledge that he wanted much more than friendship with Lizzy.

He shook his head. He couldn't think like that. She was

married and she had vowed before God to be faithful to her husband. She belonged to another man and there was no chance she could ever be his.

The thought pierced his heart like a knife.

Please take these feelings from me, Father, he prayed again. *I don't want them.*

After listening to her for a few more seconds, he opened the gate and pushed the wheelbarrow inside. Lizzy stopped singing and turned to look at him. Her smile made his heart thud.

"Oh, thank goodness," she said. "For a moment I thought you were Mrs. Lassiter come to scold me for bringing the chair out here."

He couldn't help but smile back. "I won't t-tell. What are you doing?"

"Singing to the pigs." She said it as if it was the most normal thing in the world.

"I can see that. Why?"

"They seem to like it." She looked down at the piglet in her arms. "I know God provided us with animals to eat and that they will be going to slaughter one day, but until that happens I just want them to have a happy life. They deserve it, don't you think?"

"They do," he said quietly.

She was the most wonderfully confusing person he'd ever met. On the one hand she could beat just about anyone in poker and rushed to the vociferous defense of anyone she felt was being wronged, and on the other she was utterly sweet and guileless. It would have been so much easier to ignore his feelings for her if she didn't intrigue him so much.

For a few seconds he watched her as she stroked the piglet, until one of the pigs nudged his leg as it stretched up to investigate the contents of the wheelbarrow. He dropped his gaze and swallowed.

170

"I'd better get this spread," he said, waving vaguely at the pile of leftover cabbage leaves he'd brought. "You can keep singing if you'd like."

She looked at the pigs who were now all showing an interest in the wheelbarrow. The piglet on her lap began to squirm and, laughing, she placed it onto the ground. "I think my audience is more concerned with filling their stomachs than listening to me."

He tried not to appear disappointed. He'd wanted to hear more.

She stood and walked over to him, joining him in taking handfuls of the leaves and scattering them amongst the pigs. He tried not to stare at her, but he couldn't keep his eyes from straying to her every now and then. He loved the expression of happiness on her face as the pigs crowded around her and snuffled into the dirt to find every bit of food.

When the wheelbarrow had been emptied, she stood with her hands on her hips and watched them eat. Dirt covered her hands and arms and the skirt of her dress, but she didn't seem to mind. He didn't think he'd ever seen anyone look prettier.

"I have to admit," she said, looking out over the field, "I never would have thought I'd enjoy farming so much. I know I'm probably more a hindrance than a help, but it's all made being here so much more fun. I don't know what I'd do with myself all day if it wasn't for you."

He rushed to assure her. "Oh n-n-no, you are a b-big help. I get through my work much quicker now. I feel like I should be p-p-paying you some of my wages. You could be a farmer."

She turned to look at him. "You really think so?"

How could she not know how amazing she was?

"I think you can do whatever you want to."

Her answering smile took his breath away. He tried to

convince himself it was simply because they were friends and he was proud of her. If he thought it enough times, maybe one day he'd believe it.

"There he is!" The angry shout came from behind him.

Lizzy focused beyond him and he looked round to see Mr. Bowman, one of their neighbors, striding towards them along the track from the direction of the house. He was followed by his foreman, Bert Garrett, and two of his farmhands, Snyder and Pratt. Elijah opened the gate and pushed the wheelbarrow out after Lizzy, securing the latch behind them and leaving the pigs to their meal.

As he approached, Elijah could see Mr. Bowman's face was twisted in fury. He stepped forward, placing himself in front of Lizzy. He couldn't imagine what had the man so angry. He'd done some work for him and he'd always seemed like a personable type.

"Is s-s-something wrong, Mr. Bowman?"

"Is something *wrong*?" he growled. "I should pound you into the ground for what you've done."

Elijah raised his hands, glancing at the other three men warily. "I-I-I don't know w-what..."

"What I'm talking about?" Bowman snapped.

Elijah clamped his mouth shut. He hated it when people finished his sentences for him.

"I'm talking about that death trap you designed for me!" he said, raising his fist. "It almost killed my grandson!"

Elijah retreated a step and felt Lizzy's hands touch his back. He was suddenly afraid, not for himself but for her. He wasn't sure he could protect her from all four men at once.

"M-Mr. Bowman, I d-don't understand."

"That windmill thing!" Bowman shouted. "The blade came off and hit my Bobby!"

Elijah stared at him in disbelief. It couldn't be true. He'd used the same design as the one he'd built on the ranch. It

172

was a solid construction. Something like that just couldn't happen.

"I-Is he all right?"

"No he's not all right. His arm's broken!"

"I-I-I'm sorry, but it couldn't be the design. I could check it and s-s-see..."

"You're not going anywhere near the farm, you stammering freak," Garrett spat. He stepped forward, Snyder and Pratt on his heels. "Never should have trusted someone who's not right in the head. Now you're going to pay for hurting the boy."

"No!" Lizzy ran in front of Elijah, her arms out in front of her as if she could push them back through sheer force of will alone. "There's an explanation. You can't just accuse him. If you let him..."

"Get out of our way, girl," Garrett snarled.

Grabbing her shoulder, he shoved her aside, sending her sprawling onto the ground.

Elijah's heart hit his throat. "*Lizzy!*"

Before he could move, Garrett's fist was coming at his face. A lifetime of being a target for bullies who thought slow speech meant a slow body kicked in. He ducked, the blow missing him by barely an inch. Springing back up, he slammed the heel of his hand into Garrett's gut, sending him staggering backwards and gasping for breath.

He glanced at Lizzy to see if she was all right, but she was already back on her feet, appearing shaken but unharmed. He turned his attention to Snyder and Pratt who were advancing on him. Bringing his fists up, he rotated into a fighting posture without even having to think about it. It had been a while, but some instincts never left.

"No, stop this," Bowman said. "We should wait for the marshal."

No one listened.

173

Pratt reached Elijah first and threw a punch at his head. Elijah bobbed out of the way and pivoted, using his momentum to slam his fist into Pratt's face. Pratt staggered back, raising his fingers to where red seeped from his nose.

The sight of the blood broke through Elijah's haze of anger. This wasn't who he was anymore. This wasn't who God wanted him to be.

He straightened, dropping his hands to his sides. "I-I-I won't fight you."

"Fine by me," Garrett growled, advancing on him and raising his fist.

Lizzy exploded past Elijah, shrieking, and barreled into Garrett, throwing them both to the ground where she punched at his chest. Snyder grasped her waist and lifted her off, kicking and screaming. Garrett pushed to his feet.

"Put me down, you *brute!*" she screeched, hammering both fists back into Snyder as he struggled to hold onto her.

"L-l-l-leave her alone!" Elijah roared, rushing towards them.

Garrett's fist slammed into his jaw.

He stumbled sideways.

A gunshot split the air, startling everyone into inaction. As one, they turned towards the source.

A horse slowed to a stop beyond Bowman and Marshal Cade dropped to the ground, his revolver in his hand.

"I thought we'd agreed you would wait for me, Mr. Bowman." His gaze swept over the assembled group, coming to a stop on Lizzy and the man still holding her. "I'm going to have to ask you to put Mrs. Shand down, Mr. Snyder."

Snyder lowered her to the ground and she immediately spun around and slapped him.

He clamped a hand over his cheek. "Ouch!"

Lizzy gave him a final glare before marching away to join Elijah.

"A-are you all right?" He wanted to reach out to her and take her hand, but in the presence of the others he didn't dare.

She brushed several wild strands of hair from her eyes and nodded. "Are you?"

He moved his jaw from side to side, trying not to wince. It was in one piece, at least. He'd had worse. "I'm okay."

"Now," Marshal Cade said, "would someone like to explain this brawl?"

Lizzy whirled from Elijah and jabbed her finger at Bowman. "He came here throwing around completely unfounded accusations and these... these *apes* attacked us! I demand you arrest them!"

Elijah had to clamp his mouth shut to stop himself from smiling, immediately regretting it when his aching jaw protested. He loved it when she came to his defense.

The marshal moved his gaze to their neighbor. "Mr. Bowman, when you came to my office and told me about what happened to your grandson you agreed to let me handle the situation."

Bowman blew out a breath, throwing a reproving look at Garrett. "I know, Marshal. Things just got a little heated. My men are very fond of the boy."

"A *little heated*?!" Lizzy looked like she might explode. She marched to Garrett and jabbed her finger into his chest. "*He* pushed me over and punched Mr. Griffin, and *he*," she strode up to Snyder, "grabbed me in the most appalling way. You saw it!"

Snyder took a step away from her, appearing afraid she would slap him again.

The marshal looked around the group. "I think we're all going to have to take a trip back to my office."

"All?" Lizzy said. "We've done nothing wrong!"

"Ma'am, Mr. Bowman has brought a very serious

accusation against Mr. Griffin and I can't just ignore that. You don't have to come, but I'm afraid I'll have to take him in until I can get to the bottom of it all."

"But he has no proof!"

The marshal looked at Elijah. "Did you design that windmill and provide Mr. Bowman with the instructions on how to build it?"

He knew there was no way this could have been his fault, but he couldn't deny that fact. "Yes, sir."

Cade returned his attention to Lizzy. "I'm sorry, Mrs. Shand, but I have to do this. You have my word I will conduct a thorough investigation."

She shook her head, her lips pressing together. Elijah's heart broke to see her upset.

"It will be all right," he said softly, "y-y-you don't have to worry."

She looked up at him. "It's just so unfair." Her gaze turned to steel as she moved it to the marshal. "But I'm coming with you. To make sure everything is done properly."

One side of Cade's mouth twitched. "Yes, ma'am."

It took a few minutes to sort out the travel arrangements, but eventually they decided to hitch up the buggy for Elijah and Lizzy to ride in while everyone else used the horses they'd arrived on. When Lizzy pointed out that any one of Bowman's men could simply ride off, the marshal assured her his aim was good enough to take them down if they tried. She pointed out she only had his word for that and wouldn't back down until he took aim at a plum hanging from a branch twenty feet away and shot it straight through. Elijah had to bite back a grin when she then thoroughly berated him for scaring the pigs.

After all that had happened, she was unusually quiet as they drove towards the town.

"Are you truly all right?" Elijah said to her quietly. "D-d-did they hurt you?"

She sighed and looked down at her hands. "Only my pride. I just don't understand how they can get away with this. I know nothing you did could have hurt that boy."

He didn't understand why she had such faith in him and part of him wanted to tell her how unworthy he was of it. The rest wanted to let her continue to believe he was the man she thought he was.

"Thank you," he said.

She looked up at him. "For what?

"F-f-for believing in me."

She held his gaze until his heart was beating double time and his thoughts were straying into territory they shouldn't have been anywhere near. Then she looked away and he had to take a deep breath to calm himself. They spent the rest of the journey in silence.

On reaching the marshal's office in Green Hill Creek everyone went inside. Marshal Cade waved Elijah and Lizzy into the two chairs in front of his desk, leaving the other four men to stand. Elijah didn't know what to make of that.

"Right," Cade said, lowering into the obviously well-used chair behind his desk, "let's get this all sorted out. I've heard what Mr. Bowman has to say about the accident..."

"Wasn't an accident," Bowman snapped. He hadn't stood still since they'd entered, instead pacing the width of the room. "It was negligence, plain and simple."

"Now I want to hear what you have to say, Mr. Griffin," the marshal continued, ignoring the interruption.

Elijah swallowed, acutely aware of every person in the room. Speaking in front of more than one person he didn't know well made him uncomfortable. He couldn't help feeling like they were judging him for his speech. Not to mention that this time it wasn't just his stutter they were judging.

"Th-th-th-th-" He stopped, squeezing his eyes shut in

frustration.

"This is stupid," Garrett said. "He can't even talk right, let alone make anything. He's just slow."

Before he realized what he was doing, Elijah was on his feet and facing him, the old familiar anger coursing through him.

"Mr. Griffin, you'd do best to sit back down." Marshal Cade's voice was calm and he hadn't moved from his seat, and yet the implied authority was unmistakable.

Garrett's mouth twisted into a smirk that in the old days would have earned him a bloody nose or a cut lip. Before Elijah found a better way in a Savior who loved him no matter how he talked.

He unfurled his fists and deliberately turned away, sitting back down beside Lizzy without looking at her. He didn't want to see her face filled with disappointment in him.

He focused on a pen lying on Cade's desk and spoke slowly. "Th-that windmill design has been used on Mr. Shand's ranch and f-f-five others. N-n-none of them have ever broken before. I d-don't know what went wrong, but it wasn't m-m-my design."

Mr. Bowman strode up to the marshal's desk, glaring at Elijah. "That thing was built exactly to your instructions. I had my doubts that you could do it, but after I spoke to Shand and the others who have them I decided to give you a chance. Now my grandson has a broken arm because of it. I should never have trusted someone like you."

Someone like you. All Elijah's life he'd had to deal with the attitude that because he couldn't speak well he couldn't think well. And despite all his best efforts over the past three years, it still made him angry. He stared at the pen and prayed silently for restraint. From the corner of his eye he could see Lizzy, her lips pressed together like she was struggling to keep from speaking as she glowered at Bowman. She looked to be angrier than he was. At least *she* was on his side.

Marshal Cade leaned back in his chair. "I reckon the only way to get to the bottom of this is to go and see that windmill and find out what went wrong. Now Mr. Griffin is the one who designed it so he'll come..."

"You can't bring him!" Garrett shouted. "He'll just lie and make it look like it isn't his fault. You can't trust him."

"He's right," Bowman said. "I'm not letting him onto my property."

The marshal blew out a breath. "Mr. Bowman..."

The door to the outside opened and Deputy Eric Fielding burst in.

His eyes took a moment to take in everyone in the room before settling on Cade. "Lee, Fleming is at it again. Fred's got him cornered, but you know he won't listen to anyone but you."

"This early?" Cade pinched the bridge of his nose, closing his eyes for a moment. "All right. You stay here, I'll go." He looked at Elijah. "I'm sorry, Mr. Griffin, I'm going to have to lock you up while I deal with this."

"*What?!*" Lizzy shrieked.

"It's only until I've got this under control. Soon as I'm done, I'll be right back." He looked at Bowman. "You can take your men and go home, but I need your word that none of them will leave your place until this is settled. If they do, I'll hold you accountable. Do I have your word?"

Bowman gave a sharp nod. "You do."

Lizzy leaped to her feet. "This is so unfair!"

"Sit down and leave this to the men, little girl," Garrett said.

Fists clenching, she slowly rotated to look at him, her voice lowering to a deadly hush. "What did you call me?"

Elijah reached out to touch her arm, afraid she'd do something rash. "Don't, p-please."

The marshal stood and walked around his desk, placing himself in front of Lizzy and facing Garrett. "Go home, Mr. Garrett."

"Let's go," Bowman said, heading for the door with Snyder and Pratt on his heels.

Garrett's eyes flicked to Elijah, narrowing for a moment before he turned to follow his boss out.

Elijah breathed out.

"I don't like that man," Lizzy said.

"The look you gave him, I feared for his safety for a minute there," Marshal Cade said, fetching a ring of keys from a hook on the wall behind his desk and opening a door in the back wall. Elijah could see bars on the other side. "I'm sorry, Mr. Griffin, but I have to keep you in here. Shouldn't be for long, then we can get this all sorted out."

Elijah stood and walked through the door to where three empty jail cells waited for him. Cade used one of the keys on the ring to open the closest and Elijah stepped inside. The clang of metal on metal as the door closed made him flinch. It was more than three years since he'd been in a jail cell. Although that time he'd deserved it.

"Stay as long as you want, Mrs. Shand," the marshal said, picking up a chair and moving it to beside the cell bars. "Eric will be in the office and I'll be back just as soon as I can." He left, closing the door behind him.

Lizzy slumped into the chair and leaned against the bars of Elijah's cell. He dragged one of the narrow cots across the small space so he could sit next to her.

She wrapped her fingers around the bars. "You shouldn't be in here, locked up like a common criminal. This is all wrong."

He could have told her it wasn't his first time in jail, but he knew he wouldn't be able to take letting her down. He needed her to believe in him, at least for now. "It'll b-be

180

okay."

"Do you know the marshal? Is he an honorable man? My daddy said he is."

"I guess so. I d-don't know him well. People seem to like him." He stared at her hands on the bars, just inches from his. All he had to do was move his fingers a little and they'd be touching.

She let go of the bars and stood. "I have to do something. I can't just sit here."

"But what can you do?" He wanted her to stay, where he could be sure she was safe.

She began to pace the small space between the cells. "There has to be a way to find out what caused the blade to break off. If you could just see it... but Mr. Bowman won't let you. He could even get rid of the evidence before the marshal goes there. Anything could be happening and no one would be able to prove a thing." She stopped pacing and turned towards the door. "I'm going to get you out."

His apprehension turned to panic. "No, w-wait, Lizzy!"

"Don't worry," she said, pulling the door open and looking back at him with a smile. "It's all going to be all right." And then she left.

Elijah grabbed the bars to his cell. "*Lizzy!*"

CHAPTER 18

Lizzy didn't like making the horse gallop while pulling the buggy, but she needed to get back to the ranch as fast as possible. There wasn't much time if she was going to save Elijah from jail. And she was definitely going to save him.

She pulled into the yard twenty minutes after leaving the marshal's office, jumped to the ground and headed straight for the bunkhouse.

She knocked on the door first, just in case. The last thing she wanted was to walk in on one of the men in a state of undress. Only when there was no reply did she venture to open the door.

The long, wide room was much more of a mess than it usually was when she visited in the evenings. Maybe Mrs. Lassiter hadn't been in to tidy up yet. Lizzy found a new admiration for Richard's housekeeper as she walked between beds covered with unwashed clothing and tables covered with unwashed mugs and plates.

"How can they live like this?" she wondered aloud.

Were all men this untidy? She only had experience of four, her father and brothers, and they wouldn't have dared to leave the house in this kind of state no matter how hurried they were in the mornings. Her mother would have... oh. That was how the world functioned, because God had given men wives. She smiled at the thought.

Elijah's corner, however, was like an oasis in the disarray, bed made and free of clutter. Her haste momentarily forgotten, she sat and ran her hand over the cover, imagining him sitting propped up against the pillow, a book in his lap, sketching another design or creating another engineering marvel, the glow of a lamp casting light and shadow across his handsome face and reflecting from his tousled hair.

Casting a glance at the door, she picked up his pillow and held it to her face, filling her lungs with his scent as she closed her eyes.

A sudden realization of what she was doing jolted them open again. Leaping up as if the bed had grown thorns, she rapidly put the pillow back in place. She couldn't think like that of a man who wasn't her husband.

"Father, forgive me," she whispered.

Tears burned at her eyes and she brushed at them in annoyance. This wasn't the time. She had more important things to do than lament her sad predicament.

Hoping Elijah would forgive her for invading his privacy, she opened the locker next to his bed and found the portfolio, quickly flicking through the pages inside until she found the design for the windmill. As she'd hoped, it was extensively annotated in his neat handwriting. She replaced the portfolio in the locker and folded the page into her pocket. It wasn't as good as having him there, but it was the next best thing.

With one last look at Elijah's corner, she left the bunkhouse. It occurred to Lizzy while she was climbing back into the buggy that the only knowledge she had of the location of the Bowman farm was when Richard had commented at a junction in the road on their way home from church that it was in that direction. She considered riding out to find either Richard or one of the men to ask, but immediately discounted the idea. They'd want to know why and if she told them, they wouldn't let her go. Besides, she didn't know exactly where Richard was. Surely a whole farm would be easier to find than a few men and a herd of cows.

She'd just have to head down that road and pray she got there before anything happened that would make her quest to free Elijah even harder.

~ ~ ~

In the end it turned out to be relatively easy to find Mr. Bowman's farm, thanks to Elijah's windmill.

About a mile after the turning onto the road she spotted the tall structure above the trees and headed in that direction. She left the buggy hidden in the wood, tethered by a patch of lush grass for the horse, and made her way on foot towards the windmill. Half a mile or so from the road she reached the far edge of the trees and flattened herself against a wide trunk, peering out across the grassy expanse between the edge of the forest and the windmill.

Away to her right, up a shallow incline, sat a two storey farmhouse and a cluster of outbuildings. The wind pump was straight in front of her, roughly fifty yards away. One of the wooden paddle blades lay on the ground a short distance from it.

There was very little cover between Lizzy and the windmill, just a few lanky shrubs and a collection of wooden barrels by a stone well which must have been the source of the water the pump was moving to the buildings.

She raised her eyes to the top of the windmill. It looked a long way up. At least there was a ladder attached to the latticework structure enabling people to get to the top, but it still looked frighteningly high.

She drew a deep breath in and out. *Please, God, help me to do this. Help me to help Elijah.*

She took another careful look at the house and barns to make sure no one was about, prayed that no one would look out a window, and left the cover of the trees. Picking up her skirts, she sprinted across the open ground and threw herself behind the barrels when she reached the well. She lay still, listening for any sign she'd been seen. After half a minute she dared to raise her head and peek over the top of the barrels. All was quiet.

With another deep breath and another quick prayer, she launched herself for the windmill.

Reaching the broken blade, she threw herself flat into the long grass, hoping it was enough to hide her. She pulled Elijah's diagram from her pocket and unfolded it, being careful to keep it as clean as possible. He was so neat that she was sure he wouldn't like dirt on the page. Sadly, what with the pigs and the fight and now being on the ground, she wasn't anywhere near clean. But she did what she could.

She studied the blade from where she lay in the grass, comparing it to the expanded diagram on the paper, but couldn't tell where the problem lay. The blade seemed intact, which meant whatever had caused its separation from the main structure most likely lay at the point of its attachment.

She rolled onto her back to look up at the windmill towering above her. She was going to have to climb. But if she did, she'd be in full view of anyone who happened to walk outside or glance out a window.

"For Elijah," she whispered to herself. "I'm doing this for Elijah."

She pushed the diagram back into her pocket, took a few moments to gather her courage, and pushed herself to her feet.

She hadn't scaled a few rungs before she wanted to rip off her dress. Her skirt was constantly in the way, threatening to trip her with every step. Gathering the offending fabric, she hooked it over one arm and resumed her ascent, not caring if anyone saw her exposed calves. There was a time for modesty but this wasn't it.

After what felt like hours she reached a narrow platform just below where the blades made a creaking sound as they rotated slowly in the slight breeze. The constant movement made the tower vibrate and she clung even more tightly to the ladder, not daring to look down.

Leaning against the structure, her feet on the platform and one arm hooked around a handle set into the side of the box surrounding the mechanism, she stared at the blade assembly a few feet away. It wasn't easy to see details with it moving, but she had no idea how to stop it and wasn't sure what would happen if she did. So she hung on and ran her eyes over each component, having to squeeze them closed every few seconds to counteract the dizziness that threatened from watching the moving parts.

At first she wasn't sure she'd be able to see anything useful, but after half a minute or so she grew used to moving her eyes around with the blades. And then she saw it, the break that must have caused the blade to tear free. She pulled Elijah's diagram from her pocket and studied it, finding the corresponding part. She looked between the paper and the real thing, frowning.

"That's not right." Her eyes widened in realization. "That's it. That's it!"

"Hey, you! What are you doing up there?!"

Lizzy started at the voice yelling at her and Elijah's design slipped from her fingers. She grabbed for it desperately as it floated out of her reach, grasping onto the handle when she almost slipped from the platform.

"Get down from there!"

Past the blades she could see Mr. Garrett running towards her. Her heart thudding in her throat, she scrambled onto the ladder and began the climb down as fast as she could, her fear of him eclipsing her fear of falling.

186

She heard more voices shouting and running footfalls but didn't dare look away from the ladder as she took the rungs at twice the speed she had coming up.

The footsteps halted. "What's this?"

She glanced behind her and saw Garrett thirty feet away, stooping to lift something from the ground. He straightened with a piece of paper in his hand.

"Leave that alone!" she shouted, desperate not to lose Elijah's design.

Her foot hit thin air.

She cried out.

And then she was falling.

CHAPTER 19

Lizzy hit the ground hard. Pain exploded in her left wrist. For a few seconds all she could do was lie still, her eyes closed, panting for air and waiting for her head to stop spinning.

A shadow fell across her, blotting out the sun. She looked up at Garrett standing over her, the piece of paper with Elijah's windmill design on it clutched in his hand.

Anger burned through her at the sight of the neat drawing being crumpled so carelessly. "Give that back," she snapped, reaching for the paper.

He stepped back, lifting it out of her reach, and looked up at the windmill. "What are you doing here?"

When she didn't answer he bent down and grabbed her injured wrist, yanking her to her feet. She cried out in agony.

He leaned in close, his fingers pressing painfully into her arm. "What did you see up there?"

"You're hurting me," she said, attempting to pry his fingers away with her free hand.

He jerked her against him and growled through gritted teeth. "What... did you... see?"

Unable to free herself, wrist throbbing and heart pounding, she did the only thing she could think of, she stamped on his foot with every ounce of strength she possessed.

He yelped in pain but didn't release her. His face twisted in anger. "You're going to pay for that, you little..."

"Mr. Garrett? What's going on over there?"

She looked around him to see Mr. Bowman striding towards them from the direction of the house. Snyder was with him.

Garrett glared at her for a moment before letting her go and stepping back, stuffing the paper into his pocket. "It's Mrs. Shand, Mr. Bowman," he called. "She was climbing on the windmill."

Lizzy hugged her injured wrist against her.

Mr. Bowman reached them and frowned at her. "What were you doing on the windmill? And what's wrong with your arm?"

"She fell," Garrett said.

Mr. Bowman stepped forward, lifting his hand towards her. "Are you hurt?"

"Don't touch me!" She took a step back, searching for an escape.

He raised his hands, palms facing her. "I'm not going to hurt you. What were you doing up there?"

She lifted her chin in defiance. Whatever happened to her, she wasn't going to give them the satisfaction of seeing her afraid. "I was looking for evidence of what really made the blade come off, before you got rid of it."

"Got rid of it? What are you talking about? The evidence is that my grandson was hurt. This windmill was built just as Mr. Griffin said and it's dangerous."

"Except it wasn't," she retorted. "You didn't build it like he said."

He narrowed his eyes. "What do you mean?"

"She's just lying to get Griffin out of trouble," Garrett said. "Let me show her off your property, Mr. Bowman. I'll make sure she won't give you any more trouble and that Griffin stays in prison, where he belongs."

She looked between the two men, realization dawning. Pointing at Garrett, she said, "He's hiding Elijah's design in

189

his pocket. Look at it. You'll see."

Mr. Bowman turned his gaze on Garrett. "What's she talking about?"

He shook his head, his hand moving subconsciously to his pocket. "Nothing. She's crazy."

"Just look in his pocket!" she said, reaching for it.

He smacked her hand away.

"Hey now, there's no call to lay hands on her," Mr. Bowman said. "Just empty your pockets and show me she's wrong."

Garrett's eyes darted between them and his Adam's apple bobbed. He slid his hand into his pocket and pulled out the paper with a thin laugh, waving it in front of him. "It's nothing, just a doodle, not important."

Then, to Lizzy's horror, he ripped it into pieces.

"No!" She lunged to grab the paper as he released it to blow away in the breeze. Ignoring the pain in her wrist, she ran after the fluttering fragments. Nothing mattered but saving Elijah's drawing.

After a few seconds she became aware of someone following her as she snatched at the remains of the design. It was Snyder. Her heart slammed into her throat. She'd been wrong, Bowman did know about the windmill and now she was in serious danger.

But then Snyder began grabbing at the small bits of paper tumbling in the breeze. It took a few moments for her to realize he was helping her.

When they had collected all the pieces they could find, he handed them to her.

"I'm sorry, Mrs. Shand," he said, not meeting her eyes. "About earlier, I mean. I didn't mean to... Garrett said..." He sighed. "I'm just really sorry."

She pressed her lips together, nodded, and prayed for the grace to forgive.

As they returned to where Mr. Bowman and Garrett stood waiting for them, she carefully arranged the scraps of paper in her hands. It made her wrist hurt even more, but she wasn't going to let any one of them help. Tears almost sprang to her eyes when she realized a piece was missing. Elijah would be so disappointed in her for losing a part of his precious design. She only hoped he could recreate it.

"Here," she said to Mr. Bowman, holding up the fragment showing the damaged part she'd seen. "This is the bit that broke. If you go up there you'll see it, and you'll see why it broke. This says the rod should be made of steel, but the one up there is made of wood."

Bowman looked up at the top of the windmill then at Garrett. "You handled the construction. Is she right?"

He looked between them. "I... don't know."

"You don't know? Lewis has a broken arm and you don't *know*? I gave you enough money to cover everything; there was no reason to change the design."

"Wood is cheaper than steel," Lizzy murmured.

Mr. Bowman's eyes widened. "You did it to steal from me? Is that it?"

Garrett's fearful gaze turned to anger and his hand moved to the gun holstered at his waist. But Bowman was quicker, drawing his revolver and aiming it at Garrett's chest.

"You should know how much I want to pull this trigger," he growled, "and how lucky you are that I'm a fair man."

Lizzy thought about how unfair he'd been when he had Elijah thrown into jail with no evidence, but she didn't say anything. She very much wanted to, but she didn't.

"I'm sorry, Mrs. Shand," he said to her. "I had no idea."

She could have been magnanimous and accepted his apology, but she was in pain and angry. "Can we go and get Elijah out of jail now?"

"We sure can." He scowled at Garrett, motioning with his revolver for him to start walking. "And you'll be taking his place."

~ ~ ~

Elijah tapped a nervous rhythm with the end of the pencil in his hand against his thigh. He'd been staring at a blank sheet of paper on his lap for over an hour and had yet to draw a single line.

Dropping the pencil onto the cot beside him, he stood and walked to the door of his jail cell. "Anything yet?"

"Nothing to add to what I told you ten minutes ago, which was the same thing I told you twenty minutes ago – the marshal's not back and I can't do anything till he is."

"You could g-go and check on him, find out how long he'll be."

A sigh drifted from the front office and a chair scraped on the floor. Deputy Eric Fielding appeared in the open doorway and hooked his thumbs into his belt loops. "I can't leave you here alone. Marshal's orders."

Elijah stared at his hands wrapped around two of the iron bars, wishing he could somehow bend them apart. "I'm w-worried about Mrs. Shand. She can be a bit..." he cast around for the right word, "impulsive."

The deputy smiled. "My Lucy's the same. It's just one of the reasons why I love her, but sometimes it scares me half to death. Thing about women, though, is they're a lot stronger than we men sometimes give them credit for. I'm sure Mrs. Shand is just fine."

Elijah wanted to ask how he could possibly know that, but he stopped himself. He knew Deputy Fielding was just trying to make him feel better. It wasn't working, but he appreciated the effort.

"Want some coffee?" the deputy said. "It's strong enough to eat through iron."

Elijah looked at the bars and snorted a humorless laugh. "No, thanks."

Fielding disappeared back into the office and Elijah returned to his cot and sat. He didn't bother to pick up the pencil and paper. There was no point. Instead, he dropped his head into his hands and closed his eyes.

I know I'm meant to have faith, Lord, and I'm trying, I really am. But I'm so scared for Lizzy. Please keep her safe. I don't know what I'd do if she was hurt.

At the sound of the door to the street opening he leaped up, craning to see who it was in the limited view he had from the cell. He recognized Marshal Cade's voice speaking to Fielding and had to stop himself from calling out.

The marshal appeared in the doorway after half a minute that felt like a lifetime.

"Sorry I took so long," Cade said, walking up to the bars of Elijah's cell. "What's this Eric tells me about Mrs. Shand leaving?"

"She s-s-said she was going to get me out and I'm s-s-scared she's gone to the Bowman farm."

"Did she say she was going there?"

"No, but it's the only place I c-can think she'd go. P-please, I need to get there."

"Well, I'm heading out there anyway." The marshal walked back to the office, returning with the keys to the cell. "Might as well take you with me."

Elijah fought the urge to run out into the street as soon as he was free. His impatience must have shown.

"Don't worry, we'll get there," Cade said as he followed Elijah out of the cell room. "Mrs. Shand won't be in any danger. Mr. Bowman may be a bit hot-headed sometimes, but I've never known him to be anything other than a fair man."

Elijah gritted his teeth. "He br-brought men to the ranch who attacked us and threw me into jail."

Cade winced. "True. Okay, let's go."

He opened the door to the street and stepped out. Elijah almost ran into him when he came to a sudden halt. When Elijah followed his gaze along the road he nearly sobbed with relief.

Driving a wagon in their direction was Bowman, Garrett and Snyder in the wagon bed behind him. Behind them was Lizzy with the buggy.

Elijah's overwhelming joy changed to fear when he saw she was only using her right hand to drive, her left arm held awkwardly in her lap. He rushed to the buggy as it came to a halt in front of the marshal's office.

"Are you hurt?"

She winced as she stood. "Would you mind helping me down? I think I've sprained my wrist."

He reached up and lifted her gently to the ground. He had to force himself to let her go. If it had been up to him, he would have kept her in his arms where she would be safe.

"What happened?"

"Woman climbed up my windmill," Bowman said, jumping down from the wagon's seat. "She's lucky she didn't get herself killed."

She faced him defiantly. "I found out why it broke. And I only fell because Mr. Garrett scared me."

His expression softened. "Yes, ma'am, you did."

He glanced at the back of the wagon where Snyder and Garrett were getting out. For the first time since their arrival, Elijah noticed the rope binding Garrett's hands.

"Mr. Griffin, I owe you an apology," Bowman said. "It turned out the windmill wasn't built to your instructions and that's why the blade broke off. Mr. Garrett was using cheaper materials and pocketing the extra money. I shouldn't have jumped to blame you without proof and I'm sorry."

Elijah felt the old, familiar anger simmering, ready to erupt as it had done so many times in the past. But that was the old him, the Elijah who hadn't yet been saved by grace. A grace he was sorely in need of at that moment. He prayed for the strength to forgive as Jesus had forgiven him.

"I understand," he said, which was true. He couldn't excuse it, but he understood it.

"Looks like you're free to go, Mr. Griffin," Marshal Cade said as Deputy Fielding took Garrett inside.

Elijah bit back a reply he would have regretted and simply nodded and turned his attention back to Lizzy. Her wrist was beginning to swell and it tore him apart. He would have done anything to take her pain onto himself. She was hurt because of him.

"Y-you need to see the doctor."

"I'll pay for any treatment you need," Bowman said. "It's my fault you were injured. Just tell Doc Wilson to send the bill to me. And Mr. Griffin, I wouldn't blame you for saying no, but if you would come and oversee the fixing of the windmill, I'd be really grateful. I'd pay you whatever you think is fair."

It was the last thing he wanted to do, but he needed all the money he could get if he was to ever realize his dream of studying to become an engineer.

"I'll c-c-come round in a few days."

"I'm much obliged. Mrs. Shand." He tipped his hat to Lizzy and left them to go into the marshal's office.

Elijah gestured along the road. "Doctor's this way." She was unusually quiet as they walked and it scared him. "D-does it hurt a lot?"

She looked down at her wrist. "No, not too much."

"Did you really climb the windmill?"

"It was the only way I could think to find out what

195

happened."

They walked on for a few more steps. Lizzy's eyes were fixed on the ground in front of her.

"I was really w-worried about you," Elijah said softly.

She raised her eyes to look at him. "I was really worried about you too."

"I know." He didn't know why, but he knew she cared about him. It filled him with joy and ripped at his heart all at the same time.

After Doctor Wilson checked Lizzy's wrist, pronounced it sprained but not broken, and bandaged it for support, they returned to the buggy and started for home.

Lizzy was as quiet as she had been since returning from the Bowman farm and Elijah was becoming more and more worried. Had something happened to her that she hadn't told him about?

Halfway through their journey he brought the buggy to a halt, unable to stand not knowing any longer.

"What's wrong?" he said, laying the reins down and swiveling on the seat to face her. She didn't look up and he ducked his head to see her face. "Please t-talk to me."

She closed her eyes for a few seconds and he had to stop himself from wrapping his arms around her and telling her everything would be all right. He couldn't stand seeing her so subdued.

Finally, she slowly turned to face him and reached into one of the pockets in her dress, pulling out a handful of something. Her fist unfurled to reveal several pieces of torn, crumpled paper.

"I'm so, so sorry. I needed it to compare to Mr. Bowman's windmill so I could tell if anything was wrong, but Mr. Garrett took it and tore it up. I didn't mean for it to get ruined." She sniffed and wiped the back of her hand across her eyes.

He took the pieces of paper and straightened them, finding what was left of his windmill design. "You got this from my portfolio?"

She nodded miserably. "Are you angry?" she said, raising her eyes to his.

His mouth dropped open in astonishment. "Angry? Of course not. You s-s-stood up for me. You put yourself in danger and got hurt helping me. I'm grateful, m-more than I can say."

She looked at the fragments of paper. "But it's all torn and there's a piece missing."

He touched his finger to her chin, raising her face to look at him. "This isn't the only copy I have. I keep copies of all my designs in a safe deposit box at the bank. It's all right, I p-p-promise."

Her blue-gray eyes searched his for the truth of his words, apparently finding it when the corners of her lips turned upward a little. Realizing he was still touching her chin, he lowered his hand to his lap.

Her smile grew. "I'm not sure *everything's* all right. I left the chair in with the pigs. Mrs. Lassiter's going to be livid."

"You just tell her it was m-my fault."

"Oh, I couldn't do that. Jail would be nothing compared to the wrath of Mrs. Lassiter."

He laughed with her despite knowing firsthand the horror of a real prison. He was glad she could joke about it and that she would never know that kind of experience.

As their laughter faded he found himself caught in her gaze. Even though he knew he should look away, the connection between them was suddenly more than he could resist, the urge to draw her into his arms overwhelming. Before he could stop it, his gaze dropped to her mouth.

Her lips parted, drawing in a breath.

He swallowed and forced his gaze back up, expecting to

see disgust and anger in her eyes. But what he saw there almost knocked him flat.

He saw the longing tearing at his heart reflected back at him.

Unable to stop himself, he leaned towards her.

This is wrong.

The thought was an almost physical blow slamming into his brain. Half of him wanted to ignore it and give in to the desire raging within him.

The other, rational half of him knew he couldn't.

Closing his eyes, he drew back. When he opened them again Lizzy was staring at her hands folded in her lap.

Shame washed over him. Of course she didn't feel the same way he did; she was a good person, one of the best he'd ever met. She would never betray her husband by allowing herself to have feelings for another man. Blinded by his own desires, he'd simply seen what he wanted to see. And now he'd no doubt scared her.

Grasping the reins, he set the horses in motion again and stared ahead of him. He didn't dare look at the woman sitting beside him for the entire rest of the way home.

In case she saw in his eyes the agony of his heart breaking.

~ ~ ~

Lizzy buried her face in her skirt, hugging her knees and rocking on her bed. Outside in the yard she could hear the sounds of Elijah unhitching the buggy.

She'd almost done it. She'd almost kissed him.

For a moment, sitting in the buggy, all she'd wanted to do was pour out her heart and confess her love for him. She'd wanted to feel his arms around her, his lips on hers.

If he hadn't pulled back and turned away she would

have done everything she knew was wrong, and she was sure he had seen it. Now he knew she was a shameless hussy, ready to betray her husband at the slightest provocation. What must he think of her?

Except what she felt for Elijah didn't feel like the slightest provocation. It felt like a raging torrent of provocation.

How could this have happened? All she'd dreamed of was to come to the west, live a life of adventure and romance, and fall madly in love.

And she had, but with the wrong man.

It didn't matter what Richard did now. It wouldn't make one bit of difference if her husband threw himself at her feet and begged her forgiveness and spent every waking second with her. There was no doubt in her mind that she was hopelessly and utterly in love with Elijah, and her heart felt like it was about to shatter into a million pieces that no one would ever be able to join back together.

What could she do now? Even if Elijah hadn't noticed what happened today, he would surely see her feelings written all over her face.

How could she ever face him again?

CHAPTER 20

Lizzy plodded slowly down the stairs, her mood descending as she did.

She could hear voices coming from the kitchen, but instead of being eager to spend the time with everyone as she usually was, she now dreaded joining them marginally more than she would have dreaded walking into a cave full of hungry bears.

Reaching the door, she grasped the handle. She froze when she heard Elijah's voice.

He was in there. Which shouldn't have been a surprise because he was there every morning for breakfast. On any other day she would have been happy about that. Any other day when she hadn't made a fool of herself the day before by almost kissing him.

She glanced longingly back at the stairs, wishing she could run back up and hide in her bedroom. Her injured wrist gave her the perfect excuse to stay indoors for the day, but she knew the situation would only get worse the longer it went on. She needed to face Elijah now and try very hard not to come across as the foolish, lovesick girl she was.

She went to grasp the handle again, stumbling forward when it was pulled away from her. Hands caught hold of her shoulders and set her upright and she looked up into Richard's face.

"I was just about to come and see if you were all right," he said, smiling.

"Uh... yes. Thank you. Sorry." She made a vague attempt to hide her fluster and walked into the kitchen.

Variations on the theme of "Good morning, Mrs. Shand" greeted her from the men gathered at the table.

"Good morning, everyone." Not wanting to appear rude, she raised her gaze from the floor. Her traitorous eyes were immediately drawn to Elijah where he sat in his usual place at the end of the bench. Next to *her* usual place.

He stared at her for a second before looking back down at his food.

Her heart sank. He hadn't smiled at her. He always smiled.

Silently, she took her place at the table next to him.

"How's your wrist?" he said. "Does it hurt?"

She looked at the bandage wrapped around her hand and arm. "Not if I don't use it."

"Elijah told us how you climbed that windmill," Anson said. "That was mighty brave of you."

"Sure was," Kosumee added.

"Clever too," Herman said, "the way you took Elijah's drawing and found out what was wrong."

"Mrs. Shand is real smart," Eugene said, nodding.

"I'd like to give that Garrett a piece of my mind," Alonzo said, waving his fork for emphasis.

"You'd have to get in line," Amos said. "No one hurts our girl."

There were vehement nods and comments of "Yup" and "Too right."

Lizzy's eyes burned as she looked around the table at the group of rugged cowboys coming to her defense.

"You're all so wonderful," she said with a teary laugh.

She was answered with shrugs and smiles and even a couple of blushes. Richard grinned at her from the other end of the table.

201

Mrs. Lassiter placed a plate in front of her.

Wondering how she was going to use both a knife and fork, Lizzy saw the food was all cut into bite-sized chunks.

She looked up at Mrs. Lassiter still standing beside her. "Thank you."

Her expression indecipherable, Mrs. Lassiter nodded and walked back to the range.

Lizzy glanced at Elijah and he gave her a small, sad-looking smile before focusing back on his food. She couldn't help thinking that he was disappointed in her and she couldn't blame him one bit.

It felt as if everything was twisting and turning her emotions upside down and she didn't have the first idea of what to do about it.

~ ~ ~

Elijah stabbed the fork into the bale of straw with somewhat more force than was required. It didn't make him feel a whole lot better, but it was a convenient outlet for his frustrations.

He carried the forkful of straw into the stall, shook it out over the floor, and returned to the bale for more.

He'd seen the smile that passed between Lizzy and Richard at breakfast and he couldn't help wondering if something had changed between them.

He wanted to be happy for her, he truly did. He knew how hurt she'd been by her husband's indifference at the start of their marriage, and that Richard's attitude now appeared to be thawing no doubt made her happy. But the thought of the two of them together made Elijah feel sick to his stomach and he hated himself for it.

He couldn't get his emotions straight. He wanted her to be happy, but he didn't want it to be with Richard. He was wracked with guilt for feeling that way, but he didn't want to feel otherwise because that would mean losing the love he had for Lizzy. He was happy and devastated and angry and elated and terrified all at once. No wonder God hadn't listened to his prayers for help; *he* didn't even know what he wanted any more.

Except for Lizzy. He knew he wanted Lizzy with all of his heart. And that was both the best and the worst part of it all.

He thrust the fork into the bale again and shook it for good measure before carrying another load of straw to the stall.

And now Lizzy seemed to be avoiding him. She hadn't come to the pond in two days. At breakfast she'd acted awkwardly around him and she hadn't gone with him to feed the chickens and pigs. True, she was injured, and he didn't expect her to help, but she loved seeing the animals. Before yesterday he wouldn't ever have thought she'd choose to miss it. The only explanation was that she was afraid of him after what happened in the buggy, after he'd almost kissed her. And he didn't have any idea how to explain and fix it without admitting how he felt about her.

He shook the last load of straw over the stall floor and did a final check that everything was ready for the pregnant cow Amos said they might be bringing in. He hoped they did. He needed all the distraction of work he could get.

An hour later Amos rode slowly into the yard, leading a very pregnant and decidedly uncomfortable looking heifer by a rope. Elijah left the loose post he was repairing in the pasture fence and waved him over to the barn.

"She's been in labor more than forty-eight hours now," Amos said when they'd guided the mother-to-be into the stall. "Figured we'd better bring her in, case something goes wrong."

"I'll w-watch her." Elijah stood back to take a look at her

extended stomach. "She's big."

"Might be twins or might just be a big calf. It's not going to be an easy birth, either way. You want me to stick around?"

"No, I can handle it."

Amos looked around. "Where's Mrs. Shand? She's usually with you during the day, isn't she?"

His mouth went dry. "G-g-g-guess her wrist is hurting. I-I-I think she's inside." He pressed his lips together against a sigh of exasperation. How was he ever supposed to hide anything when the more flustered he was, the worse his stutter became?

Amos stared at him for a few seconds, his eyes narrowed. "It wasn't your fault she got hurt, Elijah."

He pushed his hands into his pockets and looked at the heifer. "But it was because of me."

Amos let out a long sigh and glanced out the open door. "You've been a friend to her when she needed it, I know that much. Whatever happened yesterday, I reckon she still needs that."

Elijah nodded carefully, unsure how to respond. He was sure Amos couldn't know what had happened in the buggy. He wasn't so sure, however, that his feelings for Lizzy were as well hidden as he wished. There were times when he suspected he might as well have been wearing a sign. It scared him.

Amos looked down at his shoes, scuffing one against the flagstone floor. "What I'm trying to say is, things may not be as straightforward as they appear, and Mrs. Shand is going to need a good friend like you."

Elijah had no idea what that meant, but he was afraid to ask. So he nodded again.

There were a few seconds of silence during which he got the feeling Amos wanted to add something more on the subject. But then he said, "Well, I'll be getting back out. If you need anything, I'll be over north, by the black rocks. Got a couple more in labor, but they all seem to be doing well. Still, I should be there, just in case."

Elijah nodded for a third time.

Amos nodded back and then left. A few seconds later Elijah heard his horse leaving.

"Well, that w-was strange," he said to the heifer. "What did he mean, things may not be as straightforward as they appear?"

He waited, but she didn't appear to have anything to add to the conversation, focused as she was on munching the hay in the feeding rack. Probably just as well. He was confused enough as it was.

"I saw Amos leaving. What's going on?"

He looked round to see Lizzy standing in the open doorway, her dark hair shining in the sun. She was so beautiful it made his heart hurt.

He turned back to the heifer, mostly so he wouldn't have to keep looking at Lizzy. "He b-b-brought this girl in. She's been in labor for more than two days and he wants me to k-keep an eye on her."

She walked up beside him and leaned her arms on the stall door. "Two days? Poor thing. That sounds terrible."

The heifer glanced at her briefly before turning back to the hay.

"It's not uncommon for a first calf. Gets easier the more they have."

"So what are you going to do?"

He indicated a blanket he'd thrown over a pile of hay bales. "I'm going to k-keep her company until her little one is safely born."

She looked at the makeshift seating then back at the heifer. She didn't look at him. "Can I stay with you?"

205

That surprised him. Maybe his assumption that she was afraid of him was wrong. "Of course you can, but it could be hours. You might get b-bored."

She gave a small laugh. "I admit, that does happen quite a lot. I'd still like to stay though. I want to see the calf being born."

He tried to think of a way to express that he'd love her being there, that he'd missed her, and that everything was so much better when she was around. Without sounding as inappropriate as it did in his head.

All he managed to come up with was, "I wouldn't mind the company." Which didn't quite convey the full breadth of his true feelings, but would have to do under the circumstances.

It wasn't the first time he'd watched over a cow in labor in the barn. It was the first time he'd actively looked forward to it though. The heifer had stopped eating and was now pacing around the stall. It was a sure sign the labor was progressing, but there was no indication the calf was ready to come out yet. Much as Elijah didn't want the animal to suffer, he wasn't averse to staying in the barn with Lizzy by his side.

They sat on the blanket, arranging it so they could lean back against the bale behind them. He couldn't help noticing how she avoided doing anything with her left hand.

"How's your wrist?"

She looked at her bandaged arm. "It doesn't hurt as long as I don't use it. It's a bit bruised and swollen, but I'm sure it'll be all right."

"I'm so s-s-sorry that happened to you because of me."

"Oh, I don't mind." She smiled. "When I was younger I had this idea that I wanted to join the Pinkerton Detective Agency. Did you know they have lady detectives? I had all these romantic ideas about adventure and intrigue. It all seemed so exciting. Yesterday was almost like fulfilling those dreams; sneaking onto Mr. Bowman's farm, climbing the windmill, getting caught by Mr. Garrett. I'm sorry to say I wasn't nearly as brave and fearless as I used to think I'd be under such circumstances, but I'm glad I did it."

"I think you were very brave. I'd probably still be in jail if it wasn't for you. I was really p-p-proud of you."

A hint of pink touched her cheeks. "Thank you. I think, however, that a career as a detective isn't really for me."

"You mean despite your superior sneaking skills?"

She laughed. "I shall have to find other uses for those. I..."

A loud moo interrupted her.

Elijah stood and went to the stall, reaching out to lay his hand on the cow's shoulder. "It's all right, girl," he murmured, stroking her gently.

The heifer gave him a look that said, *Easy for you to say, you'll never have to go through this,* and went back to her hay.

"Is she all right?" Lizzy said as he sat down again.

"Just uncomfortable, I guess."

They sat and watched the heifer eat.

"You didn't come to the pond last night," he said after a while.

"Richard was home," she replied, watching the mother-to-be tug a final mouthful of hay from the food rack before returning to her pacing.

"D-does he not know you spend time there with me?" He'd never given much thought to how her husband would feel about her meeting with another man, assuming Richard simply didn't mind. Or maybe he'd intentionally not considered it so they wouldn't have to stop. He was beginning to doubt his motives in just about everything when it came to Lizzy.

"He... I don't know. I mean, I told him at the beginning, the first night, but it hasn't come up since. I didn't really think about it."

Of course she didn't, because to her it was all completely innocent. *He* was the one with the feelings he shouldn't be having.

"I... I suppose I should have told him again." She looked at her hands twisted in her lap.

He wanted to kick himself. Now he was passing his guilt onto her.

"You haven't d-d-done anything wrong." He looked down at the flagstone floor. "But i-i-i-if you'd rather not come to the pond anymore, I-I-I understand." He closed his eyes in frustration at his traitorous stutter.

There were a few seconds of silence before she said quietly, "I like being with you at the pond. I don't want to stop."

His heart leaped and he raised his head, his eyes meeting hers. "I d-don't want to stop either."

A smile spread across her face, warming his heart.

He didn't know if it was wrong to spend time with a woman who was no more than a friend. All he knew was that when she said she liked being with him, it felt as if he could breathe again.

Really, what could it hurt?

They chatted for a while and, to Elijah's relief, it felt just as easy as it always had. His fears that the incident in the buggy would change things between them faded. Maybe Lizzy didn't realize what had really happened, how close he'd come to kissing her. How he'd almost betrayed all his beliefs, turned from God and embraced what he knew would be a sin.

As they talked, he silently thanked the Lord for the second chance, praying he wouldn't let Him down again.

~ ~ ~

As Elijah's consciousness emerged from sleep, the first thing he noticed was the weight on his shoulder. The second was the scent of lavender.

Careful to not move anything else, he opened his eyes and swiveled them left to where something pressed against him. It turned out to be a head covered in a mass of shiny, lavender-scented, dark brown waves. He had apparently fallen asleep while waiting for things to start moving with the heifer, and at some point while he was asleep Lizzy had rested her head against him. Whether on purpose or unintentionally while she slept he had no idea. If he was honest with himself, he wanted it to be the former, but he knew no good would come of entertaining that thought, so he didn't.

He swiveled his eyes in the other direction to see the heifer. She was lying on the pile of straw, her breathing coming in rapid pants. He recognized the signs that she was getting close to giving birth and knew he would soon have to go and check on her. But right now he could stay where he was and enjoy the feeling of Lizzy's head resting on his shoulder, so close it was almost like holding her.

He closed his eyes and swallowed. Barely an hour after he was thanking God for the chance to treat her with the respect he should be showing another man's wife, he was thinking about holding her. The situation was innocent, his thoughts weren't.

Taking one final moment to breathe in her scent, he whispered, "Lizzy?"

She let out a soft sigh but didn't wake.

Again he said her name, louder this time.

She moved against him, her eyes slowly opening until she was looking up at him. For a few seconds neither of them moved, then she lowered her gaze and sat up. He immediately felt the cold of her loss.

"I think I fell asleep," she said, rubbing at her eyes.

"Me too."

She looked at the heifer. "How are things going?"

"I think she's almost ready."

He stood and walked over to the stall. The heifer looked up at him accusingly, as if he were somehow responsible for the actions of all males of all species everywhere, and then went back to panting. As he watched, she tensed for a few seconds and her tail flicked out of the way to reveal a small hoof.

He beckoned to Lizzy. "C-come and see. The calf is starting to come."

She rushed over, raising a hand to her mouth when he pointed at the hoof. "I can see it! But is that right? Should it be feet first?"

"That's exactly how they should c-come out. When she pushes again we should see the other foot."

Right on cue, the heifer tensed again and a second hoof emerged to join the first.

"Do we need to do anything?" Lizzy said.

"No, she'll do it all herself. I'll only go in if something's n-not right. But so far it looks like it's going like it's supposed to."

She nodded and smiled, bouncing a little in the way she had when she was excited. "It's so exciting!"

And it was. Normally he'd have taken it all in his stride, he'd done this so many times before. But as the birth progressed she asked lots of questions, most of which he could answer thanks to Amos' teaching, and he couldn't help catching some of Lizzy's wonder and seeing it anew through her eyes.

When the little calf finally slipped out, she looked up at Elijah with tears in her eyes and whispered, "That was so amazing."

Caught up in the moment, all he could think to say was, "Yeah," accompanied by a shaky laugh.

The cow had stretched round to clean her new calf which was lifting a wobbly head to take its first bleary look at the world. Strangely though, she wasn't standing which they normally did fairly quickly. Elijah studied her belly and saw movement. Amos had been right.

"Looks like it's not over yet," he said.

"Why not? What's happening?"

He pointed to the cow's belly, tracking a small bulge as it moved beneath the skin. "There's another one."

Lizzy's eyes opened wide. "Twins? Does that happen often?"

"Nope. This is only the f-fourth time in the whole herd in the two years I've been here."

Her face lit up in a wide smile. "And I get to see it."

Apprehensive as he was about the unusual birth, he couldn't help be thrilled that she was sharing it with him.

She moved closer to him, her shoulder brushing against his arm as she watched the new calf and its mother. "How long will it be before the other one comes out?"

"No idea. This w-will be my first time too. The other twins were born out on the range."

"Well, I think she's lucky to be in here with you to look after her. There isn't anyone I'd rather have with me if I was in trouble."

Elijah's breath caught in his throat. Her gaze was fixed on the calf, which was just as well because at that moment he knew a blind person would have been able to see his feelings for her all over his face.

The cow paused in its cleaning of the calf to strain again and she gave a soft grunt of pain. He frowned, looking at her back end. Birthing cows were normally relatively silent. In

211

the wild it was the time when they were most vulnerable and any noise could attract predators. For her to make a sound, she must have been in real pain. Two years of experience and teaching from Amos told him something wasn't right.

He shrugged off his jacket and tossed it onto the bales of hay. "Lizzy, I'm going to n-need your help," he said as he rolled up his shirt sleeves.

"My help? For what?"

He'd set a bucket of clean water and soap by the door and he knelt beside it and began to wash his hands and up his right arm. "I'm sure it's nothing, but I'm g-g-going to check that the other calf is all right." He took the towel and dried off. "We're going to go in there and I w-want you to help keep the first calf safe."

Fear flickered on her face, but she drew herself up straight. "Just tell me what to do."

They entered the stall and the cow looked up at them, her hooves scrabbling at the floor as she attempted to rise. Elijah immediately dropped to a crouch beside her, laying a hand on her back.

"It's all right, girl," he said in as soothing a voice as he could. "We're here to help."

Following his lead, Lizzy lowered to her knees and stroked the cow's shoulder. "Do you think she'd be happier if her calf was up here where she can reach it better?"

He was impressed. "That's a very g-good idea."

While Lizzy calmed the cow, he moved the still weak calf closer to its mother's head and she immediately returned to cleaning it. He hoped it would be a good distraction from what he was about to do.

He moved to her back end and lifted her tail. The tip of a hoof could be seen, but nothing more.

"What are you going to do?" Lizzy said, watching him from her place at the cow's shoulder.

There was no good way to prepare her. "I'm going to push my hand in and f-f-feel what's happening inside."

Her hand stopped its stroking movement and her eyes opened wide. "Inside the *cow*?"

He nodded, suddenly acutely embarrassed. He was probably imagining it, but he could have sworn the cow's eyes widened too.

Lizzy swallowed. "Oh. Okay. Um. Okay."

He nodded again, unable to think of a thing to say. 'Excuse me while I stick my hand into this cow' didn't seem appropriate, somehow.

Acutely aware of Lizzy watching him, he pushed his fingers slowly past the hoof and into the slick birth canal. Thankfully, it didn't take him long to find the problem.

"One of the legs is caught," he said, reaching in up to his bicep to grasp the limb. "I j-just need to..."

He maneuvered the calf's leg carefully forward, inch by inch, until the small hoof joined its partner. With a final gentle rummage to make sure everything else was as it should be, he withdrew his hand and sat back. The cow immediately began to push and both hooves popped out.

He breathed a sigh of relief. It wasn't the first time he'd done it, and being a twin the calf was smaller than usual and so easier to move, but the process still made him nervous. And if something had gone badly wrong with Lizzy there he'd have felt ten times worse.

"Should be good now," he said, standing.

With a final rub of the top of the new mother's head, Lizzy joined him outside the stall. He washed his arm and hands and returned to stand by her side, watching calf number two slowly make its way into the world.

"I can't believe I got to see that," she whispered as they watched the mother lick both her new babies clean. "You were amazing."

213

He was surprised to see her eyes shimmering as she looked up at him. Without thinking, he wiped his thumb across a single teardrop making its way down her cheek. Several more took its place and, with a sob, she covered her face with her uninjured hand and collapsed against him.

Elijah's heart leaped. He looked down at the woman crying into his chest, unsure what to do. When it became obvious she wasn't about to stop, he wrapped his arms gently around her and she pressed herself closer into his embrace, her tears soaking the front of his shirt.

Not knowing what else to do but desperate to comfort her, he simply stood and held her, stroking one hand down the back of her silky hair. He'd never felt so helpless in his life.

After a while her sobs quietened and she lifted her head from his chest, looking up at him with her red, swollen, luminous, beautiful eyes.

"Tell me what to do," he said softly, gazing into her flushed face. "Whatever's wrong, t-tell me how to fix it and I will. I'll do anything."

He felt her breath hitch in her chest still pressed against him.

"I wish it had been you," she whispered. She shook her head and stepped back from him. "There's nothing you can do, but thank you for wanting to. You've been such a good friend, Elijah. I don't know what I'd do here without you."

With one last glance at the newborn calves, she ran from the barn.

For a long time after she left, Elijah remained where he was, unmoving, staring at the door as if he could still see her.

She wished *what* had been him?

He wracked his brain for what she could have meant, formulating theories and discarding them, over and over coming back to the only thing that made any sense – she wished it had been him she'd married.

But that didn't fit either. She'd wanted her husband from the beginning. It was Richard she'd come for, Richard she really wanted to spend time with, Richard she was married to. Elijah was simply interpreting the meaning of her words as he wanted them to be.

She couldn't possibly feel that way about him.

Could she?

CHAPTER 21

"Who's up for a game?" Anson swung one long leg over the back of a chair and dropped a pack of cards onto the table as he sat.

Eugene picked up the coffee pot from the stove, made a face as he sniffed it, and put it back down. "I'll play. I want to test out what Mrs. Shand taught me about bluffing. This needs replacing, by the way."

"What, you're a card sharp now but can't make your own coffee?" Alonzo said, wandering over to join Anson at the table.

"I'll do it," Amos said, taking Eugene's place at the stove. "'Bout time we had some decent coffee for a change."

"I'm going to ignore that," Anson said as he shuffled the deck. "You in, Elijah?"

Elijah looked up from the list of calculations in front of him. "Hmm?"

Anson waved a handful of cards at him. "Poker. You in?"

He'd only been vaguely listening to what was going on in the bunkhouse, focused as he was on working out the specific pressures of the plumbing for the house. "Oh. No." He pushed the paper and pencil into his portfolio and swiveled his legs off the side of his bed. "I'm going to work outside."

"Work," Eugene said, smirking. "Yeah, that's what you're going to do."

216

He paused in the tidying of his bed and straightened to look at him. "What are you talking about?"

Eugene's smirk grew. "You go off to work then Mrs. Shand goes too. Yeah, I bet you get a lot of *working* done." He looked at the others. "Am I right?"

Elijah dropped the portfolio onto the bed. "W-w-w-what are you saying?"

Apparently oblivious to the sudden tension in the room, Eugene sniggered. "Hey, I get it, Mrs. Shand's a very pretty lady. You and her working together all day long, stands to reason you'd want to... you know..."

Elijah was across the room in under a second, red edging his vision.

Eyes wide, Eugene stumbled back.

A hand clamped around Elijah's raised wrist, yanking him to an abrupt halt. He spun to glare into Amos' face.

"Calm down, Elijah." His voice was low, but it carried a note of authority no one in that room would ignore.

He closed his eyes, waiting for his breathing to calm, and nodded. Amos released his arm.

"Eugene!" Amos snapped. "After how nice Mrs. Shand's been to you I'd expect you to treat her with more respect."

He raised both hands. "I'm sorry. I didn't mean nothing by it. I was only joking. We all know Elijah and her meet a lot, but I know they ain't doing anything..."

"Gene," Amos growled, "might be best if you shut up now."

Finally getting the message, he closed his mouth and slumped onto a chair at the table.

Elijah snatched the portfolio from his bed and strode to the door. He didn't breathe again until he was outside and taking deep gulps of the fresh air as he crossed the yard.

"Elijah, wait."

If it had been anyone else he wouldn't have even

slowed, but he reluctantly stopped and waited for Amos to reach him.

"I think we need to have a talk."

Elijah jabbed a finger in the direction of the bunkhouse. "You d-d-don't think that, do you? About m-m-me and Lizzy?"

"Of course I don't, and the other men don't either. Eugene's just being Eugene. You know what he's like."

Elijah planted his hand on his waist and looked at the ground, willing his heart to slow down.

"But you going out there, spending all that time with just you and her," Amos continued, "to people who don't know you, it wouldn't look right."

"B-b-but we just talk. We're friends. We're not d-d-doing anything wrong."

"I know that, but you have to think of her. If it got around and gossip started, people wouldn't care about the truth."

He shook his head and turned away, not wanting to hear what Amos was saying.

"Elijah, her reputation could be ruined. You care about her, I can see that. We all do. But you need to do what's best for her, even if you don't want to. Even if *she* doesn't want to."

He wanted to protest. He wanted to make Amos understand, change his mind, tell him it was all right. But the words wouldn't come because he knew Amos was right.

And he hated the world for it.

Without saying anything more, he resumed walking.

~ ~ ~

Lizzy bent to pluck a buttercup from a patch of grass at the base of an alder tree, smiling at the rich yellow of its petals.

218

She hummed as she continued towards the pond, her heart full of the joy she always felt when on her way to her favorite place in the world. Of course, she and Elijah saw each other elsewhere, worked together, had shared the wonderful experience the previous day of helping the cow give birth to adorable twins, but somehow being at the pond with him was different. It felt like it was just the two of them while the whole rest of the world disappeared. A small oasis of calm when she could forget what was wrong and what was right and just enjoy Elijah's company.

She was a little early, but she would wait for him on their rock and listen to the hum of the insects and watch the sparkle of the sun on the water. It would be perfect, like it always was.

When she reached the clearing she was surprised to see Elijah already there, seated on the rock, his portfolio unopened beside him as he stared at the water a few feet in front of him. She stopped for a moment to let her gaze trace the contours of his face, the shimmer of the sun in his dark blond hair, the lines of his body strengthened through years of physical labor. He was beautiful.

She was beyond telling herself she didn't have deep feelings for him. She might not be able to do anything about it, but what was the point in pretending it wasn't so? She was in love with Elijah Griffin and it seemed that wasn't going to change anytime soon. So for now, while they were together, she was simply going to enjoy it.

"You're early," she said as she walked towards him, twirling the buttercup in her fingers.

"So are you." He spoke without moving his gaze from the pond.

Something in his tone brought her up short. He looked at her and smiled, but there was a sadness in his eyes that scared her.

She hurried to the rock and sat beside him, placing her hand on his arm. "What's wrong?"

He returned his gaze to the water. "I've always liked coming here, ever since I found the place after Mr. Shand hired me. But I've never loved it as much as I do now, when y-y-you're here with me." He let out a deep sigh. "Which makes this the hardest thing I've ever had to do."

Dread seeped down her spine and her fingers slipped from his arm. "Makes *what* the hardest thing you've ever had to do?"

His raised his hand as if to touch her, then lowered it again, his shoulders slumping. "We can't do this anymore," he said quietly.

A void opened, deep inside her. "What do you mean? Can't do what anymore?" Even though she knew what he was saying, she hoped she'd got it wrong, that he was talking about something that wouldn't rip out her heart.

"Come here. Spend time like this together."

She sat back, shaking her head, unable to believe what he was saying. "But yesterday you said you didn't want to stop! You said you liked coming here. I don't understand. Did I do something wrong?"

"No! Never. Y-y-you could never do anything wrong." Again he lifted one hand towards her, leaving it hovering in the air between them. "People will find out and they'll assume w-w-w-we're... we're..."

"But we aren't doing anything wrong!" Desperate tears pooled in her eyes and she wiped at them angrily with the back of her hand.

"But they'll think we are." He finally slipped his hand into hers, the touch sending tingles through her skin. "Your reputation could be destroyed."

She looked down at their entwined hands. "I don't care about my reputation."

"But I do."

She lifted her gaze again, seeing an intensity of emotion in his eyes that made her want to throw herself into his arms.

"I c-c-care about you, Lizzy. If I was the cause of you being hurt in any way, I wouldn't be able to live with myself."

She blinked back more tears trying to escape. "How will I survive without you?"

"We'll still be working together during the day and you'll still c-come to the bunkhouse for poker games."

"But it won't be the same," she whispered.

"I know."

She tightened her fingers around his. How could he do this to her? He'd been her lifeline since she'd arrived. Without him she would have lost her mind. He'd given her hope and happiness in the midst of the mess to which she'd come. How could he abandon her now?

Letting go of his hand abruptly, she stood and turned to go. She needed to get away, to be alone. To let the tears come.

"P-p-please, Lizzy." There was a tremor in his voice that made her stop. "I'm not d-doing this to hurt you. If there was any way I could change things, I would. You don't kn-know how hard this is for me. How much I want... things to be different."

"I don't think you know how hard it is for me," she said without looking back. "If you did you'd understand that to me, coming here is worth anything."

She fled before he could answer. And before he saw the tears streaming down her cheeks.

CHAPTER 22

It had been three of the worst days of Elijah's life, and that included his seven months in the Idaho City territorial jail.

He still saw Lizzy every day, albeit less than usual because of her injured wrist, and she'd been to the bunkhouse for poker once, although she hadn't stayed long. The only thing that had really changed was they no longer met at the pond. And yet, that seemed to have changed everything.

Or perhaps what had really changed was he'd pushed her away, however unintentionally, and it had hurt her. He was beginning to think he'd made a mistake.

By Saturday afternoon he felt as if he'd reached the end of his tether, let go, and was drifting away in the current. He'd spent the morning at the Bowman farm, carefully going over the windmill to check what Garrett had done wrong and how to fix it. The worst thing about that wasn't the memory of being wrongfully accused of creating a bad design, it was that he was there alone.

He'd become used to having Lizzy with him whatever he did, her ever present enthusiasm making each task that much more fun. But when he'd mentioned going she hadn't asked to go with him. He missed having her want to do things with him. He missed *her*, so much it felt as if part of him had been ripped away.

So he decided he needed to talk to someone about it, someone he could trust to give him good advice and not tell anyone else what he said. Someone who, he hoped, would have more insight into what God would want him to do than he himself had. Which was how he ended up at the Jones' house in Green Hill Creek at a little after two in the afternoon, hoping Pastor Jones was in.

He strode up the path to the front door, barely seeing the flowers blooming throughout the well-tended garden. Although he did notice the scent of lavender. It reminded him of Lizzy.

It was Lizzy's friend, Louisa, who answered the door. "Good afternoon, Mr. Griffin."

Elijah berated himself for not thinking of that. He hoped she didn't tell Lizzy he'd been there to talk to the pastor. He didn't want her to know how badly their time apart was affecting him.

"G-g-good afternoon, Miss Woods. Is Pastor Jones in?"

"He's in his office. Come in."

She showed him into the parlor and left to fetch the pastor. Elijah sat down for roughly five seconds before his nerves got him up again and set him pacing.

He'd thought a visit to Pastor Jones was a good idea, but now he was here he was a lot less certain. The thought of admitting to someone that he was in love with someone else's wife had his heart racing. What if the pastor didn't understand? What if he told him he was evil and going to hell? What if he...

"Elijah?"

Elijah spun around so fast his foot caught on the rug and he stumbled, just catching hold of the back of a chair before he hit a glass-fronted cabinet.

"Oh, hey there," Pastor Jones said, rushing forward to steady him. "You all right?"

He straightened with an embarrassed laugh. "Yes, uh, s-sorry." He pushed the rug back into position with his foot.

"Can I get you anything, Mr. Griffin? Pastor?" Louisa

said from the doorway.

"N-no, thanks."

"No, thank you, Louisa."

She nodded and disappeared back along the hallway.

"So, what can I do for you?" Pastor Jones said.

Elijah looked at the door where Louisa had been moments before, wondering how thick the walls were.

The pastor watched him carefully. "You know what? How about we take this conversation to the church? I need something from there anyway."

He breathed out. "That w-would be great, thanks."

The short walk to the Emmanuel Church along the road was accompanied by small talk that went partway towards calming Elijah's nerves, but nevertheless he was still anxious when they got inside and Pastor Jones showed him to a chair.

"No one can hear us in here," the pastor said with a gentle smile. "Whatever it is, it won't go beyond the two of us."

Elijah guessed that overseeing a large church gave the pastor a sense of when a person needed to talk privately. Not that he was exactly being hard to read. He was a nervous wreck.

He clutched his hands together in an attempt to still the shaking and leaned his elbows on his knees, staring at the floor. "Is it a s-s-sin to want something that would be wrong, even if we d-don't do anything about it?"

"That depends on what it is you want and what your definition of not doing anything about it is."

Elijah raised his eyes. "You w-won't repeat anything I tell you to another soul?"

"No. You have my word on that."

"Not even Mrs. Jones?"

"Not even her."

He searched the pastor's face for any sign of deception

but found none. It wasn't that he distrusted him, but if anyone found out about his feelings for Lizzy lives could be ruined. He had to be sure.

Nodding, he lowered his gaze to the floor again. "I'm in love with another man's wife."

He experienced a small amount of surprise that his stutter hadn't appeared at all in his confession. He would have expected to barely be able to get the words out. But maybe getting the words out was what he needed. Keeping to himself the one thing that was destroying him inside was exhausting.

When Pastor Jones didn't say anything, Elijah glanced at him. He'd anticipated surprise, shock, outrage, disappointment, disgust, or any combination of the five, but the pastor simply sat, his expression calm, and waited for him to continue.

So he did.

He told Pastor Jones everything, from the Friday afternoon fifteen days previously when he'd first seen his boss' beautiful new wife, to the last few days when he'd missed her desperately, and everything in between. He held nothing back. He didn't think he'd be able to if he tried. Once he started talking, he couldn't seem to stop. Even his stutter barely troubled him.

He told him how Lizzy had been bored and lonely and he'd simply wanted to help her. How they'd begun meeting at the pond which had also started out as completely innocent, two friends enjoying each other's company. How he'd come to realize that his feelings were turning into much more than just friendship and how he'd begged the Lord to take them away. What Amos told him about protecting Lizzy's reputation and how he'd stopped the meetings at the pond as a result, and how losing that closeness with her was tearing him apart.

225

And at the end he looked to Pastor Jones, waiting for condemnation.

Instead, his expression was one of sympathy and compassion. "Elijah, I'm so sorry for what you're going through."

"Y-you don't think I'm sinning?"

A small smile touched the pastor's face. "I know what it's like to adore someone you can't have. Believe it or not, I was once as young as you and desperately in love with a wonderful girl. Sadly, her father didn't like me at all."

"I would have thought any father w-would be happy for his daughter to marry a pastor."

"Oh, I was very far from being a pastor back then," he said, chuckling. "Let's just say I was somewhat rough around the edges. I also had no idea what to do with my life and no way to support a wife or family. All I knew was I'd found the girl who made me want to be a better man and who I knew I couldn't live without."

Forgetting his own troubles for a moment, Elijah sat up, intrigued. "What did you do?"

"I had to ask myself the question of what I wanted more, the girl I loved or my life of itinerant work and... other pastimes. I chose love."

"So you changed and got a job and proved yourself to her father?"

"Actually, no. I tried, but I just wasn't very good at being responsible, no matter how strong my motivation. What really changed my life was getting a job replacing window frames at the local church. The pastor there saw something in me, or I guess God did and prompted him. He would stay in the church when I was working. At first I thought it was to make sure I didn't steal anything, but later I realized it was so we could talk. At the end of the two weeks I was there I asked Jesus into my heart, and it was Him who made the real change."

Elijah nodded in understanding. The same thing had happened to him, only he'd been in jail at the time. "So what happened with the girl?"

"I eventually convinced her pa I could be a good husband. Or at least not the reprobate I had been. Took me two years though, before he allowed us to marry. And that two years was torture, believe me."

"So that girl was M-Mrs. Jones?"

"Sure was. It's more than thirty years ago now, but I still remember the agony of wanting a woman I couldn't have. I understand what you're feeling."

Elijah moved his gaze back to the floor. He would wait years for Lizzy if he had to, but that wasn't an option. He didn't even have that hope. All he had to look forward to was a future of seeing her every day, his aching heart heavier than iron.

"But Lizzy won't ever be mine." He sat back and ran his hand over his hair. "I don't even know if I w-w-want to stop loving her. It hurts more than anything sometimes, but when I'm with her it's like I'm standing in the sun and when I'm not it's like being under a cloud. I kn-kn-know it's wrong to feel like this, but I don't want to stop."

It was the first time he'd admitted it, even to himself. He *wanted* to love Lizzy. Because as bad as it made him feel, it also filled him with joy.

"Does Mrs. Shand know how you feel?" Pastor Jones said.

"I don't know. I haven't said anything, but I don't know if I'm hiding it very well."

"Do you think she feels the same?"

He paused for a moment, remembering what she'd said in the barn about wishing it had been him. But then he shook his head. "She wouldn't. She's a good person."

"You're a good person, Elijah, in as far as any one of us is good. But you have Jesus in your life. You are good because He was punished in your place. God has forgiven you all your sins."

He huffed out a frustrated breath. "B-b-but feeling this way is a sin and I can't stop. How c-c-can God forgive me if I keep on sinning?"

"Elijah, feeling isn't a sin. God knows you can't help how you feel. What matters is how you act on it. You did the right thing in stopping meeting her at the pond, even though it's causing you so much heartache now. I think you know that was acting on your feelings in a way you shouldn't have."

The pastor was right. It had taken Amos to make him see it, but Elijah knew those times, however innocent their actions, had only deepened his feelings for her.

He dropped his head into his hands and groaned. "You're right. I wish you weren't, but you are. But w-w-what do I do now?"

"Keep praying and be open to hear what God tells you. And willing to obey Him even when it's not what you want to do. He knows your heart and how you want to do the right thing. He will lead you through this. Like it says in the Bible, all things work for the good of those who love Him, even things that are unpleasant at the time. In the future you'll be able to look back on what's happening now and see how God used it to shape your life for the better. Just give it to the Lord and let Him work it out."

Releasing a long breath, Elijah nodded and sat up.

Pastor Jones was smiling. "The Lord is the one Who's right. I just wait for Him to speak through me. Mind if I pray for you?"

"Please do." Elijah leaned his elbows on his knees and bowed his head, closing his eyes.

Pastor Jones' hand rested on his shoulder. "Father God, I thank You for Elijah, that he belongs to You, and for his integrity and desire to do Your will and act honorably. You know exactly how he feels and how difficult it is for him. Lord, fill him with Your Spirit, surround him with Your love and give him the strength to obey You in whatever You want him to do. And I pray that one day he will find happiness and joy with the woman You've chosen for him, whoever she may be. I pray all this in the Name of the Lord Jesus, Amen."

"Amen," Elijah whispered, wiping at his eyes. He felt as if a huge weight had been lifted from his shoulders. God was in control. He just needed to remember that more often.

"I probably shouldn't do this," Pastor Jones said, "but the ladies of the quilting circle baked a huge batch of raisin cookies for after church tomorrow and brought them here this morning. I'm sure no one would notice if we appropriated one or three."

Elijah laughed, somewhat surprised he was able to. "I w-won't tell if you don't."

CHAPTER 23

Lizzy brought her horse to a stop outside Pastor and Mrs. Jones' house and slid to the ground, leaving the black mare tethered to a nearby hitching post next to a brown gelding that looked just like one of the horses at the ranch.

She pushed the gate open and looked in trepidation at the pretty cream painted home and its garden bursting with color.

She'd come out of desperation, knowing she would explode soon if she didn't tell someone about Richard and Elijah and everything that was going on. Since she and Elijah had stopped meeting at the pond she'd barely had any sleep and only picked at her food. Her wrist was improving, but she still wasn't doing much on the ranch. Spending time with Elijah hurt too much.

She knew she couldn't go on as she was, but now she was here she couldn't help being nervous. What if Louisa was disgusted at her for falling in love with a man who wasn't her husband?

She'd chosen Louisa largely by default. Amy was locked up at the marshal's office where Lizzy planned to visit her after this, she didn't want to bother Sara after the burning of the barn two nights before, and despite having visited Jo with Sara and Louisa two days previously she wasn't at all sure she could get back there on her own.

The problem was, although she loved her new friends it was only three weeks since they'd first met and she really had no idea how any of them would react. But she couldn't wait any longer. The last three days since Elijah told her they could no longer meet at the pond had been torture. She was beginning to fear for her sanity.

She took her time walking up the path that made its way through the riot of brightly colored flowers, breathing in their scent and listening to the hum of insects. She guessed that Mrs. Jones must also take care of the pots of flowers that adorned the front of the church. The pastor's wife had enviable green fingers. It made Lizzy think of the vegetable garden on the ranch where there were flowers planted to encourage the bees to the various crops. And that made her think of Elijah. Everything seemed to make her think of Elijah.

She wondered where he was now. He'd disappeared after lunch. That was part of the reason she'd come now, when he wouldn't notice she was gone.

To her relief, it was Louisa who answered the door when she knocked.

"Why aren't you out with Jesse?" Lizzy said, smiling.

"He's doing some extra work at the bank going through all the accounts after what happened." She stepped back to let Lizzy inside. "Are you here to see Pastor Jones?"

"Nope. I came here to see you." She gave her a quick hug and walked past her into the house.

"Oh." Louisa closed the door. "Did you come with Mr. Griffin?"

Lizzy spun around from where she was peering into the parlor to stare at her, her heart pounding. "Elijah's here?"

"Yes. Well, not here, he went with Pastor Jones to... oh." She walked rapidly past Lizzy towards the kitchen "Would you like some tea? I made scones this morning."

"Wait, hold on," Lizzy ran to catch up with her. "He went with Pastor Jones to what?"

231

Louisa was lifting a cloth over a plate on the table. "Nothing. Would you like honey with your scone? It's delicious. Sara's husband makes it. Or his bees make it, I should say."

"Forget the scones for a second," Lizzy said. "Elijah went with Pastor Jones to what?"

"So you don't want a scone?"

"Of course I want a scone! But first I want you to answer my question." She stood with her hands on her waist, silently daring her friend to evade her again.

Louisa sighed. "I shouldn't have said anything. I just assumed, since you came so soon after he did, that you'd come with him."

So the horse tethered outside didn't just look like the one from the ranch, it *was* the one from the ranch. "Where is he now?"

"Pastor Jones said they were going to the church which I think meant whatever they were going to discuss was private. That's all I know, I swear. And if I knew more I wouldn't be able to tell you anyway because obviously this is something that is, as I said, private. So you shouldn't be asking me." The last was said in a mildly reproving tone that made Lizzy feel guilty.

"I'm sorry, you're right. It's just..." She sank onto one of the chairs at the table in the center of the kitchen and sighed. "Elijah's the reason I came to talk to you. Part of the reason, at least. A big part. Most of it, if I'm truthful. Although there is more to it than just him. But mostly it's him. And I just really need to tell someone before I burst and lose my mind."

Louisa sat on the chair opposite her. "What's wrong?"

She folded her arms on the table and lowered her head onto them to hide her face. She didn't want to see Louisa's expression when she admitted her terrible behavior. "I'm in love with him."

"I'm sorry, I can't hear you. Your voice is muffled."

Lizzy heaved a sigh into the table and raised her head. "I'm in love with him."

Louisa frowned. "With who? Richard?"

She pressed her lips together and shook her head.

Louisa's eyes widened. "*Elijah?*"

She nodded and dropped her head onto her arms again.

There were a few seconds of silence before Louisa said, "Do you want to tell me about it?"

She looked up. "Could I do it over that scone?"

It took her roughly twenty minutes and two scones to tell Louisa everything. She probably could have done it in less time, but she wanted her friend to understand precisely why and how it all happened. She may also have got a little carried away in describing how wonderful Elijah was.

At the end of it all she sat back, sucked the honey from her fingertips, and waited for Louisa's take on the whole situation.

"Does Elijah know how you feel about him?" she said, handing her a napkin.

"I don't think so. I hope not." Lizzy rubbed at her sticky fingers. "I don't want him to think I'm the kind of wife who would run after other men. I intended to fall in love with Richard, I really did." She put down the napkin and sighed. "I feel awful about how I blamed Elijah when he said we shouldn't meet at the pond any more. I know he was only thinking of me. It just hurt so much. It still does."

"But he was right," Louisa said. "If the gossips here found out, they'd be spreading all sorts of lies about you. You know what happened to Amy."

She nodded. She knew very well. "So what do you think I should do?"

Louisa leaned her elbows on the table and clasped her hands together in front of her chin. "What do you *want* to

233

do?"

"I want... I want..." What did she want? She realized she'd never really thought about it. "I want to be with Elijah, but that's impossible. I'm married to Richard."

"Well, it seems to me that before anything else happens, you need to find out where you truly stand, why Richard advertised for a bride and then ignored you when you arrived. And why he told his parents they forced him into it. Have you asked him where he's going at night? And where he was when he was spending all that time away from the house, like when it had been raining but his coat was dry?"

"I haven't really asked him anything. We've been talking more lately, but it still feels like we don't know each other." And maybe she was afraid of finding out the answers.

"Then there's the first thing you should do, sit down with him and have an honest discussion. If he's... well, if that changes things then you can go on from there."

Lizzy nodded slowly. "You're very practical. Not like me." She pushed a crumb across the plate with her fingertip, following it with her eyes. "I think I might have made a mistake in coming here."

"What? No!" Louisa reached across the table to take her hand. "I know you're confused over Richard and Elijah, but you can't give up. God will work things out."

"That's just it," she said quietly, staring at the plate through increasingly blurry vision, "I don't think He will. I wanted to come here so much that I didn't... I didn't..." She wiped at her eyes with the napkin. "I was scared that if I asked Him whether or not I should come, He'd say no. And I so wanted to come."

"Oh, Lizzy." There was no condemnation in Louisa's voice, only sympathy, but Lizzy carried enough self-condemnation for both of them.

"I can't help thinking this is all my fault. That if I'd just asked, if I'd been willing to do whatever God wanted rather than what I wanted, I wouldn't be in this mess."

Louisa took the napkin from her hand and replaced it with a clean handkerchief from her pocket. "I don't know about all that, but here's what I do know - God loves you and He only wants the best for you. Even if you messed things up, He can still turn it around. Nothing is impossible for Him."

Lizzy dabbed at her eyes. "Not even me?"

She laughed softly. "Not even you. He's got wonderful things in store for you, I know He has. Just like for all of us."

Lizzy smiled despite her tears. "Thank you. You're very wise."

"Yes, I am," Louisa said, nodding.

She laughed and handed her back the slightly damp handkerchief. "And very practical."

"Practical isn't always such a good thing," she said, smiling. "My mama would be horrified to hear me say that."

"It'll be our secret," Lizzy said. "Thank you for listening to me. I truly was at my wits' end."

Louisa reached out across the table to take her hand again. "That's what friends are for. I'm here for whenever you need me."

"Me too." She lowered her eyes to the plate of scones between them. "Um, how many...?"

"You want *another* one?"

"I haven't been eating much lately. I'm hungry."

CHAPTER 24

Lizzy placed her palm against the mare's smooth neck, whispering, "It's all right, Meg. Not much longer now."

Meg stopped shuffling her feet and bent her head to tug up a tuft of grass growing beneath the spreading branches of the tree that hid them.

Lizzy returned to staring at the stables. How long could it take to saddle a horse? She could have done it in half the time Richard had been in there, even with her injured wrist. She was feeling antsier than her steed.

It had taken her two days to work up the courage to do this and now she was here, waiting for her husband to take off into the darkness the way he did every night, every part of her was longing to give up, go back to bed, and ignore whatever he was doing. And that's what she had done on both Saturday and Sunday. But now it was Monday night and the events of the day – Amy's trial and Sara and Daniel's trouble with the man from back east – had spurred her into action. Around her, her friends were settling into their lives, their somewhat rocky beginnings turning into their happily ever afters. Lizzy wanted that for herself.

She'd already tried asking Richard, in a veiled, roundabout way, if there was anything going on that he wanted to tell her. His answer had been no, just as she'd expected. She could have tried being more direct, but her courage had failed her at that point. So this was her only way to the truth. But despite her youthful desire for action and adventure, the prospect of sneaking after Richard in the middle of the night to who knew where was making her more than a little nervous, and she just wanted it to be over.

"Come on, Lizzy," she whispered to herself. "A Pinkerton detective thrives in these kinds of situations. Where's your sense of adventure?"

The light in the stable extinguished and her stomach knotted. Quietly, she pulled herself onto Meg's back and waited.

The door to the stable opened and Richard emerged, leading his horse out into the moonlit yard. He carried a lantern, but it was unlit. With a near full moon and clear night there was enough light for both of them to see by. That could be good or bad for Lizzy, good because she and Meg would be able to see where they were going, bad because if Richard looked back they would be visible. But there was nothing she could do about that.

He mounted his horse and looked up at her dark bedroom window, his shoulders rising and falling in what could have been a sigh. Perhaps he felt guilty for whatever he was doing. She hoped so. She didn't want to think too badly of him.

He turned his head, sweeping his gaze across the yard, and she clamped her gloved hands over her face, freezing as he looked in her direction. She'd worn the darkest clothing she owned, was wearing navy gloves, and had chosen Meg because she was black, but that didn't mean they were invisible. For what seemed like minutes she held her breath, waiting to be discovered. But then Richard started off.

She breathed out, willing her heart to slow, and waited for him to get far enough ahead to not hear her. Then she urged Meg after him.

They rode north in the direction of the mountains, towards where the cattle grazed, and for a while Lizzy thought she may have misjudged him. Maybe he really was spending the nights taking care of the herd. But then he veered to the right and she knew that wasn't the case because she could hear the vague distant sounds of the cattle somewhere to her left.

There was very little cover and any second Lizzy expected to be discovered. What she would say then she had no idea, other than the truth, but she very much didn't want to have to tell him she was spying on him, probably without cause.

After fifteen minutes of riding at a slow walk, however, he hadn't looked back once, and he entered a wood that she was fairly certain marked the boundary of his land and disappeared from sight. She urged Meg to pick up speed, as much as she could in the low light, and came to a halt at the edge of the trees.

She could hear Richard's horse rustling through the dry leaves on the forest floor and knew she'd make just as much noise if she took Meg in. After a few seconds of indecision she slid to the ground, looped Meg's reins around a low branch, and made her way on foot into the trees. If Richard went too far or she lost him, she'd just have to try again another night. With a better plan.

She hurried after the sound of the horse, trying to ignore the unnerving noises of the night around her. If something happened to her, she could always scream for Richard. Hopefully he'd save her first and ask questions later.

After a couple of minutes Lizzy spied a light ahead and Richard came to a halt and dismounted. She waited for him to move on ahead then lifted her skirt, mindful that she no longer had the sound of the horse to cover her movements, and crept forward. She stopped again at the sound of Richard's voice.

"I don't know how much longer I can keep sneaking

away like this. I think she's beginning to suspect."

A woman's voice answered him. "What makes you think that?"

"Questions she's been asking the past couple of days. Nothing outright, but I know something's made her suspicious."

"You mean apart from you sneaking away every night?"

"I don't think it's that. I'm very careful."

Lizzy rolled her eyes. She'd noticed him leaving without even trying.

The woman sighed. "You knew this wasn't going to be easy. Perhaps... perhaps we should stop meeting for a while."

There was a pause. "I can't do that. I can't go without seeing you."

Lizzy suddenly wished she hadn't come. She wasn't ready for this, not now. Not after losing her heart to Elijah and then losing his friendship. She wasn't ready to also find out her whole motivation for leaving her family and crossing the country had been a lie.

She almost turned to leave before stopping herself. She couldn't live like she was. She had to know for certain what was going on.

Taking a deep breath, she crept closer to the light.

She reached the shadows at the edge of a small clearing in the trees. Richard's horse stood on the far side, grazing next to a gray mare. Richard himself sat with his back to a rock near the center of the clearing, the lit lantern beside him. In front of him, nestled between his legs and leaning back against his chest, was a beautiful Indian woman. An obviously pregnant Indian woman. His arms were wrapped around her, his head leaning against hers in an intimate, loving pose.

Lizzy's gut dropped through the ground.

"I could say I told you so," the woman said.

"Please don't. We don't have much time together. I don't want to spend it arguing."

She sighed and nodded. "Neither do I."

Richard's hand moved to rest on her swollen stomach. "How's my boy doing?"

"Your son *or daughter* is still making me sick every morning," she said with a smile.

He kissed the side of her neck. "I wish I could be there to help you."

She turned in his arms to look at him, her expression one of pure love. "So do I."

He stroked one hand down the side of her face and slid his fingers into her hair as their lips joined.

Lizzy backed away, not wanting to see any more. She moved back the way she'd come as fast as she dared, found Meg where she'd left her, and headed for home.

Home. That was a joke. Home wasn't a place you shared with a husband who spent his nights with another woman, a woman who was carrying his child.

As she rode, she thought she should be crying, but for once in her life there were no tears. She didn't even feel any sadness, or anger, or disappointment, or anything else she would have expected. Instead she felt almost as if she were floating, detached from her body, mind and soul.

On arriving back at the house she took Meg to the stable, removed her saddle and halter, gave her a drink and returned her to her stall. All without thinking, without feeling, her actions mechanical and automatic.

On her way to the house she looked at the dark, silent bunkhouse and a desire broke through her deadened emotions. With everything inside her, she wanted to run into that room where all the men were sleeping and throw herself into Elijah's arms. It took every ounce of willpower she possessed to keep her feet moving in the direction of the house. The big, dark, empty house. The place she'd once thought would be her home for the rest of her life.

Without lighting a lamp she went directly to her bedroom and closed the door, then she stood still for a few seconds, wondering vaguely what to do next. Her eyes went to the bed.

Bed. It was night time so that was as good a place as any to be.

Curling up on top of the covers, fully clothed, she waited numbly for sleep.

CHAPTER 25

The next morning found Lizzy still lying on the bed where she'd been since returning from following Richard.

She thought she'd slept, but she wasn't sure how much. Now she lay listening to the sounds of breakfast coming from the kitchen below. Voices of people she'd thought were her friends.

Did they all know? Were they all secretly laughing at the stupid girl who'd come thousands of miles to marry a man who already had a woman?

And what had she come for? Asinine ideas of adventure and romance and cowboys and Indians. A childish fantasy culled from dime novels and her own ridiculous notions.

It was her own fault. She'd always looked at the world with a relentless, misguided optimism, a yearning for more excitement and adventure. And this is where it had got her; alone, miles from home, rejected by a husband who'd never wanted her, trapped in a marriage that was such in name only, in love with a man she couldn't have. There couldn't have been a bigger fool than her anywhere in the world.

A soft knock sounded on her door.

"Elizabeth, are you all right?"

She squeezed her eyes shut at the sound of Richard's voice. "I'm not feeling well. I'm just going to stay in bed for a while longer."

"Can I do anything? Do you need the doctor?"

She almost laughed at the undoubtedly fake note of

concern in his tone. "No. I'll be all right."

"Can I bring you anything? Are you hungry?"

"No, thank you."

There was a pause. "I'll ask Mrs. Lassiter to keep an eye on you. Just ask her for anything you need."

"I will."

There was another pause before she heard his footsteps walk away and the creak of the stairs.

She didn't move for another hour, only rousing from the bed when her stomach began to grumble and everyone was gone, the house quiet other than Mrs. Lassiter as she worked.

She immediately regretted looking in the mirror. Dark circles ringed her eyes, her hair was knotted and wild, her skin pale. But then, what did it matter what she looked like? It wasn't as if there was anyone who would care.

She splashed some water onto her face, more to wake herself up than anything else, dabbed herself dry with the towel, and headed out.

Mrs. Lassiter was in the kitchen when she got downstairs, peeling potatoes at the sink. She glanced at Lizzy as she walked in.

"Mr. Shand said you were ill. Is it anything catching? Because if it is, don't come near me. I've got too much work to do to get sick. I'm not making anything special for you to eat either. It's your regular breakfast or nothing..."

After a night of not feeling anything at all, a single, burning emotion blossomed in Lizzy's gut.

Anger.

"Did you know?" she said quietly.

Mrs. Lassiter's tirade came to a halt. "What?"

Lizzy focused on a corner of the table. "Did you know what Richard was doing?"

"I have no idea what you're talking about. Do you want breakfast or not?"

"Did you know about the woman? The one carrying his child?"

The color drained from her face. "I... don't know..."

"Get out."

Mrs. Lassiter frowned, placing her hands onto her waist. "I don't know what you think you know, but this is my kitchen..."

Deep inside Lizzy, something snapped. "*Get out!*" she shouted, advancing on Mrs. Lassiter. "This is not your kitchen, it's mine! I may be his wife in name only, but until I'm not this is my house and my kitchen and I can do whatever I want in it and I want you *out! Now!*"

Mrs. Lassiter stared at her with wide eyes. "Well, I never..."

"*Get out!*" Lizzy screamed, thrusting out her arm to point at the door. "*Get out, get out, GET OUT!*"

Mrs. Lassiter lifted her chin, wiped her hands on her apron, and walked to the back door without another word.

Lizzy stood in the middle of the room, shaking. A bubble of pain rose in her chest.

Gasping in a breath, she crumpled to the floor, tears pouring down her face and great, despairing sobs wracking her body.

~ ~ ~

Mrs. Lassiter was marching across the yard muttering to herself when Elijah brought his horse to a halt at the barn.

He dismounted and raised his hand in greeting, but she didn't even glance in his direction. He caught "...not my fault he married her..." and then she disappeared behind the bunkhouse and out of earshot.

Shrugging, he looped the rein loosely over the fence and patted the side of Fred's neck. A sound from the direction of the house caught his attention. Someone was crying.

With a jolt, he knew it was Lizzy.

Breaking into a run, he charged across the yard and through the open back door. What he saw in the kitchen brought him to an abrupt halt.

Lizzy sat on the floor, face buried in her hands, her whole body convulsing in deep, frantic sobs. The sight of her in such agony ripped at Elijah's heart like nothing else ever had, robbing him of his voice, his reason, even his ability to breathe.

He lowered to his knees beside her and touched her arm. When she didn't respond, he shuffled closer and hesitantly circled his arms around her shoulders. She immediately turned towards him and pressed her face into his shirt. He tightened his hold on her and closed his eyes, praying for the wisdom to know how to comfort her.

"I'm... such... a fool," she sobbed against him, her words punctuated by tearful gasps for breath.

"No! Who t-t-told you that? Was it Mrs. Lassiter?"

She shook her head against his chest. "I... followed Richard... last night... I'm so... stupid... Shouldn't have... come here."

A fresh burst of tears erupted and a minute passed while she wept into his chest and his mind raced with questions.

"Lizzy, what happened?" he said when her sobs eased a little. "What about Richard?"

"He met a woman... last night... in woods... Pregnant... his baby."

He felt every muscle in his body tense. Had he heard her right?

He gently slid his fingers beneath her chin to raise her face and she looked up at him with red, puffy eyes. The anguish he saw broke his heart.

"D-d-d-did you just say that you followed Mr. Shand

last night and saw him m-m-meet with a woman who is carrying his baby?"

She pressed her lips together and nodded. And then she burst into tears again, flinging herself against him.

"I'm such a foolish girl," she sobbed, her voice muffled in his shirt. "I always believe things will work out if I want it hard enough and I do stupid things without thinking them through and I'm just... I'm so childish. How could I marry a man I don't even know just so I could have adventures and see cowboys and Indians? Who else would do something so ridiculous? I'm just stupid and childish and scatterbrained and I ruin *everything*."

Elijah closed his eyes, feeling the old, familiar rage surging. He knew he should ask the Lord to take it away, but this time he didn't. Richard had everything he could want. He would never have to wonder where his next meal was coming from or where he was going to sleep, and if he did if he would wake in the night with a knife in his gut when someone decided they wanted his shoes. But most of all, he had Lizzy as his wife. And instead of treating her as the most precious thing in the world, he had betrayed and hurt her.

He waited until her crying eased and then slipped his hands into her hair, gently lifting her face to look at him.

"N-n-none of that is true," he said, holding her gaze. "You are the bravest, most wonderful, incredible, smart, loving, b-beautiful woman I have ever met. You make everyone around you happy. You make *me* happy. Don't ever let anyone m-m-make you feel like you are anything less than perfect just the way you are. And don't ever stop believing you can have anything you want, n-not for anyone."

She stared up at him, tears forgotten, her eyes wide in shock.

He dipped his head to press a kiss to her forehead, for the briefest moment savoring the feel of her skin against his lips. Then he released her and rose to his feet.

Without saying another word, he left the kitchen and strode across the yard towards his horse.

CHAPTER 26

It almost felt comforting, giving in to the anger and letting it take over. Elijah leaned forward over Fred's neck, the wind rushing past his face as he gave the horse free rein.

What he would do once he reached the men, he had no idea, but he was in no frame of mind to plan his actions anyway. He didn't want to think. All he knew was that he wasn't going to allow Richard to cause Lizzy any more suffering. A small voice in the back of his mind told him he needed to calm down before he did something he'd regret, but he pushed it aside. This had to end now.

It didn't take him long to find the herd and the smoke from the small fire they always kept going led him straight to Richard, Amos and Alonzo some way from the cattle. He couldn't see Kosumee, Anson, Herman or Eugene, so they were probably off riding the boundary fences and checking for any animals that might be in trouble, their usual morning routine.

His anger flaring at the sight of Richard, he leaped to the ground almost before the horse had stopped.

Amos stepped forward to intercept him. "What's..."

Elijah didn't even spare him a glance, shoving him aside as he marched towards where Richard was rising to his feet by the fire.

He opened his mouth to speak.

Elijah drove his fist into his face.

Richard crashed to the ground with a grunt.

"How c-c-c-c-" He shook his head, releasing a growl of frustration, and tried again. "How c-c-could you do that t-to her?"

"Elijah!" Amos grabbed his arm. "What the..."

Elijah shook off his hand and advanced on Richard again. "All she w-w-wanted was to be your wife, to love you, and y-y-you betrayed her."

"Elijah," Amos said, "you need to calm down."

He spun to face him. "Did you know?" he said, his voice rising further. "About his m-mistress?"

Amos stared at him for a moment before his eyes flicked to Richard.

"And she thought you were her friend," Elijah said in disgust.

Richard scrambled to his feet and backed away. "You don't understand..."

"D-don't I?" he shouted, jabbing his hand in the direction of the house. "So you didn't m-m-marry Lizzy while you had another woman pregnant?"

He came to a halt and drew himself up defiantly. "It's not what you think."

Elijah moved forward, itching to punch him again. "All she did was try to make you happy. You d-d-don't deserve her."

"And I suppose you do?"

That brought him up short. "What?"

"You think I don't know about all the time you spend together? That you sneak away to meet almost every evening in the wood?"

"We haven't d-d-done anything wrong. Lizzy would never betray you."

He took another step towards Elijah, pointing at him. "You can't tell me it's all innocent. Nothing may have happened, but I know you want it to. I see the way you look

249

at my wife."

"If you paid your wife any attention at all," Elijah growled, "she wouldn't need to spend time with another man."

"If you were a real man, you wouldn't need to go after another man's wife!"

Elijah launched himself forward, grabbing Richard's shirt and throwing them both to the ground.

A fist connected with his side, but he barely felt it. He aimed another punch at Richard's face, but hands grabbed at his arm and he hit his shoulder instead. Amos shouted their names, but they were both beyond listening as they rolled away, grappling each other across the grass. Richard shoved him onto his back and drove a fist into his stomach, knocking the wind from him.

"Stop it, you two!" Amos roared, but neither listened.

Then Alonzo yelled the one word that was guaranteed to get the instant attention of anyone who worked around cattle.

"*Stampede!*"

Elijah froze, breathing hard as he stared at Richard's angry face above him. The thundering of hundreds of galloping hooves finally entered his consciousness.

Richard pushed away and Elijah scrambled to his feet, looking around.

A wall of cattle was bearing down on them.

Amos and Alonzo were already mounted and galloping their horses out to the sides of the approaching herd, preparing for an attempt to turn the panicked cattle.

"Hurry!" Richard shouted as he clambered onto his horse.

Elijah ran for his horse and vaulted into the saddle, but at the sight of the herd Fred reared beneath him. The pommel slipped from his grasp and he crashed to the ground. Pain exploded in his right arm. Fred took off at a gallop.

Elijah pushed himself to his feet with his left arm, stumbling to escape the path of the oncoming herd. All he could hear was thundering hooves and frantic lowing.

"*Elijah!*" Richard screamed, struggling to turn his frightened horse towards him.

For a brief, strange moment Elijah wondered that he seemed afraid for him when they'd just been fighting.

And then the herd crashed into him.

A steer clipped him and he was thrown to the ground. He tried to rise but was rammed again.

Curling into a ball, he wrapped his arms over his head.

Hooves pounded over his body.

Agony exploded in his leg, his torso, his arm.

Lord, save me!

And then everything went black.

CHAPTER 27

Lizzy stood at the kitchen door, staring out across the yard as she had repeatedly in the past half an hour. But just as with each previous time, there was nothing to see.

Sighing, she returned to the table and sat, taking another small chunk of cake from the plate and chewing it slowly.

She was desperately worried about Elijah. He'd left so angry and she was afraid he would do something reckless that would get him hurt. She thought back to the previous Monday when she'd done the same thing to him, leaving him in jail to go off to the Bowman farm. Now she understood how he'd felt. Not even cake, which usually calmed her, was working.

For what must have been the twentieth time she considered saddling one of the horses and going out to find him. The problem was, she wasn't even sure where he'd be. She felt certain he'd gone to confront Richard, but she didn't know where Richard was either. Plus with her wrist still healing, saddling a horse was a slow procedure. The previous night when she'd done it in preparation for following Richard it had taken her almost an hour and she'd had to persuade Meg to lie down just so she could get the saddle onto her back. It would probably be quicker to walk.

Pushing the half full plate away, she closed her eyes and rested her head on her arms on the table. "Father, please keep Elijah safe and from doing anything reckless. It's my fault he's angry and I don't want him to get hurt because of me.

Please give him peace. And if he reaches Richard, please keep Richard safe too." Tears seeped from between her closed eyelids. "I'm sorry for making such a mess of everything."

At the sound of hoof beats outside she raised her head and leaped up, wiping at her eyes as she ran for the door. Richard, Herman and Kosumee were riding into the yard. Between them they carried a makeshift stretcher that they were obviously being careful not to jostle.

And on the stretcher was...

"Elijah!"

She dashed across the yard towards them, her heart pounding in terror.

Elijah lay unmoving, his clothing drenched with blood, cuts and abrasions scattered over the exposed skin of his hands and arms.

All the air fled from her lungs and none seemed able to replace it. She could hardly choke out the words she needed to say. "Is he...?"

"He's alive," Richard said. "Let's get him inside."

They carried the stretcher in through the kitchen and Lizzy ran up the stairs ahead of them.

"In here," she said, beckoning them into her bedroom and thrusting back the covers on her bed.

They laid the stretcher on one side of the wide bed and gently moved Elijah from it.

"Eugene has gone for Doc Wilson," Richard said. "He'll be here soon. He'll fix him."

By the way he stared at Elijah, she wasn't sure if he was talking to her or himself.

"I'll go take care of the horses," Kosumee said. He touched Lizzy's shoulder on his way out. "He's strong."

She nodded, her eyes on Elijah's broken body. All she could do was keep repeating the same prayer over and over in her head.

Please don't let him die, please don't let him die, please...

"Reckon I'll go into town and see if Gene needs any help," Herman said. "If the doc's not in his office, we might have to go looking."

"What happened?" she said when she and Richard were alone.

"Stampede. His horse panicked. Threw him. He couldn't get away in time. I tried to get to him. I tried..."

For the first time, she noticed how pale he was. "You should sit down."

"This is my fault. We were fighting. Probably spooked the herd. This is my fault." He clutched his shaking hands together in front of him and shook his head slightly. "I'll be back in a few minutes."

Lizzy gaped at him in horror. "What? No, you can't leave me. You can't leave *him*."

He turned his haunted eyes to her, his gaze so intense she took a step back. "I'm going to get someone who can help."

With one more glance at Elijah, he hurried from the room.

All alone, Lizzy fell to her knees at the side of the bed and reached out for Elijah, her hands hovering over him, afraid she would do even more damage if she touched him. There was so much blood.

"Please, Father. Please don't take him." Tears streamed down her face but she couldn't bring herself to wipe them away. "I know I've sinned against You and Richard and Elijah, but please don't make him suffer for what I've done. Please save him." Needing to touch him somehow, she finally lay her hand over his where it rested at his side.

A touch on her shoulder startled her and she looked up at Mrs. Lassiter. She didn't know whether to be relieved or appalled at her presence.

Richard's housekeeper stared at her for a few seconds, an uncharacteristic look of uncertain compassion on her face. "He'll be all right. Doctor Wilson will be here soon. All you need to do is keep praying." She looked at Elijah and Lizzy saw tears glistening in her eyes. "I'll go and start some soup. He'll need something warming when he wakes up." She nodded as if confirming the rightness of what she had decided to do. "That's what I'll do." And then she left.

Lizzy returned her eyes to Elijah's face, the only part of him that seemed relatively untouched by injury, and prayed harder than she'd ever prayed in her life.

~ ~ ~

Richard returned what felt like hours later, but in reality was no more than ten minutes. Lizzy heard several pairs of feet on the stairs. She couldn't imagine who was with him, but she hoped whoever it was could help Elijah as Richard seemed to think they could.

"How is he?" he said as soon as he entered the room. His hair was wild, his face sheened with sweat.

She started to answer, but her words stuck in her throat at the sight of the two people behind him. One was a tall Indian man who looked very familiar. The other was a woman. An Indian woman.

It was her.

For a few seconds Lizzy couldn't speak. She couldn't believe Richard would bring his mistress into the house when Elijah lay injured, possibly dying.

"What is *she* doing here?" she finally managed to snarl.

"How... how do you know her?" His eyes widened in realization and his shoulders sagged. "That's how Elijah knew. You told him."

"I followed you. I wanted to know where you went

every night. I never thought..." She stopped, unable to get the words out.

The woman stepped past him. "My name is Huyana. I know this is difficult for you, but at this moment you need to know one thing – I'm a healer."

Lizzy hated that she was so calm, as if it was perfectly normal that her husband's mistress should be in her house. With every fiber of her being she wanted to scream at her to get out.

Instead, she took a deep breath, raising her chin. "Can you help him?"

"I can try."

Lizzy rose to her feet. "Then please try."

~ ~ ~

She'd always hated the sight of blood. It didn't make her light-headed like it did with some people, but she didn't like it at all. She liked it even less when it was Elijah's. And it was everywhere.

Huyana worked swiftly, using scissors to cut away Elijah's shirt while Richard and the man who'd come with them removed his trousers. Lizzy looked away, a lifetime of modesty overcoming even the seriousness of the situation, but when Huyana asked for her help in cleaning the blood from his skin she pushed away the feelings of impropriety and did as she was asked.

His arms, legs and back appeared to have taken the worst of the damage and there was bruising just about everywhere. There were several cuts, but the worst of the blood came from two deep gashes, one on his right shoulder and the other on his left side. Lizzy had to repeatedly wipe tears from her face with the back of her hand as she worked. Seeing him so badly injured was more painful than anything she'd felt before. It made Richard's betrayal feel benign by comparison.

Huyana cleaned each wound thoroughly and sewed the edges together with a needle and thread she'd had Mrs. Lassiter boil, performing the tasks with an efficiency and confidence that was reassuring. Lizzy had to close her eyes for the sewing part.

She went to work on Elijah's broken arm next and for the first time, Lizzy was glad Elijah wasn't conscious as the bones were maneuvered back into position. If he had been awake, the pain would have been excruciating. Just watching Huyana stretch his arm and move it around until she was satisfied the bones were lined up correctly made Lizzy feel queasy.

"What's going on here?"

Lizzy moved her eyes from Elijah's face to the bearded man standing in the doorway. A frown creased his forehead above the bridge of his round spectacles.

"Doctor Wilson," Richard said, rising from where he'd been cleaning one of Elijah's smaller wounds. "Elijah was caught in a stampede."

"Yes, I know. Mr. Peck told me."

Lizzy noticed Eugene standing behind him in the hallway. He glanced at Elijah through the door then looked away again, his face pale.

Huyana stood, raising her chin defiantly. "I've cleaned and closed his wounds and set the arm bone. I was just about to start on his leg, if you'd like to assist me."

Lizzy had the strangest urge to laugh. Maybe she was becoming hysterical.

A raised eyebrow was Doctor Wilson's only reaction to the challenge. He walked to the bed to inspect Elijah. "This is good work, very neat," he said after thoroughly checking the wounds. He ran his fingers along Elijah's arm. "The bone

257

ends are aligned correctly?"

"Yes."

"And you sterilized the needle and thread?"

Huyana clenched her fists at her sides. "They were boiled."

He nodded slowly. "Ma'am, I don't think I could have done better myself. I'd be happy to assist you with setting the leg."

The tension drained from Huyana's shoulders and she retook her seat by the bed. "I think he has at least two breaks on this leg, here and here. There's also a lump on his head and some swelling on his chest, but I'm not sure if a rib is broken or just bruised."

The doctor took a seat on the opposite side of the bed. "After we set and cast his leg we'll deal with the rib."

Her help no longer needed, Lizzy withdrew to the settee in the corner of the room, tucking her feet beneath her and watching Elijah's face as Huyana and Doctor Wilson worked and discussed treatment.

She didn't understand much of what they said, so she concentrated on praying. She'd done everything wrong, but she knew God still heard her. He had to.

A hand rested on her shoulder and she looked up at Richard.

"He'll be all right," he said softly, his gaze on Elijah. "He follows God with all his heart. He won't let him down."

She didn't know how to answer, but she hoped he was right.

Mrs. Lassiter rushed back and forth from the room, bringing hot water and cold water, taking away bloody towels and cloths and bedding and bringing fresh replacements, taking news to the men gathered downstairs in the kitchen. Lizzy thought she should offer to help, but she couldn't move. She felt like if she left the room, if she let

Elijah from her sight even once, she would return and he'd be gone. Later, when he was awake, she'd thank Mrs. Lassiter for all she was doing, everything that Lizzy couldn't at that moment.

Finally, all of Elijah's wounds were treated, his broken arm and leg were encased in casts created from bandages soaked in plaster of Paris, his torso was wrapped securely, and he was lying on clean bedding.

Lizzy spoke for the first time in she wasn't sure how long, asking the only thing she needed to know. "When will he wake up?"

Doctor Wilson came to sit beside her. "I don't know. It's impossible to tell with injuries to the head. All we can do is wait and pray."

She drew in a trembling breath. "Could he die?"

"I'm not going to lie to you, it's a possibility. But thanks to Huyana's work he hasn't lost too much blood, his color's good and he has a strong pulse. I'm hopeful. You should be too."

When the doctor had left, Richard and Huyana went downstairs. Lizzy couldn't help feeling relieved. Grateful as she was to Huyana for what she'd done for Elijah, she was still extremely uncomfortable being in the same room with her. The marriage between Lizzy and Richard may have been nothing more than a sham, but it still didn't feel right having her in the house.

She moved back to one of the chairs beside the bed and reached out to touch Elijah's face. Despite the bruises, he looked peaceful, as if he could wake up any moment with a smile and tell her it had all been a mistake and he was fine.

A tear spilled down her cheek, her chest tightening. Taking his hand, she pressed a kiss to the back and wrapped it in both of hers.

"Please don't leave me," she whispered. "I need you. I...

I love you."

When there was no response, she lay her head on the bed, tucked his hand beneath her chin, and let the tears come.

CHAPTER 28

Lizzy didn't remember falling asleep, but when she woke her neck was sore from resting at an awkward angle on the bed. She was still holding Elijah's hand.

She lifted her head to study him, hoping he may have woken while she slept, but his eyes were closed, chest rising and falling in a slow rhythm beneath the bedcovers.

Reaching out, she touched her fingertips gently to his cheek and whispered, "Please heal him, Father."

Sitting back, she looked around and gasped in a startled breath when she realized she wasn't alone in the room.

"Sorry, I didn't mean to alarm you," Huyana said from where she sat on the settee in the corner of the room.

Lizzy's stomach twisted at the sight of her there, but she held her tongue. The woman had helped to save Elijah's life.

"I don't blame you for hating me," Huyana said.

"I don't hate you."

Her expression said she didn't quite believe her. "Truly?"

Lizzy started to reply that it was true, but then realized she wasn't certain of that. "I'm trying not to."

The corner of Huyana's mouth tilted up a little. "I think Richard owes you an explanation, but I'm not sure he'd be very good at giving it. He never has been so good with explaining himself. As with most men."

"You talk as if you've known him a long time."

"More than four years. But it's not what you think."

Lizzy's head was swimming. He'd been involved with this woman long before he'd even begun writing to her. "You're not in a relationship with my husband and pregnant with his child?"

Huyana winced a little. "All right, it is what you think, but there's more to it than that."

"What more could there be?"

Huyana gazed at her steadily. "Richard is my husband."

It was a few seconds before Lizzy's flopping jaw could form any words. "He's... what?"

"Not according to your law," she said quickly, "so Richard isn't legally guilty of being married to more than one woman. But we were joined in a ceremony in my clan just over a year ago. So according to our law, he is my husband. And I love him." She gave Lizzy a rueful smile. "For better or worse, as your marriage vows say."

Lizzy felt like she was going to be sick. "I don't understand. Then why did he marry me?"

Huyana sighed, leaning back into her chair. "You've met his parents so you know how..." she cast around for the right word, "determined they can be."

Lizzy nodded. She couldn't deny that.

"They didn't know anything about me until after we were married. I begged him to tell them, but..." She shrugged. "He's not accustomed to standing up to them. When he finally did tell them, they threatened to take away the ranch."

"Because his father owns it," Lizzy said, remembering her conversation with Amos on the subject.

"Yes. It's his father's name on the deeds. They told him he had to marry a white woman or lose everything."

Lizzy couldn't keep the bitterness from her voice. "So he found a girl naive enough to come clear across the country in the belief he would love her."

Huyana's face filled with pity. "It was never his

262

intention to hurt you."

She wasn't quite ready to believe that. "And what about you? Were you okay with it?"

Huyana gave a short, humorless laugh. "Not in the least. There was a lot of shouting those first couple of weeks. I even threatened to leave him."

"But you didn't."

She breathed out a long sigh and rubbed a hand across her swollen stomach. "No. I love him, what was I supposed to do? He's not a bad man, he just found himself in a bad situation and did the only thing he thought he could." She lowered her eyes to where her hand rested on the new life inside her. "For me and this little one."

Lizzy leaned back in her chair and closed her eyes as she considered everything Huyana had told her. Instead of being the one whose husband had been unfaithful, *she* was the one with whom he was being unfaithful. At least, she would have been if they'd ever truly been man and wife.

She opened her eyes and looked at Elijah's unconscious form. "Nothing happened between me and Richard. He was never unfaithful to you. In fact, most of the time he barely even spoke to me. I understand why now. I don't think he wanted us to get close at all."

"He told me that," Huyana said, smiling. "I knew he was telling the truth. He's a terrible liar."

Lizzy tried not to reflect on how he'd been lying to her since they met and she'd barely suspected. "How did you meet him?"

Her gaze moved to the window. "He came onto the reservation. It wasn't long after he'd moved onto the ranch and he wanted to get to know the neighbors. That actually impressed me. Most white people wouldn't have bothered with us."

"Did you like him straight away?"

Huyana laughed, a rich, warm sound. "Oh no. I found him extremely annoying, especially when he kept coming to the reservation with some vague excuse or other. I wasn't naive, I knew that he was interested in me, but I had no intention of even being friends with a white man, much less more. And my brothers, well, they weren't happy with him at all."

A thought came to her. "Wait, that man who came with you earlier, was he...?"

"Elsu, my oldest brother."

"I've seen him before. He was with two other men Richard spoke to on our way to visit his parents."

"My other brothers. I apologize for them. I only discovered what they'd done afterwards. They were hoping to intimidate you into returning home. I had a very thorough talk with them when I found out."

"No need to apologize," Lizzy said with a small smile. "I have three older brothers myself."

"Ah, so you understand."

She nodded. "Very well. To be honest, I wasn't scared of your brothers until Richard took out his rifle."

"His rifle?" Huyana rolled her eyes. "*Men.* I think my brothers know he's not so bad as they think, and he knows they wouldn't ever actually hurt him, but none of them want to be the first to back down."

Lizzy remembered how awed she'd been at her first glimpse of real life Indian warriors. "I just wanted to talk to them. They looked so magnificent."

Huyana pursed her lips, fixing Lizzy with a calculating stare. "I had thought Richard was exaggerating about you, but I can see he wasn't. You're a formidable woman."

"No one's ever called me that before," she said, surprised. "If you think it would make your brothers feel better, you can tell them I was very afraid."

She grinned. "Oh no, I'd much rather tell them the truth."

Despite everything, Lizzy giggled. She suspected she could grow to like Huyana. "So what changed your mind about Richard?"

"After more than a year of trying to ignore him, one day he just came straight up to me holding a bunch of flowers and said, 'I know you won't consider me because of the color of my skin, but I think you're the most beautiful, charming, intelligent, graceful woman I've ever met and I have just one thing to ask you – if you couldn't see me, would you allow me to court you?' And I realized the answer was yes. Without knowing it, I'd begun looking forward to his visits, and I found myself thinking about him much of the time. I knew then that I was no better than any white person who would reject me because I'm the wrong color. So I took the flowers and told him if he could get my parents' permission, he could court me. We were married six months later."

It wasn't so much the words that convinced Lizzy, but the sincerity with which they were said. In spite of being the one legally married to Richard, she had no claim to him. He belonged to his wife. His *real* wife.

"I'm so sorry," she said. "None of this is right."

"It's not your fault. We can't choose who we love, but I think you know that." Huyana's eyes went to Elijah.

Lizzy followed her gaze. "I do. I won't ever be able to thank you enough for saving him."

She simply nodded.

"You know," Lizzy said, "it would be easier for me to dislike you if you weren't so nice."

Huyana smiled. "I was just thinking the same thing about you."

~ ~ ~

Lizzy and Huyana talked for another half an hour and she discovered she liked her husband's other wife very much.

In many ways, it was a relief. If she'd been awful, it would have been a lot harder to come to terms with the situation. As it was, Lizzy found her anger melting away in the presence of the kind, charming woman who clearly loved Richard very much.

When he appeared at the door, Huyana excused herself and left, placing her hand briefly on his arm as she passed.

"How is he?" Richard stood in the doorway, arms wrapped around his waist, glancing at Elijah and then back at her.

"The same, I suppose."

Nodding, he lowered his gaze to the floor. He straightened his arms and then clasped them around himself again, looking behind him and then back into the room.

Finally, he took a deep breath in and said, "Could I come in?"

"Of course."

He pulled a chair up to the other side of the bed and sat. It must have been a full two minutes before he spoke.

"I remember the day I met him," he said, his eyes on Elijah's still face. "The man who did his job before had upped and left in the middle of the night without a word. I found out later he'd had gambling debts he couldn't pay and there were people who weren't happy about that. Anyway, I was in town to put a notice in the mercantile that I was looking to hire and Elijah was right there. He'd just arrived in town and he overheard me talking to Mr. Lamb and asked me for a chance then and there. Said it was God's guiding had brought him there right at that moment." He rubbed the back of his neck. "I didn't know about that, and his stutter, well, I'm ashamed to say it gave me pause. He also looked really young and his clothing had seen better days and he was so

266

skinny he didn't look like he could lift so much as a shovel, although he was carrying this old knapsack full of books. But there was something about him, something so open and earnest. I told him I'd try him out for a week and it turned out to be one of the best things I ever did. He's a good man. A much better man than me."

Lizzy tried to imagine the young man Richard described, but Elijah had changed a lot in the two years since then. He was still young, but now he radiated health and strength. But the books, that was Elijah through and through.

Richard sighed. "This is all my fault. If I hadn't panicked when my folks threatened to take away the ranch, if I hadn't done what I did..." He shook his head. "All I'd ever wanted was this ranch. I had no idea what I'd do if I lost it, and with Huyana expecting I didn't know what else to do." He moved his eyes to Lizzy. "I know you have no reason to believe me, but I never meant to hurt you. I thought if I could just keep things going long enough to get a loan from the bank and buy the ranch from my parents then everything would be okay. I figured I could do it in another two or three years. That's all I needed."

"What were you going to do then? What did you plan to do about us being man and wife?"

"I thought we could get a divorce. I figured that wouldn't be hard, what with me being married to Huyana. And as for anything happening between us... I'll be honest, I thought any woman who would come clear across the country to marry wasn't looking for romance or anything like that. It was either going to be that she needed to get away from something or that she needed a roof over her head or had some other practical reason. Whatever it was, I figured giving you whatever you wanted would be enough, and I would have provided for you afterwards, for as long as you needed." He gave her a faint, rueful smile. "I didn't count on

267

you wanting the one thing I couldn't give you."

"Love," she said quietly.

"Yes."

She sat in silence for a while, watching the slow rise and fall of Elijah's chest as she considered everything she'd heard. She understood why Richard did what he did. She even understood his reasoning, flawed as it was. But most of all, she knew she was anything but innocent in the whole thing.

"I owe you an apology," she said.

Richard stared at her, his mouth dropping open. "You owe *me* an apology? You didn't do anything wrong."

Her gaze went to Elijah. "Yes, I did."

She closed her eyes for a few seconds, gathering her courage. She'd asked God for forgiveness and she knew that in His ever present mercy He had granted it, but admitting her sins to Richard was difficult on a whole new level.

"I didn't know about Huyana or the baby or any of it, and yet when things didn't go like I wanted them to I did what I knew was wrong. I may not have actually done anything, but in my heart I was every bit as unfaithful to you as you were to me. I fell in love with another man, and because of that he might not... he might..." Tears welled in her eyes and she stopped.

Richard waited patiently, the sympathy on his face saying it all.

"Can you forgive me?" she said finally, wiping at her eyes.

"'Course I forgive you. I drove you away. I don't blame you at all." He looked down at his hands in his lap. "Do you think there's any way you could...?"

"Yes," she said immediately. "I understand why you did it. And I forgive you."

He looked up, their eyes met, and she knew they finally understood each other.

"If it means anything," he said, "if I hadn't already been married and I had asked you to come here for the right reasons, I would have been honored and very, very happy to have you as my wife."

She smiled at that. "Thank you. At least I know I'm not completely impossible to love."

"Far from it." He touched his fingers to the bruise on his jaw and nodded at Elijah. "And judging by the way he punched me, he certainly doesn't think so."

Lizzy's heart did a little skip. She wanted to ask if he truly thought Elijah loved her, but it probably wasn't an appropriate topic for discussion between them, in spite of their newfound mutual understanding.

"Would you mind if I stayed for a while?" Richard said.

"I'd like that very much."

So they sat either side of Elijah's bed and talked.

In some ways it was just like she'd longed for at the beginning of their marriage and in others it wasn't. And by the time Mrs. Lassiter brought them supper, Lizzy knew that although she'd lost a husband, she'd gained a friend.

~ ~ ~

It was early evening and the sun was just setting, casting a pink glow around the room, when a knock sounded on the open door. Lizzy looked up from the Bible on her lap to see Amos standing on the landing.

She beckoned him in and he took the other seat at Elijah's bedside.

"How are you holding up?" he said.

Her first instinct was to tell him she was fine, but it wouldn't have been true. "I'm trying to trust God that he'll be all right, but I'm scared."

"I can understand that. We all are. Elijah's well liked by

269

every one of us." He sat back in the chair and picked at a loose thread in the arm's fabric. "I reckon I owe you an apology. For Richard."

She'd suspected as much. "You knew about Huyana."

He nodded, his eyes on Elijah. "I tried telling Richard it was a bad idea to send for a bride, but he was convinced it was the only way he could keep the ranch. He always has been stubborn, since the day he was born."

His affection for Richard was obvious. He'd known him all his life, Lizzy could hardly have expected him to abandon that loyalty for a woman he'd only known for a couple of weeks.

"I understand," she said, smiling to show she really did. "And I don't hold it against you. Did everyone know but me?" It was a loaded question. She was fairly certain Elijah hadn't, but she needed to be sure.

"Oh no, no one but me knew. Richard never brought Huyana to the house. He planned to, once he'd told his parents, but their reaction to the thought of him being with an Indian woman put a stop to that. He was too afraid it would get back to them that he was still with her."

She looked at Elijah and let out a breath she didn't know she'd been holding. He hadn't known.

"Forgive me if I'm being out of line here," Amos said, watching her, "but would I be right in thinking you feel more than just friendship for Elijah?"

She bit her lip and nodded.

"In that case, I reckon you need to know some things about him, so you can think on what you want to do after he wakes up. Now that it looks like you aren't going to be a married woman for much longer."

CHAPTER 29

There were a few precious seconds, floating in the transition between sleep and wakefulness, when there was no pain. Just a warm, comfortable twilight when he wafted on a cloud of blissful ignorance.

And then he drifted into full consciousness and the pain came from everywhere, all at once.

Elijah opened his eyes and looked up at a ceiling. It didn't look like the bunkhouse ceiling he was accustomed to waking beneath. Since moving anything else felt like it would be unwise in the extreme, he swiveled just his eyes to look around the room. It seemed familiar. He'd been in here before. And then his gaze came to rest on a mass of dark, loose curls by his left hand and he remembered. He was in Lizzy's bedroom, in the house. He'd helped carry her luggage in the day she arrived. The day his life turned upside down.

She was sitting in a chair beside the bed where he lay, her head resting beside him and her hand wrapped around his. It didn't look comfortable, but she nevertheless appeared to be fast asleep.

What was he doing on her bed in her bedroom? Had he really woken, or was he dreaming? He turned his head to get a better look at his surroundings and a gasp wrenched from his lips at sharp pain on his right side.

No, not dreaming. The pain was definitely real.

Lizzy's eyelids fluttered slowly open, blinking blearily and then opening wide when she saw him watching her. She

271

jerked upright, her unfettered hair spilling over her shoulders. Despite the extra pain it would probably cause, he had to stop himself from reaching out and touching it.

"You're awake." Tears shimmered in her eyes. "You're awake!"

He attempted a smile. "Hey." The word came out rough and he realized how dry his mouth was. At least he hadn't coughed. He got the feeling coughing would be a very, very bad idea. "W-w-water?"

"Oh, yes. Yes."

She took a glass from the nightstand he could just see from the corner of his eye. It was an awkward, painful procedure getting his head up enough so he wouldn't choke when he drank, although when Lizzy slid her hand beneath his head to help him her touch did a fair job of distracting him from the discomfort.

"What happened?" he said when he'd taken as much water as he could.

"You were caught in a stampede."

A stampede? A vague memory of hooves and terror and falling and agony came to him.

"When Richard and the others brought you back you were unconscious," she said. "There was so much blood. I was so scared..."

She lowered her eyes as her voice broke, a tear sparkling in the light as it dropped to the bed.

Not caring how much pain it caused him, he reached out and took her hand. "Don't cry. Not over me."

She wiped at her eyes with her free hand and he couldn't help but smile. She never did have a handkerchief with her.

"I was so scared you wouldn't wake up," she said. "I've never been so scared in my life."

Despite the pain and the fact that he had no idea how badly he was injured, an indescribable joy rose inside him.

She cared about him. "How long have I b-been out?"

"Over a day. I've never prayed so much before. But Jesus has been right here with me the whole time, I know it."

It seemed their Savior had been with both of them. He couldn't believe he'd survived an actual stampede.

"Are you in pain?" she said.

He didn't want to admit it, least of all to Lizzy, but there was a time and a place for stoicism and he was at least smart enough to know this wasn't it. "Yes. A lot."

"Doctor Wilson left laudanum. I'll get you some. And I'll bring Huyana to check on you." She stared at him for a few seconds and swallowed. "I... I..." Letting out a frustrated little huff of air, she lifted his hand and pressed a lingering kiss to his knuckles. "I'll be right back."

And then she practically fled from the room.

Elijah closed his mouth after a few seconds. He raised his hand to look at it, half expecting to see it glowing. It wasn't, but the skin where her lips had touched was tingling. She'd kissed him. Only on the hand, but still. What did that mean?

And who on earth was Huyana?

Lizzy returned a few minutes later, followed into the room by Richard and a pregnant young Indian woman. At the sight of his boss, Elijah's memories came flooding back - finding Lizzy crying in the kitchen, angrily confronting Richard, the fight, being thrown from his horse and overrun by the panicked cattle.

"How are you feeling?" Richard said.

"Like I got caught in a stampede." His eyes were drawn to the large purple bruise on Richard's jaw. "I'm s-s-sorry I punched you." Even though the pain he'd caused Lizzy was still fresh in Elijah's mind, he had always respected Richard. He'd given him a chance when others wouldn't.

"I'm sorry I punched you back," Richard replied,

smiling.

That was a good sign. Maybe he wouldn't actually get fired for attacking his boss.

The Indian woman sat in a chair beside the bed. Her glossy black hair was swept into a long braid that she flicked back over her shoulder as she leaned towards him. "My name is Huyana and I'm a healer among the Miwok. I've been helping to treat you."

"She saved your life," Lizzy said, smiling at her.

Elijah got the feeling there was a story there. "I should thank you then."

Huyana nodded with a small smile. "Your right arm is broken. So is your right leg, in two places. And you may have a fractured rib. Beyond that, I'm not sure, so before Lizzy gives you the laudanum we're going to find out where else you have pain. I'm sorry, it's not going to be pleasant."

He would have taken a deep breath if breathing hadn't been uncomfortable. "Better get it over with then."

Being prodded and poked in search of broken bones turned out to be not quite as bad as he was anticipating after Huyana's warning. She was gentle and seemed to know what she was doing and, to his relief, nothing else turned out to be broken, just badly bruised. And things definitely improved after he'd taken the laudanum.

Amos and the rest of the men came to express their relief that he was awake and tease him about throwing himself in front of a stampede just to get out of work. Hearing how Amos and Alonzo had managed to turn the herd just enough so he was only caught by the outside edge made him even more amazed and grateful how God had saved his life. It could easily have been so much worse. He spent the entire time silently giving thanks.

Finally, just Lizzy and Richard were left in the room with him.

Richard heaved a sigh and looked at the floor. "Look, you had every right to be angry with me. I know what I did was stupid and wrong and it almost cost you your life and I'm really sorry. But Lizzy and I have been talking a lot and we've worked things out, so I hope you can forgive me. You're a good man, Elijah, and a good worker, and I'd rather not lose you."

"I... uh... y-you won't." Maybe it was his injuries playing with his mind, but he had no idea what was going on.

Richard nodded, exchanged smiles with Lizzy, and left.

Elijah's heart sank. Lizzy and he had worked things out, he'd said. Then they'd smiled at each other. He had no idea what was happening with the woman Lizzy had seen Richard with, but he tried to be happy for them. At least, for Lizzy. It was what she'd wanted all along.

"He's trying to do the right thing," she said, sitting beside him. "I misjudged him, sort of. Not in everything, but I didn't know the whole story."

He looked at the blue sky outside the window behind her. "So, I g-guess that's why I'm here, in your b-b-bed. Because you're not using it anymore."

She frowned in confusion. "Not using it anymore? I don't..." Her eyes widened and a blush stained her cheeks. "Oh! You mean you think that Richard and I are... are... sharing, um, living as man and wife now."

"You aren't?"

Her hand went to her mouth, a smile lighting her eyes. "No, he's going to give me an annulment. He only married me to make his parents happy because they threatened to take the ranch from him when he told them about Huyana."

Realization finally dawned. He definitely wasn't working at one hundred percent. "Huyana? You mean she's Richard's other woman?"

"His wife," she said. "At least, they were married in her

clan."

Elijah was aware his mouth was hanging open again. That seemed to be happening a lot. "So y-y-you aren't, you're not..."

"I will soon no longer be a married woman," she said, looking at the bedcovers between them.

A pause stretched into a silence that seemed to wrap itself around every dream, every longing Elijah had had in the past two and a half weeks. Lizzy would be free to do whatever she wanted.

The question was, would she want him once she knew everything? There was only one way to find out.

"I think I need to t-t-tell you about my past," he said, closing his eyes and hoping it would be easier if he didn't see her look of disappointment once she knew. "After I was rejected for the scholarship, I left home and wandered around for a couple of years, supported myself by taking odd jobs and g-g-gambling. I was carrying a lot of anger and I got into a lot of fights. In one of those f-f-fights I injured a man badly and I spent seven months in jail. That's when I met the pastor who led me to accept Jesus as my Savior. After that I made my way down to California w-w-where no one would know me, and I eventually ended up here." He opened his eyes again, steeling himself to see her look of horror. Instead, she appeared perfectly calm in the presence of a convicted criminal. "You d-don't seem surprised."

"Amos already told me. Not details, but he said you'd been in jail for hurting someone. But what you did before doesn't matter to me. I know who you are now and I would trust you with my life."

He didn't know whether to be annoyed at Amos for revealing something he'd told him in confidence or relieved that she already knew. But the knowledge that she still trusted him despite what he'd done was more soothing than the laudanum.

"Please don't be angry at Amos," she said. "He knew, well, since I'm not going to be married to Richard for much longer, he thought I should know about... about... that is to say, since, um, after the annulment there won't be anything to stop..."

Elijah watched, entranced, as she floundered, her cheeks turning an adorable shade of pink.

"To stop...?" He left the question hanging in the air between them, holding his breath as he waited for her answer, an answer that could change his life.

She raised her eyes to his and spoke so softly he could barely hear her. "Us."

His heart leaped so hard he was surprised it didn't hurt his ribs. He had to clear his throat before speaking again. "I g- guess this means I owe you two dollars."

She frowned in confusion. "What for?"

"Because you bet me two dollars you'd be able to tell when I was bluffing within two weeks and it seems like I can't hide anything from you. E-e-especially not how I feel."

She bit her lower lip. "Truth is, I don't know. Not really."

"Oh." He slid his hand across the covers and entwined his fingers with hers. "In that case, w-w-would it be wrong to tell a still-married woman that I'm completely in love with her?"

The most beautiful smile he'd ever seen lit up her face. "Only if it would be wrong for a still-married woman to admit she's madly in love with you too."

As Elijah lay there, in pain, barely able to move, and with several broken bones, he knew without doubt that he was the happiest, most blessed man alive.

CHAPTER 30

Lizzy spent the next few days taking care of Elijah, tending to his wounds, bringing him his meals, keeping him company, helping him do all the things he couldn't with only one working arm and leg and less than a full complement of working ribs. Well, not *all* the things. Amos helped him with washing and dressing, although when Mrs. Lassiter stated very firmly that Lizzy wasn't to be in the room unless he was fully clothed, the mischievous look Elijah gave her, a look that conveyed the promise that one day there would be no such rules, made her face heat and her heart beat faster.

Eight days after the stampede, she and Richard and Huyana travelled to Auburn for the annulment of her marriage. She couldn't help feeling a little sad as she signed the papers that put an end to the dreams she'd been convinced of just a few weeks before.

It hardly seemed possible it had been such a short time. She'd changed so much. In many ways, she felt as if she'd grown up. She was no longer the girl with stars in her eyes and unrealistic dreams that everything would be wonderful just because she thought it would. She'd matured into a woman who knew that she had to work to make dreams come true, she had to follow what she knew in her heart no matter what, and most of all she had to seek God's guidance, because He knew everything when she knew nothing.

Not that she was sad for the end of the marriage. It had never been real anyway, no matter how much she'd wanted it to be at the start. With Elijah she had something that was as real and solid as the mountains around her.

As soon as Lizzy's marriage was dissolved, Richard got a marriage license and legally made Huyana his wife, with Lizzy as a witness. Lizzy was thrilled for them, especially Huyana who was practically glowing as she said her vows. Richard also looked happier than she had ever seen him. It wouldn't be an easy life for them, but they would have each other, which was what they wanted most of all. And maybe one day attitudes would change and they'd be able to live out their lives together free of the cruel condemnation so many threw their way.

When they reached home after the long day, Lizzy was happy but exhausted. She went straight to Elijah's room, her former bedroom, and was almost run over at the door when Mrs. Lassiter bustled out, a scowl on her face.

"Good, you're back," she said when she saw her. "Maybe you can talk some sense into him. Fool man near killed himself getting out of that bed, but he wouldn't listen to me. Oh no. No one listens to the voice of reason around here..." She continued to mutter to herself about being the only one who used her brain as she walked down the stairs and slammed the kitchen door.

Lizzy walked into the bedroom, half expecting Elijah to be sprawled on the floor or curled up somewhere in pain and wondering if she'd have to run straight back out and go for the doctor. But what she saw was the settee, which had been moved to the window, with Elijah sitting on it and looking out. He was facing away from her and for a few moments she just stood in the doorway and gazed at the sun shining in the dark blond waves of his hair.

Always before there had been a barrier between them, her marriage to Richard preventing anything more intimate than holding hands. Now there was no such impediment. It

279

was what she'd longed for almost since they met, but now it was here she was a little nervous.

"You gonna c-come in?" he said without turning his head.

She moved across the room to stand by the settee.

Elijah looked up at her and she could have sworn his hazel eyes were seeing right into her soul. "Is it done?"

For some reason, she could barely raise her voice above a whisper. "Yes."

"You okay?"

"Yes."

He raised his eyebrows and his glance flicked to the empty seat next to him. "W-w-would you like to sit?"

Her voice chose that point to desert her completely, so she simply lowered onto the settee and folded her hands on her lap, trying not to look like her heart was pounding its way out of her chest.

His good arm was towards her and after a few seconds of silence he slowly reached out to take her hand. Her eyes followed the movement as he brought it to his lips and pressed a soft kiss to the back, his eyes closing as if he was savoring the moment. When they opened again, the depth of feeling she saw amazed her.

Everything she'd thought she wanted, excitement, adventure, the life of a heroine in a dime novel, vanished in an instant. This was the only thing she'd truly wanted, a love so deep it stole her breath away. From a man who made her heart soar.

A man she would cross continents for.

Still holding her hand, Elijah drew a slow breath in and out. Then he said, without stuttering once, "I love you, Elizabeth Cotton. Will you marry me?"

Tears pricked at the back of her eyes. "Yes. With all my heart, yes."

For a few seconds they simply stared at each other, until Elijah cleared his throat. "I really want to k-k-kiss you right now, but I'm going to need you to move closer, 'cause I can't come to you."

Dropping her gaze, a blush heating her cheeks, she inched her way along the seat until they were so close she could feel the heat of his body through her dress and she was sure he must be able to hear the pounding of her heart.

He released her hand and touched his fingers to her chin, raising her face to his.

She held her breath.

He tilted his head, she leaned into him, their lips met.

And everything else disappeared as his kiss became her whole world.

Lizzy had been kissed before, but she had never, ever in her life been kissed the way Elijah kissed her. Even with the use of only one arm and barely able to move, he made her feel as if he was wrapped around her, surrounding her with his warmth and strength and love. Heat spread all the way to her toes and she had to remind herself to not hold him too tightly. Every instinct urged her closer.

When their lips finally, slowly parted, he touched his forehead to hers and sighed. "There were times when I thought I'd never get to kiss you. But that was worth the wait."

She cupped his jaw, moved her lips back to his, and whispered with a smile, "I'm not so sure. Better do it a few more times, just to be certain."

CHAPTER 31

The following weeks at times seemed to Elijah to drag interminably, but at others seemed to race by in a flash.

Richard went to his parents and somehow managed to convince them to allow him to keep the ranch. Elijah suspected it may have had something to do with Huyana, who went with him. Maybe Mr. and Mrs. Shand realized that if they didn't let go of their prejudices they would not only lose their son, but also miss out on having a charming daughter-in-law, not to mention giving up their chance to know their grandchild when he or she arrived.

Huyana moved into the house and, despite the unusual start to their friendship, she and Lizzy became close. It filled Elijah with relief. He believed Lizzy when she told him she loved him, but he couldn't help feeling just a tiny bit worried that she still felt something for her former husband. Even though he hadn't wanted to admit it to himself at the time, he'd been more than a little jealous of Richard ever since she'd arrived. But the fact that Lizzy had no bad feelings towards Huyana helped convince him that she had no lingering attraction to Richard.

As she told Elijah, her heart belonged to him. Which was just as well because he now knew his heart hadn't been his own since the moment he'd first seen her.

It took five more weeks for his broken bones to heal enough for him to walk, but as soon as he could he was summarily returned to the bunkhouse by Mrs. Lassiter who had taken it upon herself to ensure nothing inappropriate happened when Lizzy was with him in the bedroom. This included creeping up the stairs at random intervals to burst into the room unannounced. Fortunately, one of the steps had a creak and Lizzy and Elijah developed an almost supernatural hearing for the sound, able to go from an embrace to demurely sitting at opposite ends of the settee within two seconds flat. They were never doing anything more than kissing, but Mrs. Lassiter frowned upon even that much contact.

He was ecstatic to be on his feet again, but he missed not being able to spend so much time alone with Lizzy. He also missed the private bedroom. He'd gotten used to sleeping without the sound of six other men breathing and, in Anson's case, snoring.

He was more than eager to get married, but he and Lizzy were waiting for two reasons. The first was that he wanted to be able to stand unaided at her side for their wedding. The second was the letter she had received from her parents after she'd written telling them everything that had happened.

Now she sat beside Elijah on the bench outside the ticket office at the station, her foot tapping a staccato rhythm as she peered along the railroad tracks.

"You can g-get up if you'd like," Elijah said, looking down at the movement.

She stilled her foot and moved her hand from where it was wrapped around his arm to entwine their fingers. "No, I like sitting with you."

He lifted her hand and kissed the back. "I like sitting with you too, but you seem to need to move."

"I'm just nervous. Well, not nervous, but... you know."

He did know. Over the weeks they'd become closer than he'd ever thought it was possible to be to another person. He felt as if he knew her better than he knew himself, and he loved her even more for it.

She leaned her head against his shoulder and they sat in silence for a few seconds.

"You're not nervous, are you?" she said.

He'd already decided to always be honest with her, even when it didn't reflect well on him. "I'm downright terrified."

She raised her head to look at him. "You're not, are you?"

"Of course I am." He gave her a small, somewhat forced smile. "I'm about to meet the parents of the woman I love. Right now, I'd rather f-f-face another stampede."

She wrapped his hand in both of hers. "You mustn't be scared. Daddy and Mama will adore you."

"I hope you're right." He wasn't entirely convinced.

She sat back, affecting a look of shock. "Elijah Griffin, if you're going to start doubting that I am right in all matters I think we need to have a long talk before we get married."

He laughed quietly and leaned towards her, lowering his voice. "If we weren't in pu-public, I'd kiss you."

Her answer made his stomach flutter. "If we weren't in public, kissing you would have been my preferred method of distraction from the moment we got here."

She was the most perfect woman on the face of the earth. He was going to love being married.

At the sound of a train's whistle his happiness evaporated, replaced by fear. Despite her reassurances, he truly was scared. He never liked meeting new people in the best of circumstances. Meeting Lizzy's parents, the most important people in the world to her, was very far from the best of circumstances. He prayed for the hundredth time that his stutter wouldn't be bad.

Lizzy leaped to her feet and rushed to the ticket booth window. "Is that it?"

"Yes, Miss Cotton," the stationmaster said with a smile,

"that's it."

They moved closer to the tracks to wait for the train Elijah could see approaching in the distance. It seemed to arrive much too fast, the clouds of steam trailing into the air behind it as it slowed to a halt in front of them. Lizzy bounced on her toes as the passengers began to disembark, craning up to search the windows.

"Elizabeth?"

Elijah looked round at the sound of a woman's voice to see an older couple stepping to the ground from a carriage further along.

"Mama!"

Letting go of his hand, she flew into her mother's arms and burst into tears. Her father's arms engulfed both of them and they stood that way for a long time. Not knowing what else to do Elijah waited, trying not to invade the private moment. After a while he had to take out a handkerchief to surreptitiously dab at his eyes. Lizzy's tears tore at his heart, just like they always did.

"I'm sorry for leaving you," she sniffled. "I know how childish I was being."

"Oh, darling," her mother said, "you're you and I wouldn't have you any other way."

Lizzy looked back at Elijah and wiped at her eyes with her sleeve. Smiling, he stepped forward to pass the handkerchief to her. She broke away from her parents and moved to stand at his side, slipping her arm around his.

"Mama, Daddy, this is Elijah."

This was it, the moment he'd been dreading. Taking a deep breath, he held out his right hand. "It's a p-p-pleasure to meet you, Mr. and Mrs. Cotton." Only one stutter. He was going to call that a victory.

Lizzy's father narrowed his eyes. "So you're the young man who wants to marry our daughter right after she escapes her first ill-advised marriage."

He lowered his hand, his heart sinking with it. If Lizzy hadn't been holding onto him, he would have taken a step back. "I... uh..."

She reached forward to give her father's arm a playful slap. "Oh, stop it. Don't listen to him, Elijah. He likes to act tough, but he's a sweetheart."

Sweetheart. Right. He didn't look like a sweetheart. He looked like he wanted to extract Elijah's internal organs with a spoon. At least Lizzy's three older brothers weren't there. Small mercies.

Mrs. Cotton stepped forward and held out her hand with a smile that looked very much like Lizzy's. "It's lovely to meet you, Elijah. Elizabeth has told us a lot about you in her letters, but we're looking forward to getting to know you in person."

Mr. Cotton looked nothing of the sort. Elijah kept his attention on Mrs. Cotton as he shook her hand. "Thank you, Mrs. Cotton. I'm l-l-looking forward to that too." *And hopefully I'll survive the experience.*

Mr. Cotton's stern expression didn't budge.

"Let's collect your luggage and I'll show you the hotel," Lizzy said, either ignoring or oblivious to her father's unrelenting hostility towards Elijah. "It's very grand."

~ ~ ~

"I'm pretty sure your father hates me," Elijah said as they watched the flies dancing over the surface of the pond. He was sitting with his back against the rock, Lizzy in front of him.

She rested her head back against his shoulder and he tightened his arms around her, nuzzling his face into her hair.

"He doesn't hate you," she said. "He's just feeling

286

protective of me after what happened with Richard. Mama and I will talk to him. He'll come round, you'll see."

"Are you sure about that?"

"Absolutely, positively certain." She shuffled around to face him and took his face in her hands. "In two days I'm going to become Mrs. Elijah Griffin and nothing is going to stop me. You do believe that, don't you?"

He traced her cheek with one fingertip. "I'm trying to. I want to m-m-marry you more than anything."

She leaned forward to kiss him and smiled. "Nothing can stop us from being together, not a stampede, not me being married to another man, and not my father. Only God can stop us and He won't. He wants us to get married."

He tilted his head to one side. "How d-do you know?"

"I asked Him, the night you woke up after the stampede. I didn't want to make any more mistakes so I asked Him if we should be together, even though it was the hardest thing I've ever done. I was so scared He'd say no, but I knew I had to ask this time. And He said yes."

Elijah stared at her for a few seconds and then wrapped his arms around her, pulling her into his lap and holding her close.

"I love you so much," he murmured into her hair, marveling all over again that God had blessed him with such a wonderful woman.

She sighed and snuggled into his embrace. "I love you too."

CHAPTER 32

Elijah stood outside the parlor door and ran one finger around the collar of his shirt. He wasn't used to wearing a suit and he was hot and uncomfortable, although that may have been more to do with his nerves than the clothing.

The last time he'd worn a suit, borrowed just like this one was, he'd made a fool of himself in the interview for a scholarship and destroyed his chance to study engineering. It didn't bode well for today that he was more scared now than he had been on that occasion. Back then, it had just been his career that was on the line. This time, it was his heart.

Despite Lizzy's assurances the evening before at the pond, he was still afraid something could go wrong. God may have wanted them to be together, but sometimes people did things God didn't want them to. For example, Mr. Cotton could ignore His prompting and say no.

Closing his eyes, he sent up what must have been his hundredth prayer for courage and calm since he'd woken. Then, taking a deep breath, he knocked on the parlor door.

"Come in," a deep voice responded.

Heart thudding so hard he feared it could be heard all the way into town, Elijah opened the door and stepped inside.

Across the room Lizzy's father stood with his back to him, looking out the window. He wasn't an especially imposing man physically and Elijah was at least three inches taller, but he had an air about him that made him seem like he filled the room. Considering Elijah was about to ask for his only daughter's hand in marriage, Mr. Cotton would have been slightly less terrifying if he'd been a huge, fire-breathing dragon.

He stopped just inside the door and waited silently, unwilling to speak unless he absolutely had to.

"I can see why Lizzy loves it so much here," Mr. Cotton said without turning. "It is beautiful. Although she also loves the area around our home. I think my daughter could find something to love in anything. She has a heart as big as the sun."

Something to love in anything. Was he talking about Elijah? It wasn't a confidence-boosting remark if he was.

Mr. Cotton turned from the window, his stern gaze coming to settle on Elijah. "Have a seat, Mr. Griffin."

Elijah didn't move for a couple of seconds, a little worried that if he did, he would trip over his stomach which was currently residing somewhere around his feet. When he finally managed to coax himself into action, he walked stiffly to one of the wingback chairs by the bookcases and sat on the edge, clasping his hands together on his lap.

Mr. Cotton took a seat opposite him and for a split second Elijah thought he saw a hint of amusement on his face, but then it was gone and he was sure he must have imagined it, his mind grasping for a lifeline in the storm.

"So, Mr. Griffin, what can I do for you?"

Elijah opened his mouth and closed it again. He could feel the stutter lurking, waiting to pounce and tear his carefully prepared speech apart, just like it had years ago.

"Mr. C-C-Cotton, I w-w-w-w..." He closed his eyes and swallowed. He could do this. He had to.

When he opened his eyes again, Mr. Cotton's flinty expression had softened.

"Mr. Griffin, much as I would like to intimidate the man

who wants to marry my daughter as far as humanly possible, I won't. The truth is, the whole episode with Richard Shand hasn't made me very well disposed towards any man who goes anywhere near Lizzy, but both my wife and daughter have very forcefully pointed out to me that I am holding you accountable for another man's actions, and I admit that may be unfair of me. I'm used to dealing with young men in my profession which may also have made me somewhat wary of their motives, but for Lizzy's sake I will try not to treat you in the same way. I remember how afraid I was when I asked my wife's parents for her hand. I didn't stop shaking for a week." He smiled, although the warmth didn't reach his eyes. "So maybe this would be easier if you know that whatever you say, my answer will be yes. If I did otherwise, neither my wife nor my headstrong daughter would speak to me again, and Lizzy would undoubtedly go ahead and marry you anyway."

Somehow, the assurances failed to make Elijah any less nervous. "Th-thank you, sir."

Mr. Cotton nodded and sat back in his chair, crossing one leg over the other. "Go on then."

He licked his dry lips. His speech had vanished completely from his head, but maybe this wasn't the time for speeches anyway. This was the time for honesty.

"S-sir, Lizzy is the m-m-most wonderful woman I've ever m-met. She's not just b-beautiful outside, she's beautiful inside too. I've never been as happy as I am when I'm w-with her. I love her with all my heart and if, w-w-when, you give us your blessing to m-marry, I give you my word I'll spend the rest of m-my life providing for her, keeping her safe, and doing everything in my p-p-power to make her happy."

He breathed out, silently thanking God for getting him through.

Mr. Cotton stared at him in silence, his eyes boring into

him until Elijah began to squirm. Wasn't this when he shook his hand and welcomed him to the family?

"No."

Elijah's mouth dropped open. "W-w-w-what?"

Lizzy's father burst into laughter, his guffaws echoing around the room. "Oh, you should have seen your face! I just couldn't resist. Had to get a little bit of torture in there. You'll understand when you have daughters of your own."

Elijah nodded slowly, gave him a tentative smile, and tried to push his heart down out of his throat.

Mr. Cotton's laughter reduced to a grin. "And I trust you will thoroughly terrorize any suitors for my granddaughters' hands when the time comes."

Granddaughters. Was that a yes? "So... Lizzy and I can m-m-marry?"

"Yes, you have my and her mother's permission to marry our daughter."

Elijah slumped back in the chair. He felt as if he'd just climbed a mountain in five minutes flat.

"Now, about your promise to provide for her..."

"Yes, sir." Elijah sat up again. "I've b-been saving up and I think I-I can..."

Mr. Cotton waved his hand. "Hold on there. This is where I believe Lizzy and I can help you."

He frowned in confusion. "Sir?"

"As you know, I teach at Cornell in upstate New York. It's a new university but already very well regarded. Before we came here, Lizzy sent me some of your work."

He'd noticed there were some designs missing from his portfolio, but he'd never imagined Lizzy had taken them.

"I showed it to my colleagues and they were very impressed, especially given you have no formal training. They feel you are a very talented young man. The upshot of this is, a brand new engineering department is due to open at

Cornell this fall and I've been authorized to offer you a full scholarship to be one of the first students. If you're agreeable."

For a second Elijah couldn't breathe. Had he really just been given the chance to fulfill his dream? "I... I can become an engineer?"

"If you'd like to."

He couldn't quite believe it. Tears suddenly burned at his eyes and he looked down, embarrassed.

Mr. Cotton rose and came to stand at his side, placing a hand on his shoulder. "I think you are going to be a wonderful addition to our family and our school, Elijah. Lizzy chose well this time."

"Th-thank you, sir," he whispered, before his voice deserted him completely.

~ ~ ~

When he emerged from the meeting with Mr. Cotton, Elijah made for the kitchen, slowing only enough to throw off the constricting jacket and tie and unbutton the top of his shirt as he headed for the door.

Mrs. Lassiter and Huyana looked up from the range where they were preparing lunch. A rich aroma he knew to be Huyana's cooking wafted past. Mrs. Cotton was at the table and she gave him a knowing smile as he passed.

He mouthed 'thank you' and headed for the back door.

"If you're going to find Lizzy," Huyana called after him, "she said she'd be at her favorite place and that you'd know where that was."

"Thanks," he called back without slowing.

He walked as fast as his still recovering leg muscles would allow all the way to the wood, only slowing when he reached the pond. Lizzy sat on the rock looking out over the water. She'd left her hair loose and it spilled over her shoulders and down her back. The thought of running his fingers through the dark, glossy waves momentarily drove everything else from his mind.

"Elijah?"

He blinked, startled from his hair-based reverie, and moved his eyes to her face.

"How did it go?" she said, standing and walking over to him.

For a few moments he couldn't speak as he stared at her. After being so eager to get to her, he now didn't even know where to begin.

"You... you took my designs."

Uncertainty crossed her face. "I'm sorry. I didn't know what else to do. I wanted to help you, but I didn't want to get your hopes up in case they said no. I never meant to..."

Elijah threw his arms around her, burying his face in her shoulder as the tears slid down his face. "I love you so much."

Her arms slipped around his waist. "So did my father tell you what the board said? He wouldn't tell me. Just said you should be the first to know."

He lifted his head to look into her face. "They offered me a full scholarship."

She gasped in a breath and then squealed, jumping into his arms and almost knocking him over. He held onto her tight, laughing.

"Y-you haven't asked if he agreed to our marriage," he said, breathing in the lavender scent of her hair.

She smiled against his chest. "I know he did. He knows me too well not to."

He kissed the top of her head and rested his cheek against her hair. "Don't you m-mind that you'll be going home? You wanted adventure and excitement and cowboys and Indians."

"I climbed a windmill and looked after pigs and chickens and saw two calves being born and became friends with some very nice cowboys and Indians and won lots of pennies. I'll miss all my new friends, but I did the one thing I wanted to do most of all." She raised her head to smile up at him. "I fell madly in love with the most wonderful, smartest, kindest, handsomest man in the world."

Elijah didn't think it was possible to feel happier than he did at that moment, looking into the beautiful face of the amazing woman who would be his wife. But then it seemed Lizzy made him feel that way on an almost daily basis.

"I feel like I should thank all those authors who made California sound so exciting," he said, smiling.

"I think it's very exciting," she said, smiling back at him. "Don't you?"

He dipped his head to kiss her. "I do now."

CHAPTER 33

Lizzy wondered if two weddings within two months was some kind of record. At least this time she knew for certain it would be her last.

Louisa put little blue flowers into her hair and pinned it so it stayed in place which had Lizzy proclaiming her a miracle worker, and her dress was yellow. She wondered if she should have gone with traditional white, but she wanted a color that reflected how happy she was. And she was very, very happy.

Just before they said their vows, Elijah leaned in close to whisper to her, "I love you in yellow," and she knew she'd chosen right.

The ceremony was nothing like her wedding to Richard had been. For one thing, she was surrounded by her family and friends. But most importantly of all, this time it was filled with love.

And afterwards, when she stepped from the church on her new husband's arm, she did feel different. She felt... complete.

~ ~ ~

"Where are we going?" Lizzy said, craning her head to look at the turning they should have taken to get them back to the ranch after their wedding reception.

Elijah flashed her a smile as he drove the buggy along

the main street. "You'll see."

"Is it a surprise?" she asked. "I love surprises!"

"Kind of thought you might."

He brought the buggy to a halt in front of the hotel, jumped down and handed the reins to a man who emerged from the door to meet them, saying, "Thanks, Art."

Then he helped Lizzy from the buggy and led her inside. "Remember our f-f-first time at the market?"

"Uh-huh."

"Remember Mrs. Sanchez saying you should c-come and have some of her strawberry shortcake?"

"Uh-huh."

"I thought today would be a good time."

He guided her into the hotel's dining room and she came to a halt, gasping in an awed breath.

It being the middle of the afternoon the restaurant wasn't yet open and they were the only ones there. The heavy velvet curtains had been drawn to block out the light and in the center of the room a table was topped with a pristine white tablecloth and festooned with flowers and ribbons and petals, two tall, slender candles casting a pool of flickering light over the dazzling display.

And before each chair was a porcelain plate of the most delicious looking strawberry shortcake Lizzy had ever seen, all red and white with lashings of cream.

"Oh, Elijah, it's so beautiful."

"Sara, Amy, Jo and Louisa did all the flowers and everything. I have to b-be honest, all I really did was have the idea."

She smiled up at him. "It's the best idea ever."

He gently turned her to face him, slid his arms around her waist and pressed a kiss to her forehead. "I love you Elizabeth Griffin. I can't begin to tell you how blessed I feel to have you as my wife. I p-promise to do everything I can to make you as happy as you've made me."

She'd only just managed to keep her tears at bay during the ceremony in the church, but there was only so much self-control to be had.

A tear trickled down her cheek. "I already am."

He brushed the moisture from her skin and kissed her before leading her to the table and pulling out her chair. When they were seated he reached out his hands to her. Lizzy took them and closed her eyes.

"Father," he said, "I don't have the w-w-words to say how grateful I am to You for bringing Lizzy and me together. I know I haven't done anything to deserve her, so I just thank You for Your grace and forgiveness. Please give me the strength and wisdom to be the b-best husband I can be and to love her as Jesus loves the church. In the Name of the Lord Jesus, Amen."

Lizzy was barely able to squeak "Amen" as she grabbed a napkin to dry her eyes before she dripped onto the food.

Elijah handed her a fork and smiled. "Eat. You won't be able to cry once you taste this."

Laughing softly, she took her first bite.

He was correct, the strawberry shortcake did indeed dry her tears right up.

Sometime later, when they'd cleared their plates and then cleared them again after Mrs. Sanchez emerged from the kitchen with seconds, he walked her back into the lobby.

Zach Parsons was standing at the desk.

"I thought you didn't work on Saturdays," Lizzy said, surprised to see him there after he'd been at the wedding.

"I don't. I just wanted to make sure everything got done right." He winked at Elijah and handed him a room key. "Your things are in the room. Have a good stay."

She looked up at her new husband as he walked her towards the staircase. "Stay?"

"We have two nights here," he said. "A wedding g-gift from Richard and Huyana. They thought we'd appreciate some privacy." He flashed her a not entirely innocent smile, lifted her hand and kissed the back. "Especially from Mrs. Lassiter."

She giggled, feeling her face heat. "Remind me to thank them."

When they returned to the ranch two days later she did thank them. A lot.

She was very, very grateful.

CHAPTER 34

Two weeks after the wedding, Lizzy and Elijah left Green Hill Creek.

Her parents had already set out on the return journey to Ithaca and Lizzy and Elijah would be joining them eventually, but they had decided to take their time, stop and stay at a few of the places she had wanted to see more of when the train passed through on the way to California. It was Elijah's idea for a honeymoon and she adored him for it. She may have bounced a little when he suggested it.

The gathering to see them off at the station was even larger than the welcome had been when Lizzy arrived over two months earlier. As she looked around at all her friends, she knew she could never have predicted what would happen to her when she first had the idea to become a mail order bride. It hadn't turned out at all like she thought it would, but none of it had been dull. And she was blissfully happy with the man she loved, which was exactly what she'd hoped for.

God had taken her foolish and impulsive dreams and worked them into something better than she could have imagined.

All of their friends had come to see them off. Lizzy had purposely allowed extra time for all the tearful goodbyes she knew were coming.

One by one she hugged Anson, Alonzo, Herman, Kosumee, Amos, and finally Eugene.

"Keep practicing the poker," she said to him. "You're getting better all the time. Maybe you'll even get as good as Elijah."

He looked at his shoes. "Not as good as you though."

She grinned. "No, probably not."

He smiled and wiped his sleeve across his eyes and she stretched up onto her toes to kiss his cheek, leaving him blushing furiously.

She didn't tell them, but at the bunkhouse she'd left them a big, shiny, brand new coffee pot and ten new cups along with several new decks of playing cards, bought with her winnings.

Richard took her hand in his. "Thank you for making me do what I should have done to begin with." He put his arm around Huyana next to him.

"If you hadn't advertised for a bride, I never would have met Elijah." She placed her free hand onto Huyana's extended belly, smiling when she felt movement. The baby was becoming especially restless now it was less than six weeks from coming into the world. "I'm sorry I won't be here to meet this little one."

Huyana reached forward to hug her. "Maybe one day you'll come to visit."

"I hope so."

Mrs. Lassiter stood beyond them and Lizzy had to admit she was surprised she was there at all. So she was even more shocked, not to mention somewhat speechless, when Mrs. Lassiter stepped forward and gave her a hug.

"Things aren't going to be the same without you around," she said.

Lizzy bit her lip. "Is that good or bad?"

The hint of a smile crept onto Mrs. Lassiter's face. "That remains to be seen. But I reckon I'll probably miss you anyway."

300

Mrs. Goodwin handed her a wonderful smelling package. "Lemon muffins for the journey."

Mr. Goodwin nodded and removed his pipe long enough to say, "Mrs. Griffin."

Mrs. Jones gave her a warm hug and Pastor Jones said with a smile, "It's been a pleasure to marry you. Both times."

She spoke to the husbands of the little group of women who had travelled across the country with her, and nothing could have made her happier than knowing each of the couples were as happy as she was with Elijah.

And then, finally, the moment she'd been dreading the most arrived.

Silently, Amy, Sara, Louisa and Jo gathered around her and hugged her all at once. Having successfully managed to hold back her tears up to then, Lizzy couldn't stop herself from weeping as they held onto each other.

"I'm going to miss you all so much," she sobbed, her tears soaking Amy's shoulder.

"We're going to miss you too," Louisa said, sniffing.

Sara nodded against her back. "More than anything."

"You have to write every week," Amy said. "I'll be looking for your letters every time the mail comes."

"And we'll all write to you," Jo said, "even me. We'll tell you everything. You'll get sick of it all."

Lizzy gave her a tearful smile. "Never happen."

The conductor called for everyone to board and the huddle parted reluctantly, everyone wiping their eyes. Elijah walked over from where he'd been saying goodbye to the men and slipped his arm around Lizzy's waist, handing her his handkerchief. It was already damp and she looked up at him to see moisture in his eyes. She wasn't the only one for whom leaving was a wrench. He'd been there far longer than she had.

With final goodbyes, they boarded the train and found

301

seats at a window where they could see their friends. And as the train pulled away from the station, Lizzy pressed her face to the glass, watching the people she'd grown to love disappear into the distance.

When she sat back and wiped at her eyes, Elijah wrapped his arm around her, drawing her against him and kissing her temple. She took his hand and entwined their fingers, leaning her head against his shoulder.

"You all right?" he said softly.

"I'm going to miss them all so much."

"Me too." He was quiet for a few seconds. "M-maybe when I've graduated we could come back."

She lifted her head to look at him. "Really?"

"There's lots of new towns being built out here, roads and railroads. They need engineers." One corner of his mouth hitched up. "Or maybe you'll find another adventure you'll want to go on. Or m-maybe you'll want to stay right where you are."

She began to smile back. "Or maybe I'll be happy just to be by my husband's side, wherever he goes."

He frowned, looking out the window and pretending to think about it. Then he looked back at her, tiny wrinkles appearing around his eyes. "Nah."

She burst into laughter and he hugged her close, laughing with her.

Whatever their future held, as long as they were together life would be wonderful. Lizzy just knew it.

And this time, she truly did.

THE END

DEAR READER

Thank you for reading The Wayward Heart and I hope you've enjoyed Lizzy and Elijah's story! The series continues in An Unexpected Groom. There's something Jesse hasn't told his mail order bride, something that could make her turn around and go right back home. But the more time he spends with Louisa, the more he knows he doesn't want her to leave. Can he persuade her to give him a chance? You can buy book 4 of the Escape to the West series on Amazon.

To receive an ebook of my novella The Blacksmith's Heart for free, as well as never miss a new release, sign up for my newsletter on my website. And if you're already subscribed, you are officially awesome!

If you have a moment, please consider leaving a review where you purchased the book, even just a few words. Reviews are very important for independent authors like me and they really do help others find my books. I will be extremely grateful when you do!

I know that Lizzy's story is a little more intense than the others in the Escape to the West series, and sometimes difficult to read. Thank you for sticking with her! Her story is far from easy and even her ever-present optimism is taxed. But I wanted to show that even though nothing happened as she thought it would, God brought about His own plans for her and Elijah and Richard. It's not easy to let go of our ideas for how we think our life should be, but sometimes we need to do just that so even better things can happen, which Lizzy found out!

If you'd like to contact me about anything, please do

get in touch via my Facebook page or website or at
nerys@nerysleigh.com. I love to hear from readers!

nerysleigh.com
facebook.com/nerysleigh

BIBLE VERSES

These are the verses quoted, or referred to, in The Wayward Heart, this time from the New International Version (NIV) translation.

Chapter 7 – "Truly I tell you, if you have faith as small as a mustard seed, you can say to this mountain, 'Move from here to there,' and it will move. Nothing will be impossible for you." Matthew 17:20

Chapter 7 – "Have faith in God," Jesus answered. "Truly I tell you, if anyone says to this mountain, 'Go, throw yourself into the sea,' and does not doubt in their heart but believes that what they say will happen, it will be done for them. Therefore I tell you, whatever you ask for in prayer, believe that you have received it, and it will be yours. And when you stand praying, if you hold anything against anyone, forgive them, so that your Father in heaven may forgive you your sins." Mark 11:22-25

Chapter 13 – "You shall not covet your neighbor's house. You shall not covet your neighbor's wife, or his male or female servant, his ox or donkey, or anything that belongs to your neighbor." Exodus 20:17

Chapter 18 – Bear with each other and forgive one another if any of you has a grievance against someone. Forgive as the Lord forgave you. Colossians 3:13

Chapter 21 - And we know that in all things God works for the good of those who love Him, who have been called

305

according to His purpose. Romans 8:28

Chapter 22 - Jesus looked at them and said, "With man this is impossible, but with God all things are possible." Matthew 19:26

Chapter 31 - Husbands, love your wives, just as Christ loved the church and gave Himself up for her to make her holy, cleansing her by the washing with water through the word, and to present her to Himself as a radiant church, without stain or wrinkle or any other blemish, but holy and blameless. In this same way, husbands ought to love their wives as their own bodies. Ephesians 5:25-28

Chapter 32 - Now to Him who is able to do immeasurably more than all we ask or imagine, according to His power that is at work within us, to Him be glory in the church and in Christ Jesus throughout all generations, for ever and ever! Amen. Ephesians 3:20-21